THE ALLARDS

BOOK THREE
PEACE AND WAR

Wilmont R. Kreis

THE ALLARDS

BOOK THREE

PEACE AND WAR

By Wilmont R. Kreis

Port Huron, Michigan
2008

Second Edition
2009

ISBN: 1442112387
EAN-13: 9781442112384

Library of Congress control number: 2009902691

Dedicated to my mother, Gladys Genevieve Allard-Kreis, who asked me to find my ancestors, and to my children Jennifer and Jeremy and all their cousins, for whom I am telling their story.

Acknowledgements

As before, I would like to thank Sue and Chuck Defever for all their encouragement and editorial advice. I will greatly miss Chuck's wealth of knowledge on the topic of our common relatives. Again, I would particularly like to thank my Chief Editor and biggest supporter, my wonderful wife, Susan.

PROLOGUE

The third in a series of books about my Allard ancestors, this book continues my form of historical novel, a type of *Les racines canadiennes françaises* or French-Canadian roots. To describe this period the title has been adapted from Tolstoy.

The Peace in Europe and the New World that surrounded the Treaty of Utrecht lasted over forty years, but was finally broken by the Seven Years, or French and Indian, War. As you will see in this and the next book, this war was arguably the most important event in the history of North America. Not only did it cause all of Canada and America to adhere to British culture, it set the seeds and guaranteed the outcome of the American War for Independence.

Since the books are in serial form, I recommend you read them in order. I am telling two stories, first the story of my actual ancestors and second that of the people who settled and continued to occupy New France. I have been faithful to the dates of record of my ancestors, their birth, death, marriage and other data available in abundance from the wonderfully preserved Archives of Québec, and numerous other sources. Who they married, who attended their ceremonies, where they lived and who their neighbors were form the outline of the story.

I have superimposed this on the history of the people and events of the period in question, trying to be faithful to the facts and particularly to the nature and personalities of prominent people such as Vérendrye, Washington, Montcalm, Wolfe, and Pontiac. At the end of the book I will try to confess to any fabrications of my own. Whereas Pierre* Allard may not have participated in each of these events, it is possible that he did participate in at least some. Some of our relatives, however, did participate in each historical event in the book.

Names: Unfortunately the French have few surnames. A great number of the girls had names beginning with Marie, (Marie-Anne, Marie-Charlotte, etc.). Most of the families were large and use of names of fathers, grandfathers, and siblings was common. As a result we have five second-generation Allard families each with many of the same names. Some families even used one name more than once! In their time, nicknames were common, however, I have little record of these from this period. I try to use last names and middle names to try to alleviate confusion.

Asterisks: As before, an asterisk is placed behind the first name of all ancestors. I began this to help me navigate my genealogy program, but it is also useful in the story in keeping track of which Pierre* is which. There are many ancestors who appear as characters in the story. Unless otherwise stated these are all real people in the settings in which they lived. As we look back in time, in each generation we have twice as many ancestors as the generation more recent in time. Since this story is almost three hundred years in the past, several of the people in

Québec are our ancestors, and for the most part they lived and interacted with the Allards. As we move forward there will be fewer ancestors in each successive generation. In future books we will see how these people "join" the family. I like to think of these people as families that are on a historic collision course with the Allards.

Language: These people, of course, spoke French not English, and I look at the story as a translation. If their language seems formal and some nouns, adverbs, or adjectives strange, it is to make it more the way it would have been said in French. I have not gone so far as to use gender for each pronoun (there is no 'it' in French). Even today, even semi-literate French speakers speak relatively good French. Their vocabulary and grammar is superior to the English of a similarly educated English speaker. Old French, which has endured in Québec to the modern day, is also more formal than the more modern form used today in France.

Indians: I have tried to be relatively accurate in the portrayal of Indians, although I may have used some license. Indians who lived in civilization did occasionally speak good French; they seemed to have found it easier to learn than the southern tribes found English, and the French missions made a great attempt to teach French to the Indians. Marie l'Incarnation, whom you may remember from the first book, went so far as to write an Algonquin dictionary. Although many Frenchmen could speak various Indian dialects, she found it much easier for Indians to learn French than Frenchmen to learn Algonquin.

Originally these Native Americans were relatively peaceful with some exceptions such as the battles between the Iroquois of the east and the Huron. As they became more involved with the Europeans, especially the British, they became less peaceful. In this book we begin to see some western tribes who, according to history, were more warlike.

Maps: I have included maps at the beginning of chapters where they become appropriate.

. Genealogy: At the end of the story I have also included lists of descendant (three generations) for François* Allard from the first book and Jean-Baptiste* Allard for the second and third books. I have also included the descendants of the first Henri (Indian).

THE ALLARDS
BOOK TWO: THE HUNTER
SUMMARY

At 11, the third son of François* Allard, Jean-Baptiste*, has more interest in the wilderness than farming. On a hunt, he and his Indian friend, Joseph, encounter Iroquois looking to attack their village. The boys foil the raid and are regarded as heroes.

Years later they help Antoine Cadillac start a fort at Michillimackinac. While scouting for Cadillac, they find LaSalle's lost ship, *Griffon,* filled with furs. When Cadillac returns to Charlesbourg some years later to again hire the men to start a "city in the wilderness" at the straits of *Détroit*, Jean-Baptiste* and Joseph meet Pierre Roy and Joseph Parent, voyageurs who will influence their lives.

Jean-Baptiste* marries the girl next door, Anne-Elizabeth* Pageot, and Joseph marries Monique de Baptiste, a *métis* or mixed blooded girl, and takes her last name. In Montréal François* and Jean-Baptiste* meet Elizabeth* Price, an English girl who returns the medallion François* had given an Indian many years before. François* passes it and his half of the wampum necklace to Jean-Baptiste*.

Serving with local militia, Jean-Baptiste* and Joseph take three prisoners: A poor Englishman, a slave, and an English officer who soon dies. Once again an agent of Cadillac asks the men to help on a trip to Louisiana. On this voyage they meet Jean* Casse dit Saint-Aubin who becomes a patriarch of Détroit, and Soaring Eagle, an ancient legendary Huron chief.

After their return, old François* dies in the woods. The story leaves Jean-Baptiste* pondering what will befall his family.

THE ALLARDS
To 1761

François* Allard~1671~Jeanne* Anguille
Québec
1639-1725 1647-1711
Normandie, France Loire Valley, France
I
Jean-Baptiste*Allard~1705~Anne-Elizabeth* Pageot
Québec
1676-1748 1686-1748
Québec Québec
I
Pierre* Allard~1743~Marie-Angelique* Bergevin
Québec
1716-1759 1722-1788
Québec Québec
I
Jacques* Allard
1746
Québec

THE ALLARDS
BOOK THREE
PEACE AND WAR

MAIN CHARACTERS

The Allard Family:

Jean-Baptiste* Allard: *Habitant* of Bourg-Royal in Québec.

Anne-Elizabeth* Pageot: His wife.

Pierre* Allard: Their son, an inventor and adventurer.

Marie-Angélique* Bergevin: His wife.

Jacques* Allard: Their son.

The de Baptiste Family:

Joseph de Baptiste: Algonquin, best friend of Jean-Baptiste* Allard.

Toussaint de Baptiste: His *métis* or mixed blood son, best friend of Pierre* Allard.

PART ONE

THE PEACE

Chapter 1

Anchor Bay - Michigan February 2007:

Becky Gauthier pulled her old Saturn into the parking lot of Tony's bar on the shore of Anchor Bay on Lake Saint Clair. As she stepped out she was greeted by a light hard snow hitting her face from a wind off the lake. "This is colder than shit!" she muttered to herself as she walked to the bar. This had to be the low point of her new career in journalism.

Having joined the staff of the *Detroit Free Press* less than a year ago as a cub reporter, she had been covering stories on the history of Detroit. Her editor told her that every few years it was traditional to do an article on a real piece of Detroit history and culture, the iceboat. Born in Louisiana, Becky had never really heard of such a thing, but wanting to succeed in her new career, she jumped at the chance.

Entering Tony's she found it just as anticipated, a fog of smoke, the smell of fried food and stale beer, and country and western on the jukebox. She made her way to the bar and inquired after her contact. The bartender directed her to a man in a snowmobile suit at a table drinking, of all things, coffee. She went over and introduced herself and he stood, "Ben Champine, welcome."

As they sat, he said, "I suppose the first thing we should do is take a ride."
Becky was prepared for this situation but not overly enthusiastic. Ben continued, "I hope you brought something warmer." Fortunately her boyfriend's roommate had warned her of this possibility and supplied her with snowmobile gear. She indicated she had come prepared and retuned to the Saturn for her wardrobe. She assembled in the ladies room and reappeared feeling like a cross between Star Trek and the little brother in "A Christmas Story" who was too bundled to lower his arms.

Ben indicated that she looked 'swell' and they left the bar through the back door. Although the sun was out and the sky was blue, she was greeted again with a blast of fine, hard snow. She put on the helmet with the face shield and was at least protected from the pelting snow. A number of small boats were at the shore, and several out on the bay as well as a number of small structures that looked like outhouses from her Louisiana childhood. "Fishing shanties," Ben explained.

He led her to a small blue boat with *Suicide Attempt* stenciled on the side. He directed her into the front of the two-man craft and showed her two handles. "Hold on to these," he shouted over the wind and through her helmet. Raising the single sail, he pushed forward and jumped in behind her. Becky was suddenly glad for the snowmobile suits as she realized that their arrangement in the small boat might require them to get married in some middle-eastern countries.

“Ever been in an iceboat?” Ben shouted. She nodded no and he replied, “You’re in one now.” This was the last normal thing she remembered.

The boat lurched forward and soon attained an unbelievable speed. Becky was unable to separate fear from exhilaration from disbelief. The ice surface and the surroundings became an absolute blur. Had it not been for her face shield she realized she would have lost her face. She was also very glad to have used the ladies room when she went to change.

After going about two miles in what seemed like a minute, they made a sharp turn that would have thrown her from the boat had it been not been for the handles which were now her two new best friends. The boat turned with the wind at their side as Ben shouted something that sounded like ‘hiking’. Before she could respond, the boat rose on one outrigger and the speed became unbelievable. They seemed to be at a right angle to the earth and she was certain that death was imminent. They returned to upright as quickly as they had risen and headed toward Tony’s.

Champine brought the boat to a quick but accurate stop, quickly lowered the sail, and helped Becky back to earth. After he helped her stagger back into the bar where they removed their headgear, he said, “If you come some time when there’s a good wind I can show you a real ride.” Sinking into a chair the cub reporter replied, “Could I have a beer please?”

They moved to a table in the corner where Ben ordered a beer and a diet coke. “Pilots don’t drink until the last ride is over, at least that’s the rule.”

Becky set her helmet on the table and unzipped the suit to the waist and slid out of the top part. Taking a long sip of beer she started, “I have information from old articles at the paper. As I understand it, this is a sort of club?”

Tony’s was not big on glassware, so popping the tap top on his can of coke, Ben replied, “The iceboat became popular in the Detroit area around the depression. The *Detroit News* ran a plan on how to build a small boat at home, and the *DN* iceboat, named for the paper, was born. With revisions, it has remained the classic boat in the area, in fact in the entire U. S. and Canada.

“The Lake Saint Clair Iceboat Club was formed around 1934. Typically we sail in Saint Clair Shores, but the last three winters have been so warm we have been coming to Anchor Bay where the ice is more secure. The big cove in the ‘Shores’, which the French called *l’Anse Creuse* is, however, better suited for sailing and racing.”

Becky asked, “How old is the sport?”

“No one really knows, I’ve heard it started in Holland on the canals in the late seventeenth or early eighteenth centuries. My grandfather said people here have done it as long as any one could remember.”

“Has your family always been involved?”

“Actually my father never sailed, but my grandfather did. The first time he took me for a ride I was five. I was hooked ever since. I even bought a house on the lake so I could keep my boat there, but as I mentioned, that hasn’t worked out recently.” Then pausing for a minute he said, “There **is** this board.”

“Board?”

"Actually a carved picture of an ice boat, it's very old but no one knows anything more about it. A man in the original club named Archie Allor gave it to my grandfather and now I have it."

As the waitress passed, Becky ordered another beer and continued to collect details. After finishing she was starting to relax and impulsively asked, "How about another ride?"

"Sure." And winking, "This time I'll even make it a nice ride." As they stood up she realized that Ben was very attractive and about her age. She also noticed he did not wear a wedding ring.

Ben gave her a small earpiece, "Put this on your ear and we can talk in the boat." Becky felt much more comfortable in the small boat this time, maybe the two beers had something to do with it. She also felt better snuggled into Ben now she had met him. This time they took off more slowly.

Ben began to explain, "The difference between this and a water sail boat is that there is virtually no side slipping and no forward friction. Everything is turned into speed."

They sailed along the western shore of the bay, "These were all once cottages, but each year there are more mini-mansions." They reached a long point and he explained, "Metropolitan Beach Park is on the other side of this point. We'll turn and cross the bay here to avoid the thinner ice out in the lake."

As they turned to the east, the south wind was at their side, "Now we can 'reach', and get some speed. We'll begin to rise on one outrigger, we call that 'hiking', you'll get used to it, it's the best part of ice boating." Indeed they picked up speed and the boat began to float like magic on the port outrigger.

Using her microphone for the first time Becky asked, "What do you think is our speed?"

"I have an electronic speedometer, it says 40 mph. The ice is smooth here, do you want to see what we can get today?"

Swallowing hard but being pulled by the thrill, she replied, "OK."

Ben adjusted the mainsheet and they gradually accelerated. Becky was in awe. He said, "We just hit 60, I think that's fast enough for today," and he brought the boat to a gradual stop. Indicating the flatlands to the east he said, "This is the beginning of the St. Clair Flats, the shipping channel comes through here. The two old lighthouses ahead no longer function but have been preserved as historical landmarks. Behind us is Walpole Island, an Indian reservation and hunting and fishing preserve." Then offhandedly, "Want to drive?"

Becky hesitated, "I don't think…"

"Ever steer a small sailboat?"

Letting her New Orleans accent reach its peak, "Why sir I was raised in a small sailboat."

"Then there is nothing else to know," and getting out, he pushed her back. "This is the mainsheet and here's the rudder. You control the rudder with these two foot pedals. If you go too fast, let off on the sheet or steer closer to the wind. There's only the mainsail so it's pretty straightforward. It's just that everything happens faster." He hopped in the front and the boat took off.

Becky soon got the hang of it and began to realize she was becoming an ice boater. She began to maneuver and even managed to hike and return to earth safely. When they arrived back at Tony's, she said with no lack of enthusiasm, "Thank you! That was wonderful."

Picking up his lines, he said, "It's about time to go. If you want to follow me home, I'll show you the old carved picture."

Becky agreed and helped him pull the boat up to his trailer. She was impressed at how quick and easy the procedure was.

"We'll follow Jefferson home, I'm on the lake just south of Twelve Mile Road." He handed her a card with the address. She had never been this route before. Like most people she always took the expressway. Back in her car she thought to herself, "I wonder if this is like the old 'come up and see my etchings trick'." Secretly she hoped it was.

Chapter 2

<u>Saint Clair Shores - The Same Day:</u>

Ben's house sat on a lot of about 100 feet square. The house was quite close to the lake and the main floor was high over a walkout basement with a spectacular view of the lake from the main room. Becky excused herself to use the bathroom. When she saw the mirror she almost screamed. Her hair was plastered down from the helmet, and her wind-whipped face looked like a lobster.

Returning to the main room she said, "You should have told me I look as though I was dragged behind the iceboat."

Ben laughed and handed her a glass of white wine, "You look like an ice boater. I think you look great. I hope you don't just like beer."

"Not at all, thank you, this is perfect." Looking about and trying not to be too forward she continued, "Nice house, you live here alone."

"I do now. I had a girlfriend but she didn't like the cold or going fast so she had to go." This made Becky think of her current boyfriend of convenience, Rodney, whose idea of excitement was fantasy football and watching NASCAR on television. Ben continued, "I bought this place four years ago. I learned from the deed this land originally belonged to my third great-grandfather. His name was Joseph* Champine, but then they said Champagne. His great grandfather came from the Champagne region of France to Québec. Actually the family name was Huyet, but like a lot of French names it was changed to the region of his origin and later to 'Champine'. The farm house was just to the north on the corner of what is now Lake Drive and Jefferson."

As she perused his pictures around his desk, she suddenly said, "This is in New Orleans!"

He looked at the photo, "I stop there sometimes when I go to dive in the Islands."

She looked up like he had two heads, "You dive?"

"Actually yes, I have a degree in Marine Biology from the University of Michigan and now it is part of my job."

Becky was now having trouble remembering what Rodney looked like, "My father has a dive business in New Orleans. I've been diving since I was four years old."

She then noticed the wood carving, "This is the picture?"

He took it from the wall, "Yes. As you can see it's old and the boat looks like it is very primitive."

Becky noted, "This has the rudder in the back."

"Very good. Actually all early iceboats were 'stern-steering'. Even today some larger ones are, but the small sport boats of today almost all have the rudder in front."

It showed an iceboat on a river or small lake and across the water was a cliff with a wooden fort. "I've always thought that this was supposed to be old Detroit, but the cliff seems too high."

Becky studied it; "You know, there's a guy at the Detroit Library who helped me on a piece about Detroit History this autumn. He knew all sorts of stuff and he might have an idea. His name was Jim, Jim Trombley."

Ben smiled, "I never thought of him. I know him pretty well. He has helped us on some things at work."

Becky replied, "If you don't mind, I can take it and show it to him on Monday. I have some things to do down there." Then thinking she didn't want to blow things by overstaying her welcome, she said, "I probably had better head home." Looking out the window to the darkness, she exclaimed, "Oh Shit!"

Ben looked out and said, "I should have known when the wind shifted." It was snowing straight sideways and was almost six inches of new snow covered the deck.

Becky said, "I have a confession. I have never mastered driving in the snow."

Ben laughed, "I have an idea. I have lots of food and there are three extra bedrooms each with their own bath. It wouldn't be any trouble."

Becky gave a sly smile and with her best southern belle accent, "But sir, can you be trusted?"

He raised his hand and said, "Ice boater's promise."

She smiled back and to herself, "Damn!"

He continued, "The first room on the top of the stairs is best, and I have put all the girl stuff Melinda left in there. I'm going to clean up and then put dinner together, help yourself."

Becky looked around the bedroom, well decorated, comfortable, great bathroom. It appeared that although she and Melinda did not agree on the subject of iceboats they did have similar tastes in cosmetics. Becky took out her cell phone, and getting her roommate's machine, she said, "Lisa, it's Bec. I won't be home tonight because of the snow. I'm staying with a friend, just wanted to let you know I'm not dead on I-696. If Rodney calls, tell him something has come up and I have to cancel tomorrow and next weekend, bye."

After a shower and fixing her hair, she began to think there was hope. Her Tulane sweatshirt was pretty used and Melinda had left a sweater just her size, but after thinking it over, she thought she'd play it safe with Tulane. Going downstairs she saw that Ben Champine cleaned up very nicely. He had opened a bottle of red wine and was working on steak, "I hope you're not a vegetarian."

"They're illegal in Louisiana."

"So tell me about your father's dive business."

"'Cajun Coves' business and pleasure."

"Somehow you don't look Cajun."

"You should see Daddy, mostly French trapper, some Indian, maybe a little runaway slave."

"But the blue-eyed blond thing?"

"Mama's 100% Dutch, but Island Dutch."

"Huh?"

"Mama's people came to the Islands about the same time Daddy's came to Canada. They met in college working on a dive project in Saint-Martin."

After dinner Ben poured glasses of Calvados, Becky asked, "Tell me about your job."

"I work with a guy named John Chartier, who has a boutique dive and underwater exploration operation in Northern Michigan. I do a lot of research in the winter but it also gives me enough time to go ice boating. We found the wreck of LaSalle's *Griffon* last summer in northern

Lake Michigan. Your paper had an article on it. We hope to do some more with it this summer."

At that, he arose and announced that he was exhausted and ready for bed. Becky looked up with her 'come-hither' eyes and said, "How about another Calvados."

Ben smiled and said, "An ice boater never breaks his word."

"Well, will you do one thing for me?"

"What?"

"Will you take me ice boating again?"

"Very Likely."

That night Becky's dreams were filled with exotic dives and iceboats hiking at break-neck speeds. The morning was as clear and bright as the night had been stormy. Getting a look out Ben's window she remarked on the setting. "I can see why you would like your boat here."

"Maybe next year. In the early days the boats were kept just north of here. There was a small tavern there run by a guy named Eddie Forton. I think it was Forton's Tavern, but it was torn down in the early sixties. After that they were south of here either at the Veterans 'Bruce Post' or by the Blue Goose Inn across the street."

After picking up the dishes, Becky took the carving and promised to call when she had talked with Jim Trombley. She gave him an impetuous and enthusiastic kiss that should have removed any questions of her opinion of the weekend.

Monday afternoon Ben's cell rang, "Hello."

“Ben, its Becky, Becky Gauthier,” the clarification was probably not necessary. “Jim has some interesting thoughts on the picture. He suggested that the three of us get together for dinner this week to go over it.”

“Fine with me, I’m free all week.”

“How about tomorrow? Can you pick me up outside the *Free Press* office at about six?”

“Sure fine, see you then.”

When he picked her up, she looked even better than the night at his house. Sliding onto the seat she said, “Trombley said he’d meet us at a restaurant in Windsor, *The Cajun*. He promised that it’s the real thing. Do you know where it is?”

“Every ice boater knows where it is.”

The Cajun was a short distance from the Detroit to Windsor Tunnel. It was a dark place covered with fishnets and everything else a Detroiter would expect in such a restaurant. The food was more authentic that Becky would have guessed and she exclaimed in her best Louisiana accent, “Best craw-daddies this side of Baton Rouge, Sugah.”

After dinner Trombley said that the owner had agreed to let him use his office where the light was better.

“First of all,” he started, I can’t believe you have had this all this time and never asked anybody about it.”

“Well…”

“ The piece is fairly old, I would guess eighteenth century, and the carving is typical native-Canadian style of the period. The setting is undoubtedly Québec City. If you look carefully the flag on the fort is the Fleur de Lis, which if accurate, would put it before 1760. I haven't heard of any iceboats at that time, have you?"

"No."

"And look at this in the corner, very small 'T.d.B.' if we could find anything else by this person, it would be of help. I'd like to keep it for a while and do some more research."

Ben had no concerns and with that the evening came to an end. As Ben dropped Becky off at her car he said, "How about 10 AM at Tony's this Saturday?"

"Perfect."

Saturday's weather was perfect and the sailing was even more exciting than the week before. By midday Becky Gauthier, who two years ago had never seen snow, realized that she had two new loves. This time Becky brought a change of clothes and again spent the night in Saint Clair Shores. However this time there was no snowstorm, and no ice boater's promise.

Chapter 3

Palace of Versailles - October 1725:

The Cardinal hurried down the hall and knocked at the door. It was opened by a grandly dressed attendant. The Cardinal entered and was greeted by the older man who arose from his desk saying, "You wished to see me your Excellency?"

The Cardinal replied, "Yes, Monsieur le Duc, it is of course about his Majesty."

"Ah, what now."

The Cardinal continued, "It seems that when you served as his Regent, he was agreeable with you making the decisions of state. Now, however, he is feeling pressured by you to make his own decisions."

The Duc replied, "That is exactly what I want. He has been King now three years and has yet to make a decision aside from where to hunt and which wench to send for each evening. For seven years before his coronation as Louis XV, I tried to instill into him his great-grandfather's zeal and competence for ruling. I tell you Cardinal, I am growing older and becoming weary of the job"

"Yes, well that is what this is about. It seems that his Majesty came to me three days ago and asked if I would serve as Governor and his chief minister and advisor. He said he rather I make decisions and allow him to 'live his life as he wishes.' Truly sir either one of us would be a more capable ruler, but God has not deemed it so. The best we can do is help promote the policies that will best advance the future of France."

"Your Excellency, you have my agreement. There is nothing I would rather do than retire to my country estate to live out my remaining years in tranquility."

At that moment the door burst open and a young man entered. Taller than the others, and in his late teens, he was strikingly handsome with long straight black hair and deep-set, intense dark eyes. His boots were covered with mud, which was being removed from the carpet even as he walked by two servants. He dropped into an ornate chair and propped his muddy boots up on to another. The Duc and the Cardinal grimaced. To a third servant who followed the other two but did no work, the boy said, "Maurice, have two courtesans brought right after dinner, blond and red head, none of the same from this week. And, Maurice, have them washed well."

Then turning to the older men he said, "Well, gentlemen, have you been discussing my plan or plotting my assassination?" Turning to the Duc d'Orléans, "Uncle Philippe, you have served France and me well, and I appreciate your desire to turn me into your grandfather, but it is not to be. I am the King, and can be the King, but I cannot abide with all the damned details. Cardinal Fleury here is a capable man and has no unreal expectations in my regard. I am going to announce him as my chief minister at the New Year."

Philippe the Duc d'Orléans arose, "Your Majesty, this is your decision and I will certainly abide with it, but I implore you to remember that God has made you the King of France. Your people and your country depend on your leadership. Do not forget who you are."

Cardinal André Hercule de Fleury then spoke, "Your Majesty, if you are to make me your advisor, I will serve to the best of my abilities; however, I should have at least your tacit approval of decisions. There is again the question of your colonies."

The boy returned, "Again with the colonies? Wild animals and savages. If I didn't have to take a boat, I could go there for the hunt, but as it is, they are of little interest to me."

Fleury continued, "Sir, France controls most of the New World, if we do not act prudently, we risk take over by England."

"The Hell with England! They signed the Treaty of Utrecht with my great-grandfather and now we have peace. Now I must go dine before the wenches arrive."

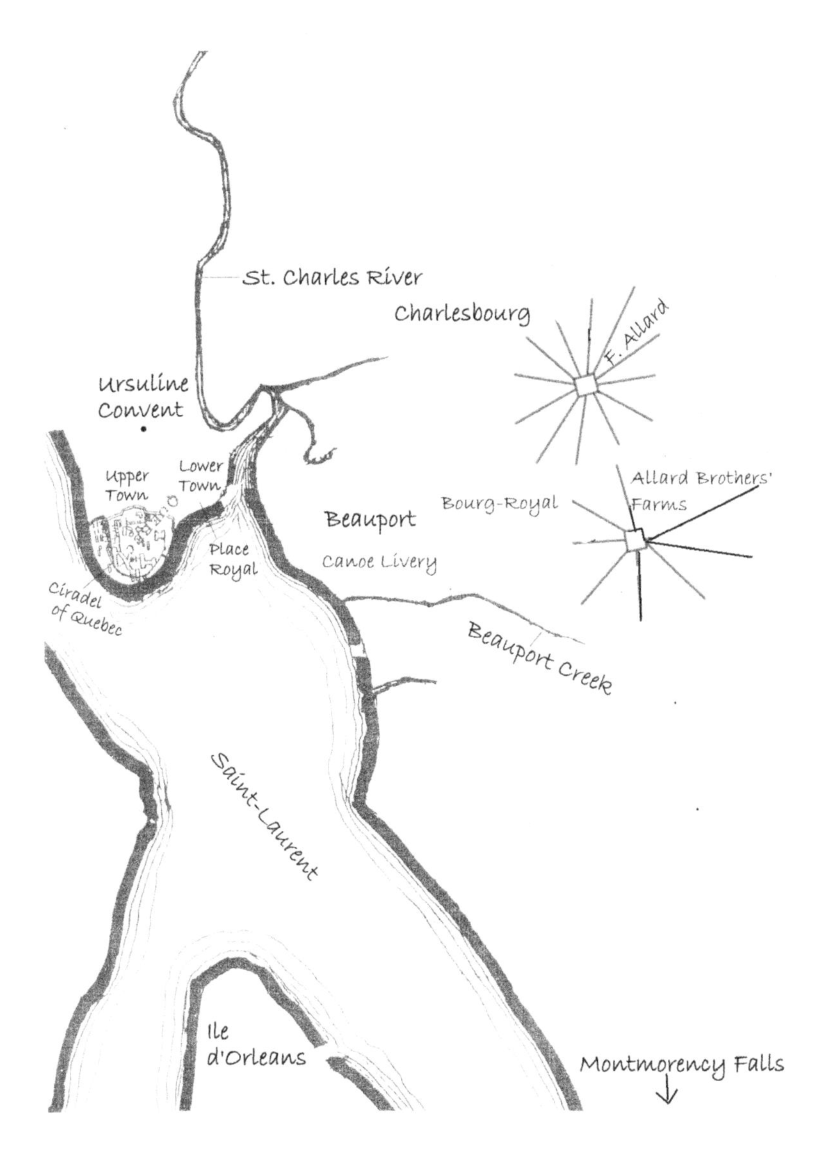
St. Charles River
Charlesbourg
F. Allard
Ursuline
Convent
Upper
Town
Lower
Town
Allard Brothers'
Farms
Bourg-Royal
Beauport
Place
Royal
Canoe Livery
Ciradel
of Quebec
Beauport Creek
Saint-Laurent
Ile
d'Orleans
Montmorency Falls

Québec 1726

Chapter 4

Pierre* Allard

There are three times of the year when Québec is spectacular by anyone's estimation: January, when the world is white, cold and clean, and the country is wild and hostile yet quiet and tranquil at the same time. October, when nature's pallet of color is beyond compare, the cool north wind blows through red, yellow and orange, and animals are everywhere. Then there is June when the world is green and blue, as the sky and the rivers compete for the true meaning of blue, and hills are covered with the deepest green imaginable. The fine season lies entirely ahead.

Québec City, the Saint-Laurent River - June 10, 1726:

This was just such a June day, when the blue river blended with the blue sky and only a faint breeze rippled its flow. The green hills surrounded the river, broken only by the gray cliffs of the upper town of Québec, rising to the imposing fort of the Citadel of Saint-Louis on their summit. The Saint-Laurent was filled with canoes of onlookers giving the appropriate festive appearance to the occasion.

As he stared intently toward his goal across the river and below the Citadel, Pierre* could scarcely contain his excitement. Today he and Toussaint were finally going to prove themselves. They had entered the race last year, but at nine years of age they were the youngest. This year they were bigger, stronger and better prepared. They watched as the men crossed the river. The older boys would be next, and last it would be their turn.

For the past one hundred years, French Canadians had managed to find fun in the hardships of the wilderness. For many years the canoe race from Beauport to Québec was a high point of the early season. Begun as a race between the various voyageurs who were home following the trapping season, it had expanded in the past few years to include the children, grouped simply into older and younger boys. It even had a sponsor. The Langlois-Abraham Ship Works provided support and prizes, but the bragging right of winning was the real prize.

Pierre*'s brothers, François and Thomas, ages twenty and eighteen were in the men's class. Although they had no chance against the real voyageurs, they still enjoyed the race. Their brother Jean-Baptiste, age sixteen, entered with his friend Pierre* Renaud, age fourteen, in the older boys' class, and Pierre* Allard and Toussaint de Baptiste, both ten years old, were in with the younger boys.

Finally their turn came and the young canoeists lined up as the starting shot was fired. During the race, adults in canoes lined the course. Their primary job was to rescue any youngster who may lose his balance. As was customary, a few of the more excited and less experienced required rescue. Pierre* and Toussaint were, however, very skilled for their young age. Using their practiced stroke and cadence, they managed to hold an early lead until near the finish line at Place Royal. Their only real opponents were the two Parent boys two and three years older. Just at the end, the older lads pulled ahead and won by a scant few feet.

The crowd cheered and Monsieur Langlois made a short congratulatory speech and gave the boys their ribbons. He remarked that Pierre* and Toussaint were the youngest ever to finish in the running as he presented them their red ribbon. Pierre* realized that he should be elated but he was already plotting for next year. Their parents collected them to go to the picnic in the town square by the cathedral. Later the boys returned to their canoe and headed home to Charlesbourg.

<u>The Abraham-Langlois Ship Works - Two Weeks Later:</u>

As Louis Langlois made his morning rounds of the yard, he was thanking God for how good life now was in Québec. He had inherited the shipyard of his father, Noel*, and now at age forty was one of the most influential men in the colony. The peace with England had continued since 1713 and business was now more important than security. He had even heard that at this years' *rendez-vous* by *Trois Rivieres,* English traders as well as a few Iroquois were in attendance.

Business was booming. Although the large ships were still produced in Larochelle in France, his yard made many smaller vessels for North American trade and fishing off the coast of Acadie and Newfoundland. They had also expanded into canoes and smaller craft and had a good relation with the Morin carriage works with whom they combined their skills to make sleds and other devices of transportation.

As he finished his rounds he saw two familiar young faces entering the yard. "Well, if it is not the two Musketeers; are you here to work or visit?"

Pierre* Allard, was the son of Jean-Baptiste* Allard, a well-known Charlesbourg habitant who had gained much early notoriety as a guard for Antoine Cadillac. Jean-Baptiste* had accompanied the great man on many of his explorations into the frontier. Pierre*'s grandfather François* had been well regarded by Louis's father, Noel*. The other boy was Toussaint de Baptiste, Pierre*'s *métis* friend who was the son of Jean-Baptiste* Allard's long-time Indian companion, Joseph de Baptiste.

The two young boys were inseparable and came frequently to the shipyard to work and learn, and occasionally take discarded material to use in their various odd projects.

Toussaint said, "We have come to work, Monsieur Langlois."

Louis congratulated them on their second place finish in the race, "You know that no one your age has ever done so well."

Pierre* replied, "Thank you, Monsieur, but we have no intention of settling for second place in the future."

Langlois chuckled to himself, realizing that these were exactly the sort of boys Québec needed. He gave them some chores and went about his own work.

At the end of the day the boys returned carrying a pile of cloth. Pierre* said, "Monsieur Biville said that you had no use for this. Could we have it in exchange for today's' chores?"

Laughing, Langlois replied, "That came from the two-masted fishing boat on the dock. It is torn beyond repair and if you will haul it away, you may have it and be paid for today as well."

Pierre* questioned further, "What are the rules of the canoe race?"

Langlois replied, "Only that there are only two people in each canoe."

"Does it matter what sort of canoe?"

"Not really but everyone would want the lightest and fastest."

The boys thanked him profusely and took off. Langlois wondered what they could possibly be up to this time.

Chapter 5

Bourg-Royal, Charlesbourg, Québec, Canada - June 1726:

Bourg-Royal had grown steadily during the past twenty years. Twenty family farms now ringed the square with the farms laid out like slices of pie in a square pan. Bourg-Royal was part of the town of Charlesbourg, a similar square directly to the west. The term Bourg-Royal was still used allowing distinction of one square from the other.

The Charlesbourg square held the church of Saint-Charles de Boromée, a few businesses and the Blue Goose Tavern and Inn. The Bourg-Royal Square was merely a village green. The farms of three Allard siblings occupied the northeast corner of Bourg-Royal. Moving clockwise, the first farm belonged to André Allard, the oldest sibling, and his wife Anne LeMarche-Allard. Next was the farm of the oldest Allard sister, Marie Allard-Villeneuve, and her husband Charles. Lastly was the farm of their younger brother, Jean-Baptiste* Allard, and his wife Anne-Elizabeth* Pageot-Allard.

The Allard complex, as the farms were collectively called, was more prosperous than most. The Allards were all ordinary *habitant* farmers but had been rich in two ways. First was a sum of money earned by Jean-Baptiste* and his friend Joseph in 1711 on a mission for the King. This had been used to secure land, buy livestock and equipment, and expand more rapidly than most other farms. The second was children; the three farms were blessed with a total of thirty-one children. André and Anne had eight children, five boys and three girls, ages ranging from 30 to 14. Marie and Charles had thirteen children, seven girls and six boys, ranging from 20 to 1 year. Their oldest daughter had died four years earlier at the age of 16. Jean-Baptiste* and Anne-Elizabeth* had ten children, seven boys and three girls, ranging from twenty years to one month.

In addition, two Indian families lived on the land. Joseph de Baptiste and his *métis,* or mixed-blood, wife with their son Toussaint and two daughters lived by Jean-Baptiste*. On André's farm lived Joseph's brother Henri with his wife and two sons. Although Henri's family lived in a traditional Indian camp, Joseph's family lived in a simple house. The French and Indian families were extremely close as their families had lived together now for three generations.

Although strip farms had developed on the periphery of Charlesbourg and Bourg-Royal, the land behind the Allard farms was vacant, and the land was theirs clear to the Laurentian Mountains. Hedgerows separated most farms in Québec, but the hedges between the Allard farms were sparse as much of the farming was done jointly. André and Charles were avid farmers, but Jean-Baptiste* was more of a hunter and trapper. However this made for a convenient division of labor. André and Anne were more bookish than the other parents and held a home school for the children twice a week.

Today Jean-Baptiste*'s five oldest boys were moving rocks. The three oldest, François, age twenty, Thomas, age eighteen, and Jean-Baptiste, age sixteen were digging and levering the large granite boulders that littered the Québec landscape. These three were the heartthrobs of all the town girls. All strong and handsome like their father, they were excellent lacrosse players and skilled hunters. Their four younger brothers also worshiped them.

The two middle brothers worked the ropes and the horse. André, age 12 drove the horse while Pierre*, age 10 along with his friend Toussaint, also 10, worked the ropes. This was particularly difficult as the ropes would frequently slip and much labor was necessary to rearrange them. At the end of the day they surveyed the collection of boulders they had pulled to the side of the field. Then they looked at the large number yet to be hauled, not to mention the holes yet to be filled. On the way back to dinner young Pierre* spoke up, "There must be an easier way to do this."

The older boys stopped and looked at their odd brother. If nothing else, Pierre* was not shy. In addition the others knew that he was a tinker and had produced the occasional good idea. François laughed, "Tell you what, Pierre* you can grow to be seven feet tall and carry them for us."

His little brother persisted, "I have an idea and I am going to work on it." Regarding the youngster, François could not help being struck by his eyes. While all the other Allards had dark brown eyes, Pierre*'s eyes were a striking green. His grandfather, François* had one brown and one green eye, it was said to run in the family, but the closest thing seen in the Québec Allards were Pierre*'s two deep-set green eyes.

Dinner at Jean-Baptiste* Allard's was served at a long table large enough to accommodate all. Jean-Baptiste* sat at the head and Anne-Elizabeth* at the other end. The five older boys sat according to age placed on one side and the other children also according to age on the other side. First was the oldest sister, Marie-Therese, age 14, then another François, age 7. He was called 'Franny" to avoid confusion with his oldest brother, also a François. Then came Jacques, age 4 and Marie-Madeleine, age 3. The youngest, Marie-Charlotte, just one month old, slept in a crib in the corner.

After dinner the four oldest boys took advantage of the long June daylight and went to the nearby stream to fish. Although he was invited, Pierre* went to get Toussaint and they went to the barn to tinker. The following morning when the boys left to face the boulders, Pierre and Toussaint had an additional piece of equipment.

When they arrived at the first stone, a particularly large pink boulder, Pierre* and Toussaint convinced the older boys to try their idea.

"We want to pull this stone south, so we will dig a narrow trench on the north and around the sides."

After they had done this, Pierre* continued, "Now put my sling around the stone," and he produced a large piece of heavy canvas. "Monsieur Langlois gave me this; it is part of an old sail."

After the sling was in place, he said, "We dig a trench on the south that is long and slopes down to the bottom of the stone. We put the dirt just removed on the north side of the stone with the sling between the dirt and the stone."

Having accomplished this, he directed the next step, "We connect the ropes to the sling where I have knotted it to avoid tearing," and he attached the ropes to the horse and the stone began to move up the sloped trench with ease. As the stone moved, the dirt fell in behind and even if the horse stopped or backed up, the dirt filled in behind the stone to prevent it from backsliding.

The stone moved with little effort to the side of the field. There was little effort required to finish filling the hole, and the project had taken less than half the time of the older method. Even better, the boys had expended about one tenth of the energy required the old way.

By noon Thomas said, "We had better slow down, Papa will never believe this."

At the end of the day surveying that they had moved more than twice as many stones as the day before, François said, "You just keep tinkering, Pierre*. It is what you do best." Pierre* and Toussaint could not have been more pleased.

Bourg-Royal - October 1726:

As autumn descended, the colors turned and the harvest was over. It was now time for the traditional *rendez-vous*, a totally Canadian event where trappers, Indians and some brave *habitants* went to a camp near *Trois-Rivieres* to trade, drink and raise hell. Jean-Baptiste* and Joseph rarely missed this event. The other men were not adventuresome enough to attend but they allowed some of older boys to go. This year André's two oldest boys who still lived at home, Thomas, age 21, and Jean-Charles, age

18, would go. Their two older brothers were now married and on their own. Jean-Baptiste*'s three oldest would go as well. The night before, they all met at Joseph's to prepare. The younger boys came to watch and dream of the day when they would be invited. After preparations, they sat by a fire and Jean-Baptiste* and Joseph told tales of their travels with Antoine Cadillac. Pierre* never tired of these same old tales, and always asked to hear his favorite which was the boat trip to Cuba where they rescued the slaves.

The following day the men and older boys left for the *rendez-vous*. After chores, Pierre* asked his mother if he and Toussaint could go off and hunt before dinner. She agreed and the boys took their bows, stopped by the barn for a sack and disappeared toward the mountains. Their mothers had agreed to let them hunt overnight after the week's chores were done. She thought the boys were going to scout out the area.

Two days later as agreed they left for the overnight. Anne-Elizabeth* asked Pierre* to try to bring home pheasant. He replied, "We are after deer."

His mother smiled wondering how these two small boys would track and return with a deer overnight, but she knew that anything was possible with these two. She watched them disappear with their bows. They would not get rifles until they were twelve; however, her boys, as their father did, all seemed to favor the bow. She was a bit apprehensive as this was their most ambitious trip to date. However, she realized that they were skilled for their age having been well instructed by their fathers.

She could not help recall the famous day many years ago when she was only three years old that Jean-Baptiste* and Joseph had foiled an Iroquois attack on the town. She realized that, fortunately, Indian attacks were now history, and the peace with the eastern Indians of the Iroquois nation and English was well established. Jean-Baptiste* had said there would actually be both English and Iroquois at the *rendez-vous*.

The following afternoon, she went out for a walk hoping to see the returning hunters. She smelled fire at the Indian camp area behind Joseph's house and went to investigate. She saw the two boys had indeed returned and were processing their kill. She was astounded at the sight. "It looks like you two were more than lucky."

Pierre* looked up with his bright green eyes and replied, "Papa says that hunting has nothing to do with luck."

She shook her head in amazement and returning to the house she saw the other boys and the men returning from the River. They were carrying a number of treasures secured at the *rendez-vous.* She greeted Jean-Baptiste* who asked how things had been in their absence. Anne-Elizabeth* replied, "Go over to Joseph's camp and see what your son has been up to."

The fathers and older boys went around in back of Joseph's house and saw Pierre* and Toussaint working on four large deer hanging from trees.

The men realized that for these two youngsters to get one deer on a overnight hunt would have been amazing, but four was unbelievable. François was first to ask, "How did you get these?"

Pierre* merely replied, "Secret method."

His brother grabbed him around the neck and easily subdued him, "I'll show you a secret."

Beginning to giggle, Pierre* replied. "OK I'll tell you at dinner," and the older group departed in amazement.

After grace was said and everyone had been served, Jean-Baptiste* said, "Well, *mon petit*, your brothers and I are all ears."

Pierre* began, "Papa always says that the hunter should go to where his prey will be and wait."

François interrupted, "But these are deer, they don't have a nest."

Pierre* continued, "Some days ago, Toussaint and I collected rotted dropped apples at the orchard and took them out to a clearing in the woods. Twice later in the week we left more apples out there. On the overnight we put more down and waited. At dusk the deer came to eat. We only shot four because we knew we could only get that many back to Joseph's camp. We waited for the prey, but this time they were trained to come."

Jean-Baptiste* laughed and said, "With all this venison, it looks as if the cows are all safe this winter."

Québec - June 1727:

As the day of the canoe race approached, Pierre* and Toussaint spent many long evenings 'tinkering' in the barn. On the day of the race, they were up well before the sun and down at the Beauport canoe livery. They had taken their canoe to the downstream end of the livery, out of sight behind some trees.

The race proceeded as usual. The men's race was run first, then the older boys'. The younger boys were gathering at the start by the time anyone saw the canoe of Pierre* and Toussaint. Onlookers tried to make out what they had done. Finally someone said, "They have outriggers on the sides, what are they thinking?"

They were paddling and almost to the starting line when the gun sounded the beginning of the race. To everyone's amazement they raised a mast and a sail. By the time they had it secure, the other boys were near the center of the river, but the Allard canoe took off like a shot. There was a fresh wind from the southwest that was directly at the side of the canoe. It began to raise onto an outrigger and the boys controlled it well and continued to gain speed.

They soon began to overtake the other canoes and the crowd responded with a combination of laughter, cheering and disbelief. They were approaching the finish one hundred feet in front of the nearest canoe and pulling even farther ahead when a large gust caused them to hike too far and the craft capsized.

The boys swam around, lowered the sail and managed to right the boat and paddle to shore well to the back of the pack but to a cheering crowd. As Monsieur Langlois delivered the awards he said, "We have no prize for originality, but if we did there is no doubt where it would go," and the crowd cheered wildly.

Afterward he came to the boys and said, "Come by the ship works tomorrow, I have a job for you."

The following night at dinner, Pierre* explained, "We modeled it after Papa's story of the Indian boats in Cuba. Monsieur Langlois gave us a large damaged sail last year. We used it for our boulder sling as well as for this sail. Next year we shall have it right."

His father added, "Next year you may have some competition."

Chapter 6

Windsor Castle, Windsor, England - Early Winter, 1727:

George looked out at the Windsor countryside. He would rather be hunting than ruling today. Now 44 years old, he had been born, raised and educated to be king. When his father died this past year, he was more than ready to take the reigns of leadership. He did, however, secretly take comfort that he still had Sir Robert to guide him.

The door opened and Sir Robert entered, "Your majesty."

"Sir Robert."

Sir Robert Walpole had been one of his father's closest advisors at the end of his reign and George II expected to count on him as well. He had known the man since he was a child and always had a good relationship with him.

Walpole continued, "Your majesty, I believe we should spend some time today discussing your American Colonies."

The new King replied, "Well yes, loyal subjects, mostly British themselves. They pay taxes, receive protection and trade. What could be a problem?"

Walpole replied, "The problem as I see it is space." Motioning to a map of eastern North America on the desk he continued." We control most of the Atlantic seaboard along with most of the more strategic ports, but we are sending enormous numbers of people to the colonies, and frankly, they are also reproducing like rabbits. We started by giving enormous tracts of land to the gentry who saw fit to settle in the colonies. They control giant estates and simply have no thought of giving that up. If I could start again, I would not have been so generous with the land, but that is in the past.

"The common colonist needs land if he is to be productive, and these mountains impede westward migration. In addition, the French have a foothold in much of the land west of the mountains as well as in the Gulf of Mexico. Then there is the Florida Peninsula here, which they control along with the Spanish." Again motioning to the map.

Beginning to grasp the issue, George asked, "What do you advise?"

Walpole returned, "The situation is not yet desperate but will soon become so. I feel we need to control this area west of Pennsylvania called 'Ohio'."

George asked, "Strange name, why not simply occupy it?"

"Well, it is occupied by some French and the Iroquois Indians. Now the Indians have often been our allies but are not likely to take kindly to our settling their land."

The king studied the map, "Encourage people to move to this Ohio, make the Indians our allies, at least for now. If we have learned anything about them it is that they can be placated, at least temporarily. As for the French, I can always deal with them on the field of battle." Then looking back out the window, "If you have no more lessons for me, Sir Robert, it is a fine winter day for a ride."

Turning back he said, “Why do we not build a few forts in this Ohio to make a presence?”

Rolling up his maps and papers, Robert Walpole reflected on the new monarch. His father had come from Hanover in the Rhineland to the throne. This was due to Queen Anne’s inability to produce a Stuart heir. George I had been a tolerable King, but he was never English. He rarely spoke the language always preferring French. His son, on the other hand, seemed to be willing to be truly English, or ‘British’ as was now the fashion after the annexation of Scotland and Wales had formed ‘Great Britain’. In addition, George II had shown the possibility of having enough of a brain to take part in the governance of what Walpole hoped to be a great British Empire.

Chapter 7

Bourg-Royal - August 1728:

Returning from the fields after a hard day of early harvest, Jean-Baptiste* Allard could not avoid a feeling of immense pride. Even though he had never regarded himself as an excellent farmer, he had one of the finest farms in all of Québec. He realized that a good deal of credit belonged to his brother and brother-in-law who were indeed excellent farmers, but he had succeeded in large part on his own merit.

Another source of pride was his wonderful family: ten excellent healthy children and seven of them were sons, each as strong, intelligent, honest and handsome as the next. It was true that Franny and Jacques were only nine and seven years old, but he was certain they would follow in the mold of their older brothers.

As he approached the house he met his two oldest boys, François and Thomas now twenty-two and twenty years old. They had been hired for the day to help unload a ship in Québec that had just arrived from France. They were full of news from the city and the sights at the ship, particularly the young women who were always interested in these two.

By the end of the week, François had developed a cough, unusual for this lad who was always the picture of health. As days passed, the cough became worse and he began to run fevers. On the fourth day he was too weak to work, something never seen before. Anne-Elizabeth* began to worry and summoned her friend Jeanne-Elizabeth Renaud-Bedard. Like her mother, Jeanne-Elizabeth was a *sage-femme,* one of the important ladies who served as doctor, surgeon, mid-wife and pharmacist in the colony. "It is definitely some form of *mauvaise-croup.* Try to get him to drink fluid, give him these herbs and tisanes and grease his throat regularly. Try to keep the children away from him."

Diseases characterized by bad coughs were common, although it was difficult at first to tell one type from another, some were very contagious and occasionally very severe. Anne-Elizabeth* began to worry at the lack of improvement. Her worry turned to near panic when the two youngest girls began to show the same symptoms. To make matters worse, the word spread that there were several other similar cases in the town. It also appeared that the source of the ailment had been a passenger on the boat unloaded by François and his brother.

Soon word spread of a few deaths in the city. Jeanne-Elizabeth paid a second visit with the bad news that this was a particularly grave variety of the croup-like diseases. The term diphtheria would not be heard for almost another hundred years, but even without a name, the *sage-femme* knew this was one of the terrible maladies that plagued the colonies.

The society of the colony stopped as people avoided each other to avoid further spread, but spread it did and soon every family in Québec was affected. The men began the awful job of digging graves to be ready to quickly accept the dead, not knowing whose children would be next to fill them. The two Allard girls improved but their brother did not, and on August 28, François Allard's throat closed and he died at the age of 22.

The plague continued into September. In spite of the horrors of the day, a farming community cannot stop in mid season and the adults and children who were able continued the harvest. Each day, Jean-Baptiste* went to the fields with the other boys and his heart almost stopped each time one of them cleared his throat. The two youngest boys next fell ill and then their oldest sister, Marie-Therese. All three of Joseph's children were stricken.

As October arrived the Allard children improved and there did not seem to be any more outbreaks. The news was not so good at the de Baptiste home as Joseph's youngest daughter, age five, succumbed. Just as things appeared over, Thomas, Jean-Baptiste, André, and Pierre* began to cough. Jean-Baptiste quickly improved but the others did not. André died on October 12 and Thomas ten days later. Only Pierre* now twelve years old made no forward or backward process. Finally at the end of the month, his fever broke and he improved quickly.

The plague had been one of the worst in recent memory; scarcely a family did not lose a child. Jean-Baptiste* saw his seven boys change rapidly to four, and young Pierre* found himself elevated from one of the 'little ones' to one of the oldest. Jean-Baptiste* sat on the porch with Joseph, Pierre*, and Toussaint on the evening of November 1, 1728, the feast of Toussaint or 'All Saints' in English. He recalled the words of the old Huron chief, Soaring Eagle, many years before, "I see great tragedy."

Even the tingle from his father's medallion, which he wore on his chest, could not console him.

Bourg-Royal - January 1729:

Pierre* approached the de Baptiste porch, Toussaint sat carving. The boy had become a skilled wood carver and produced many fine objects, which he usually gave as gifts. He had begun to carve pictures on boards that he would get from scrap from Monsieur Laforest at the lumber mill. He was finishing four such pictures, likenesses of his sister and the three Allard boys lost to the plague. Pierre* had to admit they were excellent likenesses, and the mothers treasured them. In the style of a real artist, he carved his initials TdB in the corner of each.

"How are the dogs?" Pierre* asked

"Ready to race," was the reply.

The de Baptiste dogs were legendary. Toussaint's grandmother had found a mortally injured wolf and her two cubs. She had raised the two cubs as dogs and they had bred with the other dogs. They had developed into a strain of magnificent sled dogs.

Dog sleds had been a valuable means of transportation in Québec forever. Long before the colonists arrived, the Indians had relied on them. For many years the Québecois had organized dogsled races to provide fun in the long winters. It started as a race through the woods for the women of the families. Now the most popular race was among the children.

The location of the race varied in accordance to the conditions of the particular winter. The most popular site was crossing the Saint-Laurent. This was only possible when the ice was relatively flat. Usually the crossing of the harbor from the Beauport Creek was possible as the ice in the harbor was generally protected from significant breakup into 'ice mountains'.

Pierre* and Toussaint had won their class last year. This was not a great triumph, however, as everyone regarded the de Baptiste dogs as unbeatable. The race was in two weeks and the boys were ready to begin practice. They went to the barn where the sleds were stored and retrieved their small two-man sled. In doing so they moved some of the parts of their outrigger sailing canoe. An odd thought crossed Pierre*'s fertile mind, but he ignored it.

The boys then called the four dogs who were more anxious to go than the boys. They secured the harnesses and were off. The beauty of the sled was that unlike the canoe, they could take it directly from home. They made a pass through the square and then down to the river and across to the harbor. When they landed at the Place Royal, they were greeted by Louis Langlois.

"Training for the race, I see."

"Yes sir," they replied in unison.

"I don't know why anyone else would want to compete against this team. I hope you aren't planning to put a sail on your sled."

The thought now crashed into Pierre*'s brain, and he couldn't ignore it this time.

When the boys returned to the barn, Pierre* drew a diagram of his idea for Toussaint who replied, "Pierre*, I think the croup has damaged your brain."

His friend persisted so he replied, "OK we'll talk about it after the race." They stored the sled and went up to dinner.

The race was run after mass two weeks later. The weather was perfect and the ice was smooth. The boys won handily and Monsieur Langlois suggested to them after the race that in spite of their age, they should compete with the older boys next year. Pierre* returned home with plans to work on his new invention, but the plans were dashed by the advent of one of the worst winters in Québec history. Survival and maintenance of paths and chimneys became the constant project for the remainder of the season.

Chapter 8

Québec - April 1729:

Spring came at last with an enthusiastic celebration for the breaking of the ice. Pierre* and Toussaint had arranged to work for Monsieur Langlois at the ship works when they could be spared from the farm. The shipyard had used inspiration from the sailing canoe and started to produce small sailboats. At first Langlois offered the boys work so as not to appear to be stealing their idea. However he had found that even at thirteen years of age, they were a great source of technical assistance.

The boats were not canoes but heavier wooden boats that had been propelled for years with oars. Their first attempts were stabilized with one or two outriggers, but this limited their maneuverability. Since they were to be used in the river, this was a major issue. Pierre* suggested, "Why not make them more like the big boats that sail with a keel?"

Langlois could only shake his head. Although his family had been four generations in the shipbuilding business, this youngster was always one thought ahead of him. The small keel solved their problem and Langlois was astounded at the market that developed. He told his brother, who also worked in the yard, "I believe in a few years, this could be the largest portion of our business."

By the end of the summer, they had begun to produce boats in three sizes. As the weather cooled, Pierre* and Toussaint came to him. The boys had sprouted over the summer and were now almost as tall as he. "Monsieur, we would like to start a small project. We would like permission to use scrap. If it is of value, we could barter with our work?"

Langlois replied, "That would be fine as long as you ask permission of the supervisor, Monsieur Bergevin, and it does not interfere with your duties. May I ask the nature of the project?"

Toussaint replied, "We would like to make a sled that is powered by a sail."

Langlois smiled but tried not to laugh, "I can think of a number of logistical problems."

Pierre* returned, "So have we, but we have plans for solving them."

As the boys returned to work, Langlois thought to himself, "I'm glad these two are not with the government, I hate to think of the creative means of taxation they might think of."

At the end of the day the boys went to speak with Louis Bergevin who was supervisor of construction. Pierre* knew they would do well dealing with him because Bergevin was even more fond of the two 'wharf rats' which he jokingly called them than was Monsieur Langlois. Bergevin's family had always been close to the Allards. His father, Jean* Bergevin, lived by Pierre*'s grandparents, François* and Jeanne* Allard, and Louis' brother, Ignatius* Bergevin, lived close to the farm of Pierre*s family.

Bergevin agreed to the list of materials the boys had been eyeing and allowed them to move the materials to a corner of the yard where they could work outside of their normal working hours. They spent a few evenings on the project, but it came to a temporary halt when their fathers informed them that they needed to spend all of their time at home until the end of the harvest.

The labor pool at the Jean-Baptiste* Allard farm had suffered greatly from the plague. The loss of three of his oldest sons hurt the farm almost as much as it had hurt his heart. Young Jean-Baptiste now nineteen had taken over as his strongest worker. Pierre* and Toussaint did their share of their duties and Jean-Baptiste* did not have the heart to forbid them from working at the shipyard, and with the money they were paid by Langlois, he was able to hire a *journalier*, or day worker to help.

Franny was now ten and his brother Jacques now nine were becoming more helpful each week. Their oldest sister, Marie-Therese pitched in like the boys as well. Pierre* and Toussaint approached the harvest with vigor as they knew that once it was over, they would have time to return to the shipyard.

The harvest ended, the trees were cleared, and the lumber milled for this year's projects; and the boys went back to the shipyard. They had more enthusiasm than ever. Their work was so good that Louis Bergevin gave them an extra hour to spend on their sailing sled. Winter descended and soon there was enough ice in the harbor for a trial run. Their sled sat on a wider base than a dog sled and had a frame strong enough to support a small mast. One boy sat in the sled and the other stood behind as they did with the canine variety of sled.

Pushing their prize out onto the ice, they raised the sail. It was a single cat-rigged sail that was controlled with a rope (the main sheet) by the boy inside the sled. The boy on the back did the steering. They had arranged the handles so they enabled the man in back to pivot the runners by turning them.

They started out with the wind at their back, so they let out the sail. The sled jumped forward and they were off with a holler. They attained a respectable speed and were filled with self-congratulation. Pierre* made his first attempt to turn. The mechanism worked flawlessly but the runners merely skidded and did not affect the direction of the boat. Toussaint tried to slow by letting out more sail, but with the wind at their back, this only increased their speed. The worst part was the realization they were headed directly toward thin ice and then open water!

Seeing no option other than an icy death, Toussaint let go of the main sheet causing the sled to gyrate wildly. The mast pulled out of the frame and the sled tipped breaking a runner. The boys got themselves together, gathered up their errant parts and began a humble walk, dragging their sailing sled the half mile back to the shipyard.

Bergevin and Langlois had been watching the spectacle from the dock, first with excitement, then horror and finally when they realized that the two were in one piece, gales of laughter. When the boys returned, the men appeared to be at work. Bergevin said calmly, "How was the sail?"

Toussaint replied, "We need to make a few adjustments," and they returned to their corner.

Three weeks later they had their second try. This time they had outriggers with runners that were very narrow. The pivot mechanism turned the runners again. This trip was less disastrous, but the wooden runners continued to allow a great deal of side slipping in a turn, making maneuverability almost non-existent. They had added an old pickax on a small axel that could be lowered to dig into the ice and slow the boat. When they returned, Toussaint merely repeated to Monsieur Bergevin, "More adjustments."

Québec Christmas - 1729:

No one could remember a more beautiful Christmas morning, with the exception of Jean-Baptiste* and Anne-Elizabeth* who remembered the day twenty-five years earlier when Jean-Baptiste* had proposed on the walk back to Charlesbourg. The main topic at mass was the new stained glass window in the cathedral. Although the great church had two others brought from France, this window had been made in Québec. It was one of daily reminders on how self-sufficient the wilderness colony had become.

The peace of Utrecht continued and Dutch and English traders as well as the occasional Iroquois were becoming more and more common on the streets of Québec. Colonists took time to visit on the village green after mass, as was custom. The children had built an ice pond on the green where several of the boys were involved in a game of *ah-key.* A Dutch businessman named Brinker had been watching the game with a strange set of utensils in his hand. Eventually he sat on a bench, strapped them on his boots, then stepped onto the pond and began to glide across. He was able to move and maneuver effortlessly. Pierre* and Toussaint lost interest in the game and went to investigate.

The man was only too happy to show them his treasure. "You would call them *patins* in French. We call them skates. Each skate is two thin parallel metal blades. They strap on the boot and make it easy to maneuver on the ice. In Holland we have many canals that freeze in the winter. For years we have used wooden skates, but they sideslip too much. These new ones are much more useful."

The boys looked at each other and in unison said, "*Voila!*"

Two days later, the boys were in front of Monsieur Paradis, the shipyard blacksmith. "I see what you mean," he said, "I'll have to check with Monsieur Bergevin but I'm certain I can make something out of some scrap that we have around."

Three weeks later, they were pushing their newest prototype into the harbor. This version had wider outriggers each with a fixed wooden runner with a thin metal blade mounted in the bottom. They had added a rudder much like a sailboat but also with a similar runner. The boat flew like the wind, but maneuvering remained an issue. Now the outriggers didn't slide enough, and tipping was very easy. In fact after their fourth high-speed spill, the boys returned to the drawing board.

The next version had all three runners connected by a rope and pulley system, which would turn the outrigger runners at the same time as the rudder. When he saw this, Langlois said, “I think you lads are wasting your time farming.”

They pushed version four out to the harbor and within a few minutes they knew this was the one. It ran smoothly and maneuvered effortlessly, it would hike with a beam wind like an outrigger sailboat and was as manageable. The best part was the speed. It was unbelievable. They made it to the Beauport livery and back in less than ten minutes. When they returned to shore, the break wall of Place Royal was lined with onlookers. The entire lower village had come out for a better look.

On landing they were swarmed by the curious. Everyone wanted to see the sled and how it worked. The boys were in their glory and Langlois knew that this would not be bad for business. The Dutchman, Brinker, came down and said. “Why this is excellent. I cannot wait to get home in the spring to tell everyone about it. I’m certain they will be popular on our canals.”

Three weeks later, Toussaint stopped on the porch at the Allard house. He had a board under his arm. He presented it to Pierre* saying, “I wanted to have something like this by Christmas but I had to wait until it actually worked.” Pierre* was speechless at the wonderful carving of his boat with the Cap Diamant of Québec in the background. He ran to show his mother. Anne-Elizabeth* fawned over Toussaint and hung it up in a prominent place in the main room. Next to the similar works of her three departed sons. Anne-Elizabeth* exclaimed, "We shall treasure it forever, and look! You have even signed it," referring to his initials TdB in the corner, "How wonderful."

Chapter 9

The Blue Goose Tavern and Inn, Charlesbourg - September 1734:

A group of assorted Allards and friends filled the smoke-filled room. Jean-Baptiste*, André, Charles Villeneuve, Henri and Joseph along with some of the older boys sat sipping beer and discussing the harvest. The growing season had been excellent, and the harvest was ahead of schedule. The farms had adapted to the tragic loss of the three older sons of Jean-Baptiste* emotionally as well as from a standpoint of labor.

The tavern door burst open, and two faces not recently seen in Charlesbourg entered. Joseph Parent and Pierre Roy found the Allard table and exchanged greetings while Roy ordered the obligatory round of shots and beers. After catching up and reliving old times, Parent announced, "News just arrived that our old friend Cadillac died at his estate in France last year. If we had apple brandy, we could offer a toast. It seems that after his departure from *Nouvelle-Orléans,* he and his oldest son were imprisoned for a while in the Bastille in Paris. As you would suspect, the old snake squirmed out and landed on an estate in the Bordeaux region."

Addressing Jean-Baptiste* he continued, "The news prompted us to come up here during our visit to Montréal. We have come to deliver a few items and must soon return to Détroit. We wondered if perhaps you and Joseph and maybe some of your boys would like to accompany us. We need four more men, and there is some pay involved. We could leave as soon as your harvest is close to finished and you could return before the bad weather with one of the Saint-Aubin boys who will be returning to Montréal."

Jean-Baptiste* and Joseph clearly showed interest. Although the were now settled farmers, the thrill of an adventure was irresistible. They briefly discussed it and Jean-Baptiste* asked, "Could we give you our answer in two days?"

Parent replied, "Sure, we will be staying with my brothers next to your father's old place. We have a camp in the back; the damn Belanger sisters still won't let us inside. They object to Pierre's habit of spitting his tobacco where he likes."

Launching a large brown wad, Pierre Roy added, "There is clearly such a thing as too much civilization."

After a long and raucous visit, the Allards headed home, having consumed considerably more alcohol than they had expected to at the beginning of the evening. Along the way they discussed the logistics. Charles started, "André and I can easily finish the harvest. I think it would be good for you and even better if some of your boys would like to accompany you. Jean-Baptiste*'s now oldest son, Jean-Baptiste, Jr. added, "I have little interest and I can stay with the two younger boys and you could take Toussaint and Pierre*. This is certainly an adventure more to their liking."

Jean-Baptiste Jr. who was now twenty-two had lost his love of danger when he faced death in the plague and was happy remaining a *habitant* on the farm. Pierre* and

Toussaint shared their fathers' lust for adventure. They were now eighteen, were very anxious to go. After discussions with the mothers, it was decided that Jean-Baptiste* and Joseph would go with Toussaint and Pierre*. When Jean-Baptiste* walked over to give the news to Parent, they decided to leave the third week in September.

They met at the Beauport livery and left in two light canoes. There was little in the way of cargo, so they could make good time. Parent and Roy each took the back of one canoe and the fathers took the fronts. The boys sat in the middle so that they could be instructed by the seasoned voyageurs. Both Toussaint and Pierre* had been to the *rendez-vous* near *Trois Rivieres* and to the fur market in Montréal but never any farther. The banks of the Saint-Laurent remained somewhat wild but in 1734 no longer had long stretches without sign of humanity.

They spent the night at an Indian camp where Joseph's uncle, Anuk, had been chief. The old man had died a few years before and it was now under the leadership of one of Joseph's cousins. They ate, danced and smoked. A few days later they landed in Montréal. Here they picked up a few more companions.

Joseph Parent's son, Gilbert, had been visiting friends and was returning with his father to their home in Detroit. He was 19 years old. Michel Charbonneau, at 33 a voyageur who lived in Montréal, would be accompanying the men on their return trip. Nicolas* Reaume had come as a boy twenty-three years earlier with his father Robert* on the voyage to Louisiana. He was also now 33 years old. Finally Pierre* Saint-Aubin, age 24, was the son of one of the most prominent men in Détroit who had led the trip to Louisiana. In fact, the fathers of all four of these men had accompanied Joseph and Jean-Baptiste* on that voyage to the bottom of North America in 1711.

The advent of the Canadian fall colors made the trip down the Saint-Laurent spectacular. It was equally as tranquil with no hint of the hostilities that once menaced this part of the voyage. At the end of the river, they stopped at Fort Frontenac on the eastern end of Lake Ontario and dined with the commandant.

At dinner the old soldier explained, "Our life has been quiet for the past few years. We are, however, hearing stories of more English settlers moving across the Allegheny Mountains and into the Ohio River Valley. I fear it is only a matter of time, before hostilities reappear."

The Lake of the Ontario remained wilderness with only occasional structures and these were more often than not abandoned. About halfway down the southern shore they stopped for the night at what appeared to be an Indian camp with houses. Parent and Pierre Roy went to be greeted by the inhabitants. Jean-Baptiste*, Joseph and their sons were astounded. They knew Iroquois when they saw them. The voyageurs returned and introduced the men to the Indian welcoming party. Parent explained, "These are members of the Seneca Tribe of the Five-Nations Iroquois. We have traded with them for the past few seasons."

The Seneca camp was very different from the typical Algonquin camp. The dwellings were both tent and long wooden buildings. Many of the buildings were used to store and dry grain or house animals much like the French and

English barns. The camp was clearly permanent and surrounded by fields of crops and pastures of animals. The Seneca seemed to have a very orderly life, where everyone had a job related to their place in the community.

At dinner the camp showed a more subdued demeanor than they had seen in the Algonquin camp on the Saint-Laurent. After dinner they spoke with the chief who not only spoke Algonquin but also some French. "We have welcomed the French for the past few winters. We prefer their company to that of the English who we have found to be unreliable in their promises. Although we are not primarily a hunting society, we do trap for the trade. Mainly we do this for the farming tools and other modern items the Europeans have to trade."

Addressing the boys as if wishing to teach them about his culture, he explained. "The Five-Nations live forever on their land. We do not move about. At first we felt there would be room for all, Indian and white men alike, but now we fear the English who cross the mountains and settle our land of the Finger Lakes or the Valley of the Ohio to the South. We fear they wish to push the Indian off his land and I fear this will come to a terrible end.

"The old great chief of the Mohawk has recently died. His son is an intelligent man and strong leader, but I fear that he is not willing to endure more white settlers. His Indian name has no European meaning. I believe it would be best described as meaning, *demi-roi* in French, or in English, the Half-King."

The Niagara River – Three Days Later:

Reaching the river between Lakes Ontario and Erie, Parent took them as far upstream as possible so that they could see the magnificent falls from below. Like all visitors before them, Pierre* and Toussaint were in no way prepared for this great phenomenon of nature. From this vantage point they could appreciate that there were actually two falls. The first to the east was impressive enough and then to the west, separated by an island, the larger falls that formed a curve like a deep crescent was beyond comprehension. Roy told them, "If you think this is impressive, wait until you see the portage."

Indeed the portage was unique, very long, very steep and along extremely wet rugged terrain. To make matters more difficult, they had to backtrack several miles by canoe to where the bank was short enough to climb to begin the portage. Even with their light loads, it took three days to reach the summit. At camp that night Joseph Parent suggested that they spend the next day at the falls so that the two newcomers could get a better look. The four other young men were sons of voyageurs or in Pierre* Saint-Aubin's case, a military explorer. They had all been to the falls many times, beginning when they were very young, and they knew things and places that even the older men had not seen.

After an early breakfast, the six young men headed for the falls. Having portaged on the eastern side, they came to the smaller of the two falls. They walked to the very edge of the bank and peered down at one of nature's most incredible sights. The sound of the water was deafening and meaningful conversation was impossible. Nicolas* Reaume started down the rocky cliff that formed the bank just beyond the falls. He motioned for the others to follow.

Descending slowly and carefully, Pierre* realized that one missed step would be catastrophe. It was difficult to separate fear from exhilaration. About thirty feet below the point of their departure, they encountered a narrow opening in the rocks. Reaume quickly disappeared into it and the others followed. It led to a black cave. Reaume produced a flame from a firebox and lit two small torches that he had carried in his pack. It lit the interior enough for the boys to see their way.

As they continued inward, the noise of the water was muted and Reaume said, "Each year, the contour of the cave changes some, so we must use caution." Somehow this news did not help calm the fears of the two newcomers. A hundred feet into the cave the sound of the falls became louder, and they began to see natural light. Eventually Reaume led them onto a ledge that was entirely behind the falls!

Although the thundering wall of water was quite thick, the morning sunlight managed to illuminate the cave. Once Pierre* and Joseph seemed to have recovered from the sight, Reaume motioned for them to continue. The passage became dark for several hundred feet and eventually they saw natural light at the end of the tunnel. The light was above them and they climbed to meet it and found themselves exiting on a piece of dry ground on the island between the two falls.

From here they had a perfect view of the much larger horseshoe-shaped falls on the western side of the Niagara River. The eastern falls paled in comparison to this side. They stood near the eastern end of the 'horseshoe' and looked across to the other end and to the left they could see the magnificent center of the falls.

They descended to a second tunnel and continued eastward in the darkness of the new passage. They began to see daylight but had certainly not gone far enough to be at the other side of the falls. As they went toward the light, Pierre* could see the water had been parted by something above them. Reaume produced a rope from his back and secured it to a rock in the cave. He then looped it around Pierre* and said shouting at the top of his lungs, "Careful, it's slippery."

After this obvious bit of advice, he led the boy out on a rock that went into the gap in the water like a plank on a pirate ship. Pierre* realized that he was standing in the open, one-hundred feet above the river with the falls above, below, and on each side of him. For the remainder of his life, he would remember this as very possibly its pinnacle. When he returned, Toussaint took his turn. When the amazed lad turned to reenter the cave, his foot slipped on the very slimy rock. Reaume, who had been tethering the rope, pulled it instantly and expertly and retrieved the lad before he went off. Then at the risk of being obvious, he shouted, "Like I said, careful."

Eventually they retraced their path to the mainland of the eastern bank. Reaume then led them upstream along the bank of the falls to a place about forty feet from the falls themselves. The water here was obviously deep as the surface of the water was very smooth although the force of the current was as rapid as everywhere else. Reaume again produced his rope. He secured one end to a sturdy tree and held out the loop on the free end and asked, "Who wants to be first?"

Young Gilbert Parent stepped forward, quickly undressed, placed the rope loop around his chest just below his arms, checked Reaume's bowline knot and plunged feet first into the river. The nature of the current brought him away from the bank, and of course, toward the falls, and very rapidly. In a matter of a few seconds, he was at the end of the rope that snapped taut and stopped him less than ten feet from the edge of the falls. He floated in the current for a moment then turned himself onto his back with his head downstream and pulled slowly on the rope. He was able to pull himself to a standing position facing upstream with rooster tails of water coming out of his feet. To their amazement, the boys realized that due to the speed of the current, he was actually standing on the water.

He quickly fell and was pulled to safety by Nicolas* Reaume. Pierre* Saint-Aubin went next and then Charbonneau duplicated the feat. Finally Reaume held the rope out for the two boys and asked, "Who's next?"

Toussaint slowly took the rope and carefully put it over his head. Reaume said, "Let the current pull you and let the rope stop you. Do not try to help it. Just float and we'll pull you back."

Toussaint jumped in trying to look as brave as possible, but deceit was not his strong suit. He took Reaume's instructions and was surprised at how easy the process was. He floated for a minute and began to feel the tug on the rope. He now having some confidence he turned and tried to stand. The others saw what he was doing and decided to give him a chance. The first time he fell forward, the second backward. The third time he thought he had enough energy remaining for one more attempt. To everyone's amazement, especially his, he made it to his feet if even for one second. He fell again and the others quickly retrieved him.

Pierre* realized it was now his turn. He donned the rope and entered the water with less deceit than Toussaint. He too was surprised at the ease of the entry, then further surprised by the amount of effort needed to maneuver in the current. He also realized that he was now duty bound to try to stand. He made three attempts with little success, but on his fourth he did manage to become upright for an instant. He was quickly retrieved and congratulated.

Finally Reaume disrobed and placed the rope around himself and jumped in. He quickly and easily rose to standing and then to the boys' amazement began to pull himself toward shore in the standing position. He was within three feet of the shore when to everyone's horror, the rope snapped. As he was quickly swept to the edge, everyone was paralyzed with fear, except Nicolas* Reaume. In the few seconds available, he looped the rope and caught a protruding rock. His progress stopped less than a foot from the edge. Michel Charbonneau quickly went to the pack and found that Reaume had fortunately packed more than one rope.

He ran to the bank and threw the rope. It missed Nicolas* and went over the edge. Michel retrieved it and tried again without success. The third try hit in a good spot upstream from the stranded young voyageur, but it caught on another rock and when Michel tried to pull it back, it became wedged. The rope was now stuck three feet up stream and out of reach. Nicolas* Reaume managed to turn himself with his head down stream and looking over the edge of the falls. He was then able to put his foot on the second rope, twist it and loop his foot in the rope.

He then let go of the first rope and pulled himself to where he could grab the second rope just as it freed itself from the two rocks. Michel pulled with all his strength. At this point to everyone's amazement, Nicolas* turned and again rose to his feet. He and Charbonneau pulled until Nicolas* was able to simply step ashore. He sat on the bank until he had his breath back. Then he arose and rubbed his badly rope-burned leg and began to retrieve his clothes. He looked at Pierre* and said, "That's the expert way to do it." Pierre* knew he would never doubt the capabilities of Nicolas* Reaume.

When the boys returned to camp the older men were preparing dinner, Parent asked, "What did you show them?"

Pierre* Saint-Aubin shrugged, "You know, the falls and things."

Jean-Baptiste* asked his son, "And how was it?"

He replied, "Real neat."

Lake Erie, the Mouth of the Maumee River - Late September 1734:

In the early afternoon, the group turned up the river at the western end of Lake Erie. Parent explained, "We will have difficulty reaching Détroit by nightfall. There is a large camp of Ottawa here who will welcome us." When they arrived, he explained. This group came from the area of the Ottawa River many years ago, the chief is influential with all the local Algonquin tribes."

Indeed it was a large camp and they were welcomed and invited for the night. A lacrosse game was being played by the older boys so Pierre* and Toussaint went to watch and eventually were invited to participate. Although the two boys were fairly adept at the game, the Indians were better. There was one young man in his late teens who was very strong and skillful. After the game the boys sat and talked. This particular young man was extremely fluent in French. When he asked Toussaint about his excellent French, Toussaint explained he lived in the French community and his mother was *métis*. The young man indicated his mother had been Chippewa, his father Ottawa, and his father was chief.

Just then the chief came over with Parent and Joseph and said, "I see you boys have met." Then to his son, "These men are going to Détroit tomorrow. I would like you and a few others to accompany them on some business we have."

After the older men left the boys, Pierre* and Toussaint formally introduced themselves by name. The young Ottawa replied, "I am called Pontiac."

The next day the group left with three Indian canoes accompanying them. Pierre* and Toussaint accepted the invitation to travel with Pontiac and his younger brother. Pontiac was obviously anxious to visit more with the two young Québecois. He was slightly younger than Pierre* and Toussaint but very articulate and thoughtful. He was also very engaging and charming and dressed more French than Indian.

The day of easy paddling made conversation very easy. "My father sent me to the French mission to be educated in French by the Jesuits. I even spent two years in an English mission school to learn English. I find it a vulgar language compared to French, but it has been helpful as we are seeing English traders more each year. My father believes that the Indian will survive only if he can function in the society of the European. Do you have many English in Québec?"

Pierre* replied, "We have one neighbor named Jacob* Thomas who was captured in a raid and stayed with the French. Apart from him, we see some English traders and businessmen but have little contact with them."

Pontiac continued, "Many years ago, my people came here from west of Québec. We have lived here since the time of my grandfather. The Iroquois call this land Ohio which is 'a great place' in their language. We camp for the good season on the river of the Maumee, but for trade we go to a place east of here where three great rivers converge.

They are called the Allegheny, the Ohio and the Monongahela. Each year there is a great meeting of the many tribes who live in the Ohio Country and European traders, at times French, English or Dutch. Each year, there are more and more English."

Chapter 10

Fort Pontchartrain du Détroit - October 1734:

Although it had grown since Jean-Baptiste* and Joseph had left in 1711, the great city in the wilderness had still not yet fulfilled Cadillac's expectation. The stockade area was two or three times the size it had been, but most buildings were still inside the walls. There was a second stockade nearby. Joseph Parent explained that the Huron had fortified their camp as well. "There was a Fox uprising in 1712, always a slippery group the Fox. They've pretty much left the area now but only recently have people such as Saint-Aubin and myself felt safe to build a house outside the stockade."

Cadillac's docks had been expanded, and a small sailing vessel as well as several canoes were moored where the men made their landing. The Indian presence remained impressive. Large camps were evident along both sides of the river. A familiar, but older, face came down the slope from the fort to the docks. Now in his seventies, Jean* Saint-Aubin was a spry as ever and still a guiding force of the community. He greeted his son and then made the rounds to the others. He was obviously pleased to see Jean-Baptiste* and Joseph again. He was accompanied by another man in military uniform, "Captain Boisgrévy, let me introduce Jean-Baptiste* Allard, and Joseph de Baptiste. These men were instrumental in the voyage to aid Monsieur Cadillac settle *La Nouvelle-Orléans*."

Boisgrévy was the commandant of the fort and graciously welcomed the men. They proceeded to the Fort where they were invited for dinner. Pontiac had invited the boys and younger men to join him at the Ottawa camp across the river. Jean-Baptiste* and Joseph thought this would be a good experience for the boys so they gave their permission and the groups parted for the night.

The dining room at the fort was grand by backwoods standards. That is to say it had a roof, floor and fireplace. It was, however, large and had a long table, which accommodated the number of men who had been invited to dine. Apart from the four men from the voyage, Jean* Saint-Aubin and Captain Boisgrévy, there were three other voyageur residents of Détroit. Ignatius* Vien had come with his family in 1706. Jean-Baptiste* knew his family from Québec as the Allards were close friends of the Viens. Jean* Vien's mother, Catherine* Gateau-Vien, had come as a *fille du roi* on the same voyage as Jean-Baptiste*'s mother.

Two other men were brothers, Michel and Jacques Campau, who had come with their families at about the same time as Vien. Jacques Campau had married one of Jean* Saint-Aubin's daughters. All three of the voyageurs were becoming financially successful and influential.

There were also two younger men who were officers in the military. Antoine Beaubien was an interpreter and Louis DeQuindre, his cousin, was a career officer. DeQuindre's grandfather was a rich Québec fur merchant who helped finance the voyage of Madame Cadillac to Détroit, a voyage in which Jean-Baptiste* and Joseph had played a small part along with Pierre Roy and Joseph Parent. One final guest was a man in his early thirties, Pierre* Meloche. He had come from Montréal as a soldier but now had a farm and a windmill on the south bank of the Détroit River.

As the evening progressed it became apparent to Jean-Baptiste* that although the two soldiers had come from wealthy families and the three voyageurs and Meloche from poor beginnings, they were all held with equal esteem in the community. Dinner was served by Indian servants and consisted of various game, pheasant, boar and deer along with traditional vegetables and beer, which was becoming the drink of choice in Détroit.

The conversation quickly turned to the future of the community. Boisgrévy began, "Apart from the military, the voyageurs and a few farming families, the remainder of our citizens are Indian. The primary focus of the city is Indian trade and maintenance of Indian camps. Protection of the straits is another focus, but development of a true village remains very slow. We need citizen farmers and in great numbers if we are to survive."

Antoine Beaubien entered the conversation, "Every month we are seeing more English traders. The peace of Utrecht will not last forever. The British (using the new term) are coming in ever larger numbers from the southeast and it will only be a matter of time before they decide they would like control of the strait."

Draining his first beer, Michel Campau added, "The last time I traded at the forks of the Ohio River, the English presence was impressive. My brother and I would like to increase our business enterprises and leave the trading to others, but for this we need farmers and other businesses, and we need the support of France."

Jean* Saint-Aubin, put down a pheasant leg and stood. The oldest man in the group, he was clearly the patriarch of the city in the wilderness, "Michel is correct, we need France's assistance. I hope Captain Boisgrévy can deliver this message when he returns to France next year. If I could turn all our Indian neighbors into Frenchmen, we would prevail, but as it is, without more *habitants,* and I mean many more, we shall be lost."

Finally Meloche arose, "I live on the opposite shore and have more contact with Indian than French. Our allegiance with the Indian is vital to our survival. In particular there is this young son of the Ottawa chief called Pontiac. He understands the realities of the situation and, in spite of his young age, has acquired the respect of most of the Indian leaders." Then looking at Boisgrévy, "You would do well to count this man among your friends and allies."

The discussion lasted most of the night but eventually fell to more pleasant topics such as upcoming social events and the ever popular 'who knows who'. A benefit of the small size of New France was that any two French-Canadians had some acquaintances in common.

The South Shore of Détroit - The Same Evening:

The orientation of Cadillac's village was such that when leaving Fort Pontchartrain for the other side of the river to a place then called simply 'the south coast' and today Windsor, one travels due south. This is one of the geographic peculiarities of the region that gives newcomers to Detroit even today the east-west, north-south directional confusions.

The younger men left the dock at the fort and traveled due south to the Ottawa camp. The dining room at the Ottawa camp was also grand by Indian standards. That is to say, it had neither roof nor floor, its fireplace was a fire on the ground, and there was no table but there was room for all around the flames.

Along with the six young men from the voyage were two more Saint-Aubins: Jacques*, who worked as a voyageur, and Charles*, who managed the mill started some years before by Jean* Laforest. Along with them was their close friend Niagara Campau, a voyageur and aspiring businessman.

Along with Pontiac and his brother were a few other Ottawa and several young men from other tribes. Pierre* and Toussaint soon learned that many of these men were also the sons of chiefs, thus forming a group of future leaders of the Indian community who met and socialized regularly. An unusual guest was Samuel Price, an English trader about Pierre*'s age, traveling with two other English traders who had stopped to trade with the Ottawa. Pontiac had invited him to come. After eating, smoking and discussing the voyage from Québec, the talk led to more important matters for these future leaders of the area.

Although he was among the younger of the men, Pontiac was clearly the leader of the discussion. However he did make a point of frequently deferring to the older attendees. "I believe the nomadic days of the Indian are coming to a close in this region. Already our people are finding the lack of free land and the impediments of farms in the region the English call Pennsylvania, are prohibiting mobility." Referring to an Iroquois brave in the group, "We must adopt the ways of the Iroquois, and the Europeans by becoming more stable."

The boys were impressed that not only was Pontiac's French good, it was better than theirs. The young Iroquois brave then stood. His French was not so good, but understandable. "My uncle, the chief, Half-King, believes that we must co-operate and try to live with at least one European group. Today he travels with the English, but I must tell you that he trusts no European."

Pontiac then asked Samuel Price to speak. Price rose, his French was surprisingly good, as most common English spoke no French at all. "I come from the town of Glastonbury in the British Colony of Connecticut. As a boy, my father was taken in an Indian raid along with his sister. They were taken from their home in Deerfield, Massachusetts and marched to Québec. His sister remained there, but my father returned some years later and started our family in Glastonbury. My father learned French during his years in Québec and taught it to us children. I have become a trader and have seen the things of which you speak.

"Most English colonists want their own life in this land. Most are farmers; some are tradesmen. The British Government wants the spoils of the land and the taxes of the colonists. I believe they are at crossed purposes. I do not know how this will end, but I must admit many colonists are coming to the west in search of new land. The British Crown supports them but only for its own purposes. I agree with Pontiac the nomadic days of the Indian are going."

Next a Chippewa brave stood. "Our people have always been friendly with the French. We have little use for the English and will continue to support the French presence."

Pontiac asked Pierre* Saint-Aubin what his view was of the French position. Pierre* Allard took note that Pontiac called on Saint-Aubin rather than Reaume or Charbonneau who were older. Pontiac seemed to have an attitude as to whose opinion was most valuable.

Pierre* Saint-Aubin rose and started, "I have been regularly to Montréal and also to the forks of the Ohio River. There are not nearly enough French to withstand any meaningful effort by the English to do anything. My father says that during the Queen Anne's War in the first decade of the century, the only reason the French ever prevailed was the allegiance with the Indian. Not just for the numbers but for the Indian way of battle. He says if the English would accept the Indian way, there would never be a French victory.

"If the French and the Indian stand together, we can hold the British for a time, but ultimately they will prevail and we will all become British subjects for better or worse.

During my visits to the forks of the Ohio, I have had opportunity to speak with British colonists. Many hold little allegiance to the crown. I believe it is eventually this group that will fulfill our alliance and allow us to banish the British government." Then he turned to Pontiac, "Ask our English guest what he thinks."

Samuel Price stood again, " I suppose I am in agreement. Many English will remain loyal to the king forever, but I believe many more will not. If the British king prevails in this land, those British Colonists will find they have more in common with the French and the Indian than with the loyal subjects of the king."

Then Pontiac turned to Pierre* Allard and asked, "And what do our guests who live in the very heart of French country believe?"

Pierre* had been listening intently, but did not know what to say. He was relieved when Toussaint arose, "I am *métis*. I have a unique view of both sides. Many years ago my great-grandfather, a man called Henri, said that this day would come, and the Indian way would disappear. For myself, I have always observed that the government of the Indian always represents the Indian. It does not appear to me that the government of France truly represents the French-Canadian. Now I see that the British government suffers the same shortcoming. I agree with Monsieur Price."

Pontiac stood as if to consolidate the thoughts of the group and end the formal discussion, "In the end I believe that the Indian can live with the French. Their civilizations can exist side-by-side or intermingled. However, I fear that this will not happen with the English as it seems the Indian and the English are not…" and he paused for the first time seeming to be at a loss for the correct term, then finally, "…*compatible.*"

The conversation fell to more mundane matters and later the men retired to their deerskins for the night. As the Canadians sat by themselves, Toussaint asked Niagara Campau about his unusual name.

Campau replied, "I'm surprised you waited this long, that is generally the first thing I am asked. My name is actually Nicolas. My father, Jacques Campau, and his brother Michel came to Détroit in 1706 as voyageurs and traveled regularly to Montréal. My father brought the family in 1708 to live in Détroit. In July of 1710 he took the family back to Montréal for a visit. He left with my two older brothers and two older sisters. My mother was pregnant and due to deliver after coming to Montréal.

The portage at Niagara was too hard for my mother and I was born early in that place. A voyageur that accompanied us baptized me with the water from the eastern falls. The name started early and remained."

Pierre* Saint-Aubin added, "Niagara can walk 'the falls' as well as any man, other than Nicolas* Reaume."

As the men prepared to cross back to the fort in the morning, Pontiac came to say farewell to Pierre* Allard and Toussaint. "I hope our paths will cross again. As you can see from the talk last night, our common good is going to depend on it."

As they boarded the canoes Pierre* noticed that among the Indian camps on this side there were a few houses and farms, and also a small wooden church to the south. "That is the Church of the Assumption," Pierre* Saint-Aubin told him, "It serves as the Indian mission as well as the church for the French when they are unable to cross the river to Sainte-Anne."

Once they were reunited with the rest of the group, Jean* Saint-Aubin and Joseph Parent took the two fathers and their sons on a tour. The city inside of the stockade was large enough that there were four streets running east and west. Rue Saint-Louis closest to the river and most southerly, then Rue Sainte-Anne, Rue Saint-Jacques, and Rue Saint-Joseph in order. The church of Sainte-Anne sat near the northeast corner of the fortification, a wooden structure in the traditional Christian shape of a cross.

The remainder of the structures were military and government buildings and the homes of more than half the French residents. Outside the walls were Indian camps on both sides of the river. The settlers' farms were organized in long ribbons ending at the river in the style of the early farms of Québec. Most of the farmers, however, returned to houses inside the fortifications at night. Some of the larger farms like Saint-Aubin's or the more fearless, like Parent, contained farmhouses at the river. Most of the houses like Parent's were very basic, but some such as those of Saint-Aubin and the Campau brothers were as nice as many in Montréal.

The farms ran from the fort to the level of *Isle aux Cochons* or as Cadillac had named it *Belle Isle.* Many creeks entered the Détroit River; the largest in this area was called Parent Creek for its first citizen who had occupied its bank since before Cadillac. The *Isle aux Cochons* now held two Indian camps and Parent noted that the boar hunting had suffered accordingly.

As the river entered *Lac Sainte-Claire* there was a large point which contained the small windmill run by Charles* Saint-Aubin and his brother Gabriel. Jean* told them, "The land here is quite marshy as it is everywhere in this area, but the wind is ideal. We are trying to lay log roads that will allow us to move the mill farther out on the point. We are also hoping to get better mill hands from Quebec eventually. This mill is only for grist. We must go across the river to Meloche's to mill wood." Beyond this point there was no development. Pierre* Allard asked Saint-Aubin, "How is the ice on this lake in the winter?"

Saint-Aubin replied, "As the lake is shallow, the ice comes early, is very thick and stays very smooth."

Returning to the fort, Saint-Aubin indicated the few farms on the south side of the river. "We often refer to this as 'Assumption' for the name of the small mission church there." As they approached the gates they saw two dark men coming toward the river. Jean-Baptiste* stopped and shouted, "Tom!"

The men hurried to greet each other and there was a flurry of warm greetings. He introduced the boys and told them, "This is Tom, of whom you have heard many stories." The boys were very familiar of the tales of the capture in the woods of Tom and Jacob* Thomas and the trip to *La Nouvelle-Orléans* and the slave rescue.

Tom introduced his young companion as his son Georges who had been quite young when his family left for

Détroit. Joseph explained that Toussaint and Georges were cousins as Tom and Joseph had married two *métis* sisters named de Baptiste and hence their last name. Arrangements were made for the group to meet at the Saint-Aubin farm that evening for dinner.

At dinner they were greeted by Marie-Louise* Gauthier-Saint-Aubin, a plump lady about ten years her husband's junior. They also met the other five Saint-Aubin siblings. Saying grace, Jean* Saint-Aubin prayed for their son Jean-Baptiste, who had died the previous year in a smallpox epidemic at the age of twenty-five.

Tom told them of his work, "Georges and I work periodically on the farms as *journaliers.* The rest of our time we try to help runaway slaves. We see several each year. Madame Saint-Aubin and some of the other women have been very generous in taking them in and helping them settle. Some go with the Indians, some to the northern British colonies where there is not much slavery and others farther north. We do have five African families in Détroit at present.

"Georges and I and some of the Chippewa have traveled to the southern colonies to spread the word, but the work is slow and dangerous. We shall, however, do what we can do." Much of the conversation then fell between Tom's wife and Joseph concerning her sister in Québec. After dinner, saying goodbye to their friends, they arranged to leave in the morning for Québec with Pierre* Saint-Aubin and Niagara Campau who were headed to Montréal to trap and trade for the winter.

The trip was quick as they went downstream although the Saint-Aubin canoe was heavy due to supplies. The trees were at the peak of their color. They would be bare before they reached Montréal. The first gusts of winter and early snow had arrived by the time they reached the Beauport Livery.

Chapter 11

Quebec - January 1735:

Pierre* Allard and his Uncle Georges were making a turn in the newest version of the sailing sled. Georges Allard had an interest in business and was interested in marketing the device. They had already succeeded in selling two of the early models to rich adventurous colonists. They came about and returned to the dock at the shipyard where Toussaint had been watching them.

Climbing out of the tight passenger compartment, Georges remarked, "These small sleds are fine for sport, but I think the market will be for transportation. We need a larger, more stable boat. We can sacrifice speed and maneuverability for stability and the ability to travel on rough ice such as we have later in the winter."

The threesome went up to the office and discussed some possibilities with Louis Langlois. Later the boys returned to put the sled away. Pierre* said, "This model is still too sluggish, it responds slowly to the rudder and has a tendency to want to tip over forward." His friend looked at it and replied, "Well, you just have to keep thinking, Pierre*. It is what you're best at."

Just before they reached the ramp to the shore, Louis Bergevin came to the dock with a young girl. "Toussaint! Pierre! Can you do me a favor?"

The boys left the sled and went to the dock, "Would you be so kind as to take my niece for a ride? She's been asking me all winter."

It was highly unlikely that the boys would refuse any request from the old foreman who had always been more than generous with them and their projects. They cheerfully agreed and the girl jumped down on to the ice. They immediately recognized the daughter of their neighbor, Ignatius* Bergevin. Marie-Angélique* Bergevin was about thirteen years old. She had always been an aggressive and adventurous girl. She preferred lacrosse to the girl games and was better at the sport than her brothers.

She looked at Pierre* with an enthusiastic thank-you and hopped in the rider's compartment. It was clear that she had been watching them enough that she knew exactly what to do. Pierre* turned the sled around, raised the sail, stepped onto the back and away they went. Pierre* had given rides to a few other girls, and they always squealed. Marie-Angélique* was quite calm and the first sound she uttered was asking, "Can we go faster?"

Rising to the challenge, Pierre* pointed more to the wind and picked up some speed and began to hike. His passenger looked back and asked, "How fast can it really go?" And he brought the wind to his side and sped off. Just as she yelled, "This is wonderful!" the sled came forward on one outrigger and tipped stern over bow. Both were thrown hard onto the ice as the sled came to rest in an inverted position.

Getting up quickly and realizing that he had not been severely damaged, Pierre* rushed to his passenger. He was shocked to see her face full of blood, but more shocked when she said, "Can we do that again?"

Pierre* cleaned her face and found a sizable gash above her right eye. He gave her a cloth to hold on it while he righted the sled and made ready to return to the dock. He deposited her with her uncle who dressed her wound and said he would take care of it. Marie-Angélique* said, "Thank you both, I have never had such fun!"

The following morning, Pierre* thought that it would be prudent to make an appearance at the Bergevin farm. Ignatius* greeted him at the door, "Well, Monsieur Allard, I see you have given a sledding lesson to my daughter."

"Yes, Monsieur, I am sorry."

"Well, don't be. She will mend, and who knows, perhaps it will knock some sense into that wild head of hers. Come in and say hello." They went to the kitchen where Marie-Angélique* and her younger sister, Barbe-Louise, were helping their mother. Seeing the girl without the cover of her deerskin coat, Pierre* noticed that she was not quite the little girl he remembered from the summer. She also had a bandage around her forehead and her eye was black and swollen shut.

When she saw Pierre*, she exclaimed, "Oh Mama, look it's Pierre* Allard!" Genevieve* Tessier-Bergevin looked up and said to Pierre*, "I understand you had quite an adventure yesterday."

Pierre* looked at his feet and said softly, "Yes, Madame."

She continued, "Well, no great damage, but do be more careful in the future. In spite of how she behaves, she is not Pierre." She referred to Pierre Bergevin who was exactly Pierre* Allard's age and good friends with him and Toussaint.

Like Pierre* Allard, Marie-Angélique* was a second-generation Québec native. In fact she was actually third generation on her mother's side. She was the fifth of ten children but the oldest girl. With four older brothers it was natural that she was more adventuresome than the other girls. After a few pleasantries Pierre* excused himself. As he returned home he was a little confused. He had never even thought of Marie-Angélique* as a girl, let alone a woman.

Bourg-Royal - May, 1739:

Pierre* gazed intently at the line of his plow. He was plowing the near field readying it for corn. The fields closest to the house were planted with corn to discourage varmints from raiding the field. As it was close to the house, the ground had been plowed for many years and was soft and easily tilled. It made for an easy day for both Pierre* and the horse.

However, today Pierre* was most interested in the line of the furrow. He noticed how easily he could maneuver in this soft ground and how he could turn or stay straight with very little effort. He heard his father's voice from behind and brought the horse to a stop.

"Are you plowing, or drawing pictures?" Jean-Baptiste* came from behind regarding the rows, some straight and some gentle s-shaped curves.

"Oh, I'm sorry, Papa, I was thinking."

Jean-Baptiste* replied, "I know that is what you do best, but corn rows are much easier to maintain if they are indeed rows. Do your inventing on Sunday."

As he walked away, the old man reflected on his son. Jean-Baptiste* was never the best farmer, and he knew that Pierre* was not as avid as his brothers. However Pierre* was now the oldest since his two remaining older siblings, Jean-Baptiste, Jr. and Marie-Therese were now married and gone. That left Pierre*, the two younger boys, and two younger girls at home.

Jean-Baptiste*'s oldest brother, André had died in a farming accident in 1735. His boys had taken over his farm and were expanding toward the mountains. Jean-Baptiste* and Pierre* had cleared enough of the land next to Joseph de Baptiste to build a house for Pierre* if he would ever settle down, and they were slowly working on the land behind it to make it ready for expanded farming.

At the end of the day, Pierre* ran to the orchard where Toussaint was finishing the pruning. "Toussaint! I have it!"

Getting down from the ladder, his friend replied, "You have what?"

"The answer. We steer it from the front!"

"What??"

"The sailing sled. We steer from the front. I'll work it out, and as soon as the planting is over, we'll go to the shipyard and get to work." The boys took the pruning tools and returned them to the barn as Pierre* rambled on about his idea.

That Sunday after mass he found Marie-Angélique* and explained the idea to her. Over the past few years they had become very friendly and she never missed a chance for an iceboat ride. Now seventeen, she was certainly no longer a little girl, and Pierre* was becoming more confused about their relationship. They ate on the lawn of the Charlesbourg Square. Soon after they finished, a bugle blew in the center of the square.

Pierre* announced, “I have to go, the militia is meeting this afternoon.”

The Charlesbourg Militia continued to meet occasionally. There would be a short talk on military procedure, some target shooting and then an adjournment to the Blue Goose Tavern for drinking and gossip. The unprecedented twenty-six years of relative peace had made life in the colony tranquil. In 1739 there were over 40,000 French in Québec and the number continued to grow slowly but steadily.

<u>Québec - January 1741:</u>

Over the past year, Toussaint and Pierre* had perfected the front steering method. The craft now had more the long narrow appearance of a canoe rather than a sled. The interior would now hold three people and there was no longer a stand on the back as in the dog sled. The outriggers were more widely spaced and below the passengers. Under the front of the long nose was a rudder that was controlled by a tiller mechanism under the passengers and controlled from the passenger area.

The day was clear and the ice was smooth. Pierre*, Toussaint, and Marie-Angélique* were having a fine time racing around the Saint-Laurent. There were three other such ‘iceboats’, as they had been renamed, on the bay but none preformed like this one. The speed was beyond belief and the stability and maneuverability superb. Pierre*'s Uncle Georges felt that they could sell as many as they could produce.

Today, as had become their custom, they left the boat at the canoe livery in Beauport, which made returning home simple. Toussaint left them at his house and Pierre* and Marie-Angélique* proceeded on to hers. He was now twenty-five and she nineteen. She was beginning to wonder when he would ask for her hand. It seemed improbable that he would not ask, as he rarely spoke to other girls. At her door she looked into his green eyes and he regarded the large scar, for which he was responsible, over her right eye, but again today the discussion was only about the 'iceboat'.

Chapter 12

<u>Saint Clair Shores, Michigan - May 2007:</u>

Ben Champine arose from his back deck where he sat watching the lake. He walked in and picked up the phone. "Hello,"

"Ben, Jim Trombley here. You remember that wood carving of an iceboat?"

"Yeah, sure."

"Well I have some interesting news about it. Do you ever see that girl from the *Free Press*?"

"Everyday, she's living here."

"Hey great. Let's all have dinner tonight. How about 'Fishbones' by you?"

"Why don't you come over here? Becky will make you a gumbo like you won't see at 'The Cajun'."

"Ok see you about seven,"

Trombley arrived promptly at seven. After greetings, Ben explained, "Becky and I are getting married this winter. It's going to be at Saint-Gertrude across the street. You'll get an invitation, but it might be on short notice. We want to wait until the ice is good enough that we can leave by iceboat."

Trombley shook his head, "No wonder North America speaks English."

The men took a beer to the porch and Ben asked, "What did you find out about my carving?"

Trombley took a drink, "Did you ever hear of the Vérendrye plaque?"

Becky came running to the porch door, "That's the guy who discovered the Rocky Mountains. It was found by some school children in South Dakota about 100 years ago, along with some human bones."

Trombley replied, "Wow, give the lady a beer."

Becky continued, "When I was at Tulane, we did a series on French-American history. This really got my attention because the guy's name was Gauthier."

Trombley continued, "Right again! Actually he was Pierre Gauthier de La Vérendrye, a soldier and explorer. He, his sons, and others spent a great amount of time exploring the west in the middle of the 18th century. His sons claimed to have been the first white men to see the Rocky Mountains. Their story was always under question and was further muddied by the French and Indian War that started soon after their alleged discovery.

"They said they had buried a lead engraved survey plaque documenting the trip along with a dead voyageur at the point where they left the Missouri River. In 1913 a group of school children in South Dakota discovered the plaque while digging in the fields. Gauthier's story is now believed, although little firsthand information exists today because their claim was not thought credible in their lifetime."

Ben spoke up, "What does this have to do with my carving? Did they get there by iceboat?"

Laughing, Trombley replied, "Not likely, but I sent the information on your board around. You know, the Internet is amazing."

"So I've heard, " Ben said.

"Well, a friend of mine who has worked with the plaque called and said in the corner of the plaque, almost invisible, is a definite TdB. Exactly as in your wood carving. So it would seem the same person made them both. All we have to do is connect some very old and obscure dots."

Ben asked, "And Becky is related to this guy?"

Trombley replied, "The two most common names of French immigrants were Roy and Gauthier or Gautier. There were five men of the latter who left descendants. Becky, do you know who your immigrant Gauthier was?"

"In fact, yes, he was also a Pierre* Gauthier but not the same one. Mine was called *Sanguingoria.*"

"Yes, I'm familiar with him. He and his wife were taken in the massacre at Lachine in 1689. Some of his sons became voyageurs of note. One named Jean* lived in Kaskaskia and traveled to most of the known outposts of the known frontier at that time,"
adding, "Well, stay tuned."

Becky said, "Let's eat."

Chapter 13

Charlesbourg, The Blue Goose Tavern and Inn - Early Spring 1742:

The Allard men were seated enjoying a beer and discussing the coming planting. The door burst open with what had over the years become almost a signature style. Pierre Roy and Joseph Parent entered and quickly found the Allards. Parent was now in his early seventies and limped badly. Pierre Roy, a few years younger, had fewer teeth, fewer fingers, and many more scars than in his early years. Still he lacked none of his old energy and enthusiasm. He sat down, ordered drinks around and spit a classic wad of tobacco on the floor.

This particular skill was becoming less acceptable in the Québec society. There was even a sign at the bar asking patrons to use the buckets provided around the establishment. Of course, Roy could not read, and even if he did, it would not likely make a difference. He made his first shot and beer disappear in record time and started to speak. “You boys ever hear of Pierre Gauthier de la Vérendrye?”

Hearing no response he continued, “Well, he’s some fancy military explorer who has been exploring the west for several years. Seems he’s being recalled and a small group of soldiers are going to relieve him.

“They want a few seasoned men to accompany them. Parent here thinks he can’t go just because he broke his damn leg. Well, I figure I’d like to see the far west before I die, and I'm going. I am also looking for a few more souls. I got two in Montréal and I thought maybe young Pierre* and Toussaint here might want to see if they got the same balls as their fathers." Then pointing a gnarled finger at the boys, "You better come quick before you get tied down with some woman," he said as he downed his third shot and beer.

Jean-Baptiste* began to mull this over. He would miss the boys for the planting, but it would be a wonderful adventure. He realized that Pierre* had inherited his love of the wild. Secretly he was disappointed that Roy had not invited him and Joseph. He spoke softly to Joseph then replied, "Can we let you know in a few days?"

Roy replied, "We leave for Montréal on Tuesday. You can tell us before then. We will go to Montréal where Parent will leave for Détroit with Pierre* Saint-Aubin and some boys. We will pick up our two and meet the soldiers at the fort and depart post haste."

Jean-Baptiste* asked, "Who will be the other two?"

Roy replied, "Michel Charbonneau and Nicolas* Reaume."

They agreed to meet in three days, and the Allards took their leave while Roy and Parent made further advances into the supplies of the Blue Goose Tavern. The family discussed the voyage at dinner. It was apparent that Anne-Elizabeth* was not entirely in favor, but knew the decision was not hers to make. Pierre* and Toussaint were very enthusiastic and by the end of the evening the decision had been made in the affirmative.

That evening Pierre* Allard wrestled with his thoughts. Although he had not announced anything, he had been contemplating a proposal of marriage to Marie-Angélique* Bergevin. He was now twenty-five, and she nineteen. She would not wait forever.

Sunday after mass, Pierre* sought out the young lady. This was not difficult, as they had been having lunch on the green almost every Sunday for the past two years. He explained the trip and the opportunity it posed. He could see that Marie-Angélique* did not exactly share his enthusiasm. He used his last weapon, "I will likely return before winter and if you will have me, we could be married."

Marie-Angélique* smiled broadly and agreed. He said he would come that night to ask her father.

That evening he went to the Bergevin residence where Ignatius* invited him in. Pierre* gave his carefully rehearsed speech, and Ignatius* asked Marie-Angélique* to come in.

"Monsieur Allard has asked for your hand. It seems, however, some adventure calls before hand. What do you say to this *ma petite?*"

Marie-Angélique* agreed, and her father continued, "Well, then it is settled. Fetch your mother and we shall have a toast."

As Pierre* left, Marie-Angélique* followed out onto the porch. When they were alone she said, "You knew that I would wait for you." And looking around gave him a passionate kiss and disappeared into the house. The confused young man then stepped off the porch and left to prepare himself to disappear into the frontier. That evening, Ignatius* Bergevin, a devoted farmer, wrestled with some misgivings over this voyage, but he realized that life in Québec had never been for the faint of heart.

When Pierre* arrived home, his father was waiting on the porch, an obvious sign that he wanted to talk. "I have something for you. My father gave it to me many years ago. He asked that I pass it on to the most adventuresome of my sons. It has become apparent that you are that son. I had planned to give it to you at a later date, but it carries an aura of good fortune, and you may soon be needing it."

He had an ornate Indian sack on his lap. He then removed his medallion and wampum from around his neck. Pierre* knew some things about these family treasures, but Jean-Baptiste* was determined to tell the entire story so the history might remain intact.

"When your grandfather first arrived in the new world, even before the ship landed in Québec, he was sent hunting on *Les Iles de la Madeleine.* He became lost and stumbled on an Abenaki attempting to free his son from under a tree. He helped, and the man was so grateful that he gave your grandfather this wampum. Your grandfather in turn gave the Indian this medallion.

"Originally the wampum was two identical sections which fit perfectly together. There was a young lady on the ship who had fallen gravely ill during the voyage. Sister Marguerite Bourgeoys selected your grandfather to help care for the girl. They fell in love, but she was to go to Montréal and he to remain in Québec. He gave her one half of the wampum and I suppose her family has it today, wherever they may be.

"Some years later, your grandfather and I went to Montréal on business and we met a young Englishwoman named Elizabeth* Price. She and her brother had been captured in an Indian raid and taken to Montréal. She met an older crippled Abenaki during the march who took care of them. He sold them to the Ursuline Sisters when they reached Montréal. He gave her the medallion and told her the story of your grandfather. It seems he was the same boy your grandfather had rescued on *Les Iles de la Madeleine*. Madame Price showed the medallion to your grandfather and he immediately recognized it. It was then returned to him. Later your grandfather gave the medallion, the wampum, and this sack to me.

"His father had given the medallion to him before he left France for Québec. It was said to come from the time of Jeanne d'Arc and have magical qualities. I sometimes feel a tingle when I hold it. When Joseph and I went to Louisiana, we met the legendary old Huron Chief, Soaring Eagle. He held the medallion and predicted a great tragedy for our family. I believe he foresaw the death of your brothers in the plague. The sack was dropped by an Iroquois whom your grandfather encountered during his time at the Ardouin-Badeau farm. He believed this also brought him good fortune."

Jean-Baptiste* then placed the two necklaces around his son's neck. Pierre* felt an undeniable tingle from the medallion. He looked to his father and said, "When we were in Détroit, on the night Toussaint and I spent at

Pontiac's camp, we met a young English trader who spoke French. He said his father and aunt had been kidnapped by Abenaki to Montréal. His father later returned to New England but his aunt stayed in Montréal. His name was Samuel Price."

Jean-Baptiste* looked into his son's green eyes and said, "Small world."

The next day Pierre* and Toussaint delivered their decision to Pierre Roy and the following morning the boys departed for Montréal.

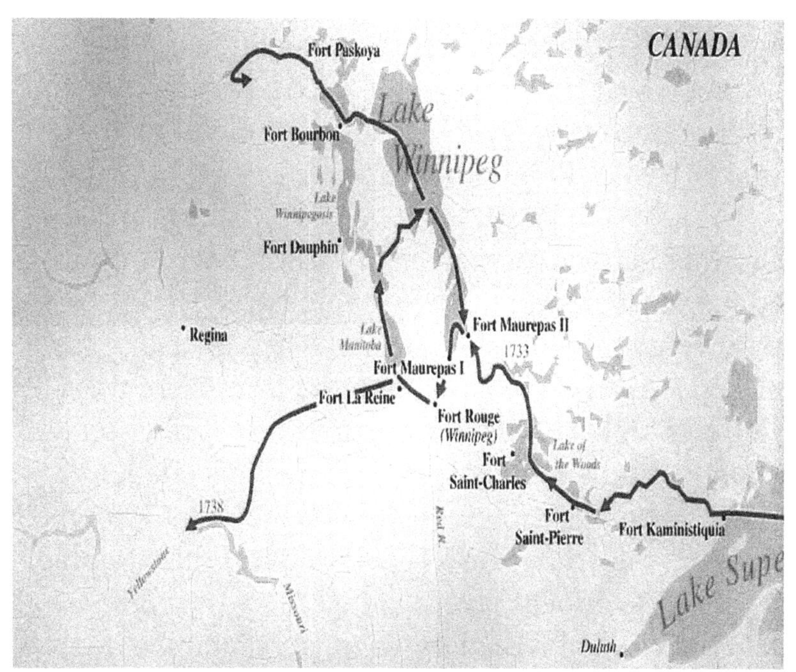

Travels of the La Vérendrye's. At the arrow labeled 1738, they proceeded down the Yellowstone River to what is now Yellowstone National Park

Chapter 14

Montréal - March 1742:

The foursome reached the hub of the frontier in good time. They traveled light and were skilled canoeists. Pierre* had, however, questioned Roy if they would be thought worthy of the job of true voyageurs. Pierre Roy simply replied, "Wait until you see the soldiers. We will be lucky if only one or two of them drown."

The weather was unseasonably warm but ice flows remained in the river, and the trees were bare. The Laurentian were still covered in snow. They landed at the Montréal canoe livery and walked to the fort where they found Pierre* Saint-Aubin who was to return to Détroit with Joseph Parent, and Nicolas* Reaume and Michel Charbonneau who were to be on the voyage west. Reaume indicated there was to be a meeting at the fort that evening. They adjourned to a local tavern called *Les Coureurs de Bois.* The tavern was favored by voyageurs, and the door to *Les Coureurs de Bois* never opened but to burst open.

The room smelled of smoke, stale beer, and the human sweat of the backwoods. The floor was covered with litter, tobacco spit and blood. Roy ordered a round of beer. Toussaint generally preferred a sweet cider, but he could see this was not the place to order such a beverage. Being seated, Nicolas* Reaume began, "Pierre Gauthier de la Vérendrye is being recalled. It seems the governor is unhappy with his work. De la Vérendrye on the other hand thinks he has done a fine job, and I agree, as do most of the voyageurs. He has spent the past several years exploring the far west and establishing small posts. He is definitely hostile at being replaced.

"His replacement is Philippe Juchereau, who is also capable. We are going with a few soldiers and Indians as far as the lake of the Winnipeg, perhaps farther. No one in the group except two of the Indians has been farther than the Lake of the Woods. It should be a grand adventure. Even with the soldiers we should be there in less than two months and will return with de la Vérendrye and some of the other soldiers. We should be home by harvest without difficulty."

As evening drew near, the men removed themselves to the fort.

At the fort they entered a large room with two Indians and eight soldiers. The men from the *Les Coureurs de Bois* constituted the entire group of voyageurs. To their surprise and delight, there was a table of food. Not being bashful, they descended upon it and devoured the bulk of the supplies. The oldest appearing soldier stood and called the group to order. Philippe Juchereau was a member of the prominent Juchereau family. A native of Québec, he had gone to France for military education and was now in charge of the voyage. He was to take charge of exploration of the west upon relieving Gauthier de la Vérendrye. Pierre* and Toussaint took an instant liking to him.

He hung a large map on the wall and then asked each man to briefly introduce himself. It seemed that the soldiers had little experience in this sort of journey. The two Indians were Huron and had been to the final destination. There would be four other Indians, two Algonquin and in keeping with the current Peace of Utrecht, two Iroquois.

"We will leave by the Ottawa River to Lake Nipissing then on to the French River and the Lake of the Huron. We will make a short stop at Michilimackinac and part through the Sault of Sainte-Marie to Gitcheegumee. On the north shore, we will find the entrance to this intricate string of lakes and follow them for over two hundred miles to The Lake of the Woods.

"Messieurs Reaume and Charbonneau have gone this route and inform me that the lakes are fine and the portages short and not so confusing as it would seem from the map. At this point our Huron companions will guide us up the Winnipeg River to Lake Winnipeg. At the north of this big lake we will rendez-vous with Commander Gauthier de la Vérendrye at Fort Bourbon. If there are no further questions, we shall meet here before sunrise."

Pierre Roy dragged the group, along with two unsuspecting soldiers, back to *Les Coureurs de Bois.* He claimed, "No self respecting voyageur leaves on a trip like this until he has drunk his last franc." The group would regret this policy in the morning.

They met at the fort where Juchereau had the curé say a brief prayer. Then they loaded their canoes. The boys were surprised at how heavily they were packed. They were also dismayed because they knew what this would mean when they reached Lachine. Indeed at the fabled rapids they began the famous portage and the weight of the canoes made it much harder than it was with the light canoes they had brought to Détroit some years before.

Pierre* and Toussaint could hardly compete with the other voyageurs but they were happy to see how well they compared to the soldiers, especially those from France. Half the men were new immigrants from France and the others born in Québec. The difference was obvious particularly at the level of complaining. One of the men called Leduc said, “I’m almost glad it’s so blasted cold, the work heats you up.”

Nicolas* Reaume laughed and reported, “This, my friend, is the warm part of the voyage.”

Following the arduous portage they entered the Ottawa River, which was more to everyone’s liking. This also signaled the beginning of the adventure for Pierre* and Toussaint as they had never been this route. Two days later they reached the trading post at Gatineau or Ottawa as it was now always called. The route had changed little since the time Pierre* and Toussaint’s fathers had taken it with Cadillac but the post was larger and a few farms actually made it a small frontier town.

Three days later they landed at the North Bay post on Lake Nipissing. Reaume led them to a nearby Ottawa camp. Nicolas* was friendly with the chief and they were invited for the night. After dinner the chief explained that they had seen more than a few English traders over the winter. “These men seem to be honorable. It is of interest that they do not regard their government well. The English are not such good woodsmen as the Indian or even as the French. These men come to trade, as they cannot live as farmers. By their claim it is because the government of the English will not give them land.”

Toward the end of the evening, the old chief pointed his finger at Philippe Juchereau, "I believe these poor English could be more allies to the French and to the Indian than we believe." The old chief had little idea of how prophetic his statement would be.

At the end of the evening the chief asked Juchereau's permission to send maidens to the soldiers. When Juchereau agreed, his esteem improved in the eyes of the voyageurs. At dawn, Pierre* thought of Marie-Angélique* and for the first time felt a little guilty about the Indian maiden.

Lake Nipissing was still frozen on the edges and the group traversed it though the melted area in the center. Fortunately they were able to cross it in one day, as landing through the ice would have proved difficult and dangerous. That night Pierre* and Toussaint spoke after dinner with Leduc and another man, Leblanc, both of whom had come from the Larochelle Region of France. "We can scarcely believe the cold. How can you endure it?"

Toussaint told them, "We truly do not find it so cold. You will become accustomed to it. Dressing warm and staying active is important. Staying dry is very important here."

Leduc asked, "What if you do get wet?"

"Either you get warm and dry quickly or you die. But I am told death by cold is pleasant."

Leduc continued, "Have you ever talked to anyone who has done it?"

Laughing, Toussaint replied, "Only people who have 'almost' died. I am told that in the very north of Québec, the old Indians go on the ice flows when it is their time to die and are very content."

Leduc finished, "I don't think I could be so deceitful."

Pierre* asked them what they had done before this voyage.

Leblanc answered, "We worked in the valley of the Ohio River burying plates."

Pierre* returned, "Plates?"

"Yes, survey plates with the particularities of the area and symbols of France. Evidently it is felt that these can be used of proof of French ownership."

Toussaint responded, "A typical European idea. I wonder if anyone has explained this to the Iroquois."

Lake of the Huron - April 1742:

Portaging to the French River, they proceeded to the large bay which would some day be renamed *Georgian* by the British. Then up to Manitoulin Island and through the North Channel of Lake Huron. The soldiers were unpleasantly surprised that although it was now the beginning of April and the songbirds were in the trees, it remained very cold and snow was everywhere, sometimes very deep snow.

Growing weary of the complaints, the Indians built an enormous campfire and placed large rocks in the pit. They then constructed a tent around it open at the top for the smoke. They threw water on the rocks and bid the soldiers and others to undress and enter. The voyageurs were quick to enter the 'Indian bath' but the soldiers were reticent. Once they had done it, however, they were thrilled at the effect. Not only were they made warm but also clean.

After a while Leduc said, "My God, I'm actually too warm."

One of the Algonquin replied, "No problem," and he dragged the naked man out and threw him in the snow. Leduc was further amazed when the others came to roll in the snow. As Leduc arose, one of the Iroquois came over and said in halting French, "More good with women." And with a sly grin he slapped Leduc on his bare rump. Leduc and the other soldiers dressed quickly as Leduc quickly calculated how many months must pass before he could return to France.

The next afternoon they made Fort Michilimackinac. This post had grown considerably since the days of Cadillac. There were many farmers and a village larger than Détroit. Juchereau met with the Commandant and obtained supplies. At dawn they headed to the Sault of Saint-Marie.

Pierre* asked Nicolas* Reaume what the 'Sault' was like and Reaume replied, "Like Niagara lying on its side."

When they reached the Sault, Pierre* began to understand. Gitcheegumee stood much higher than Lake Huron, just as Erie stood high above Ontario. The difference came in that the drop at Niagara happened suddenly, and the drop at the Sault more gradually. The result was much longer and filled with pools, rapids, whirlpools and falls large and small. In some ways this was a show of nature more impressive than Niagara.

They portaged the southwestern bank. When they stopped to rest they would go to inspect the Sault and see how very different it was at each point. When they camped for the night, Pierre Roy took Pierre* and Toussaint to a large pool where they caught sacks of trout. They brought them to camp and simply gutted each one and returned it to the sack with some snow. In this fashion they would be good for several days.

When they reached the giant lake of Gitcheegumee, the soldiers were puzzled. Leduc asked, “It is colder here than in Huron, but there is almost no ice. How can this be?” Nicolas* Reaume explained, “This is the ‘endless water’, or Gitcheegumee in Algonquin. In places there is no bottom. For many generations the Indians believed it had no opposite shore. Because of the size the water barely changes temperature between the hottest and coldest day of the year. As a result, little ice forms compared to the other lakes. In addition, the storms here would break any ice cover.”

They followed the north shore. Reaume warned them to stay close to the shore as monster storms could arise suddenly. Fortunately they were usually from the north and would be offshore here. The north coast was absolute wilderness, jagged coves with beaches alternated with high granite cliffs. Most trees were conifer and the ground remained snow covered. After a few days they could see land on the opposite coast. Reaume explained that this was not the mainland but the great *Ile Royal.* Toward the western end of the great island they saw a peninsula on the mainland that formed a large deep cove. There was a large wooden cross erected on the point of the peninsula.

They stopped for the night by the cross. That night Reaume told a story. "Do you know of Etienne Brûlé?" The Québec men did but the soldiers did not.

"Well, Etienne Brûlé came from France as a young boy on the first voyage of Champlain 135 years ago. It is said he stowed away, and Champlain found him and allowed him to stay. As he became a teenager, he went to the woods where he lived many years with the Indians and learned their ways and language as well as any native. He returned as a young man to Champlain with knowledge of the backcountry said to have been better than that of any man, French or Indian, before or after this time.

"Champlain had Brûlé guide him to the wilderness, and this was the first time the French (other than young Etienne) had ever seen the great lakes especially Gitchigumée. They made it as far as *Ile Royal* and landed for the night. They found a band of renegade Indians who killed two of the soldiers and captured Champlain. Brûlé was able to use his communication skills and Indian savvy to gain the release of Champlain but they had to flee the Island.

"They headed to the shore but a storm came from the west bringing fog and high waves. They prayed and paddled and virtually ran into this point. They were able to find shelter and safety in the cove for the night. The next morning, a Jesuit traveling with the group suggested they erect the cross in thanks for their deliverance. In the morning they explored the cove and found a large group of pigeons at the entry to a small river which they named 'Pigeon River'. This is the entry to the great string of lakes in the land of Minnesota through which we shall head tomorrow. Now the cross serves as a sign to voyageurs to find the river."

Leblanc asked, "What happened to this Brûlé?"

Reaume continued, "He lost interest in Québec society and went to live with the Huron. It is said that he fell out of favor with the chief. Some say because he had become more versed in the ways of the wilderness than any Indian."

"What did the chief do?"

"Well, they killed him, but as they considered him a great man, they did it in high fashion."

"How is one killed in 'high fashion'?"

Arising, Reaume simply said, "They skinned and burned him alive and then ate him."

The French soldiers were aghast. Leduc asked, "Does anyone have a more pleasant tale?"

Toussaint started, "My great-grandfather, an Algonquin called Henri, was possibly the very first man to walk entirely around the lake. He and my great-grandmother started at Michilimackinac and he ended the voyage one year later."

Leblanc queried, "What about your great-grandmother?"

"She died when they were exploring *Ile Royal.*"

"How did she die?"

"She was attacked and eaten by a giant brown bear."

Leblanc looked incredulous, "This is a pleasant story?"

Toussaint replied, "Oh yes, to die at the hands of the brown bear is a great honor for the Indian."

Leduc added, "More honor than I care to have." As the men retired for the night, Pierre* and Toussaint noticed that the soldiers slept particularly close to the fire this night.

At dawn they traveled to the end of the cove and the head of a small river. They were surprised to see a small cabin on the shore, and more surprised as two soldiers sat in front of it. When the men landed the two came down to greet them. The older of the two introduced himself as Jeremaye Dandonneau and said, "Welcome to Fort Kaministiquia. I'm sorry not to have a better welcome but the band has the day off." Getting no laugh he continued, "Commander de la Vérendrye has sent us to help you through the lakes. We shall leave as soon as you are ready."

Juchereau indicated that there was no reason for delay so they pushed off. By midday they were through the narrow Pigeon River and to the first lake. The lakes were narrow, deep and clear. They sat in the most idyllic wilderness setting. Best of all, as they moved away from Gitcheegumee, there was less snow and more green. Pierre* and Toussaint knew of the Dandonneau family. The family had many children who had joined the military. They had met Angélique* Dandonneau-Vien, the wife of Ignatius* Vien in Détroit.

That night Dandonneau gave them the history of the exploration. "Commander Pierre Gauthier de la Vérendrye has been here with the regiment since 1732. His three sons are also officers, but one, Jean-Baptiste was killed a few years ago. We have explored a great deal of the region and established eleven 'forts' although most are only shelters that are occupied only when the need arises. We have made good relations with the Indians. There are some Chippewa, but there are other tribes as well. The largest is called Sioux; they are, well, different than the eastern tribes we know."

The voyage became routine, long narrow lakes and short portages. Dandonneau told them, "This area is a honeycomb of such lakes, one can hardly walk a mile before happening upon another. Some of the voyageurs have a sense for traveling in them but I rely heavily on my compass." Pierre* was pleased that his father had given him his old military compass for the voyage. They passed another small-unoccupied 'fort', this one Fort Saint-Pierre. Then they came to a very large and extremely beautiful lake.

Reaume announced, "The Lake in the Woods. This is as far as I have traveled."

That night they camped on a large island in the center of the lake. Dandonneau told them, "Control of fur trade is as much of our job as is exploration. Each year we send at least 30,000 beaver to Montréal. There is a small native band on this lake called Assiniboine. They are generally friendly. The Commandant sent his oldest son, Jean-Baptiste, to negotiate with them. One of our dilemmas is that the local tribes may be friendly with us but not with each other. The Sioux were angered at this arrangement and killed Jean-Baptiste on this island.

Leduc asked, "What did they do?"

"They decapitated him, a particular favorite of the Sioux."

The next two years were looking very long to Leduc.

The next day they passed a third fort, Fort Saint-Charles, and headed into the Winnipeg River. The next few days became colder and the snow deeper. Eventually they encountered another 'fort', this one called Maurepas II as opposed to Maurepas I, which was farther south. De la Vérendrye had taken a cue from Cadillac and named these two forts after the current Governor of New-France. Here they entered a wide body of water, which they were told was Lake Winnipeg. The shore was lined with ice and the trees had become less dense.

Three days later they turned into a river to the west and by late afternoon were at the metropolis of Fort Bourbon. This fort had been built the year before and had at least a rudimentary stockade surrounding a few small buildings. The snow was frozen and the wind whipped mercilessly across the plain. Leduc asked, "Does it never thaw in this place?"

Dandonneau laughed and replied. "Oh most certainly, wait until July, you will think you are in Hell itself."

They landed the canoes and presented themselves at the fort. Pierre Gauthier de la Vérendrye was almost sixty years old, fit and agile and his skin dark leather from the years of prairie sun. He greeted the men cordially. He and Juchereau had known each other as children in Montréal and regarded one another well. As evening was upon them, he invited them to dine.

The dining room was basic enough but had candles, a fireplace, and enough dinnerware to give some vague hint of civilization. De la Vérendrye gave a summary of their work so far touching on problems and opportunities. "We have a capable and experienced staff. Ensign Dandonneau whom you have met is my nephew on my wife's side. As you may know she is Marie-Jeanne Dandonneau. Her sister, Angélique* is married to Ignatius* Vien, with whom, I am certain, you men from Détroit are acquainted."

After dinner, drinks were served and he addressed Juchereau, "Commander, there is one thing I would like to finish. We were planning an excursion to the far west this spring. Our communication with the Cree Indians to the north and the Pawnee to the south lead us to believe that we are close to the discovery of the route to the Western Ocean. My sons still wish to make this journey, with or without military support. They plan to leave soon. Some of our voyageurs are anxious to return to Montréal with me so we would like to see if any of your woodsman would care to join my sons."

Almost jumping from the table, Pierre Roy shouted, "If it's going west, I'm in!" Charbonneau and Reaume also indicated interest. Pierre* and Toussaint thought this needed to be discussed in private later. Juchereau indicated that he had no objection but could not spare any military support apart from de la Vérendrye's two sons.

In the morning, Pierre* Allard approached de la Vérendrye. "Monsieur Commandant, my friend and I would like to go on the trip west. Would it be possible to get word back with your group to our families in Québec, informing them of our plans and time table?"

The older man said, "Of course, I will try to deliver it myself. I feel very strongly about this voyage and wish I myself could go."

Pierre* wondered how this would play with his new fiancé.

Chapter 15

Northern Manitoba, Canada - May 1742:

After breakfast, the five Québec voyageurs met with the two Gauthier brothers. Louis-Joseph Gauthier was the spokesman although the youngest at twenty-five. His brother François was two years his senior but more quiet. The boys had been born raised in Sorel, a small town between Montréal and Trois-Rivieres where their father had been stationed at the small fort. They had both spent a few teenage years in France at military school, but having lived their last few years in the western frontier, they seemed as capable as the voyageurs.

Louis-Joseph had a rudimentary map of the west. "The problem with reaching the sea is a legendary mountain range that no Frenchman has actually seen. However, speaking with the Indians, there is no doubt that it exists and is formidable. The Cree who live to the north tell of a passage by way of the Saskatchewan River. I might also add that no white man has actually been to this river.

"The Pawnee to our south have indicated that we can take the Missouri River, of which we have knowledge, to a river that in the Pawnee language is called 'Yellowstone'. This will lead us to the mountains that can be crossed by a pass. We tend to regard the information of the Pawnee more favorably and have a Sioux scout who has been through the pass. We therefore favor the southern route. The weather also should be less severe than in the north.

"This will be slower and more difficult than the type of travel to which you may be accustomed. Until the mountains we have plains. Here there are few trees, no shade or cover, and the rivers go from torrents to dry beds with each rainstorm. There will be many portages. After the mountains, we have no idea of the difficulty. The Indians in the area are generally friendly, but I must warn you, much more unpredictable than those in the east."

Nicolas* Reaume stood, "I have talked to our Indians and two have volunteered to accompany us. Interestingly, one Huron and one Iroquois."

The remainder of the meeting involved details of preparation. Two days later they departed. The first day was portage to Lake Winnipegosis, which lay parallel and west of the much wider Lake Winnipeg. The trip was slow going due to dropping temperatures, blizzard condition and worsening ice on the lake. Two long weeks later they arrived at the small Fort Dauphin, which housed four lonely soldiers.

The men were thankful to get inside and warm. They waited four days until the weather cleared during which time they had a first hand look at the life of the frontier military. Two men were French immigrants and the other two Québecois. They all agreed that they could not have survived this post in winter without the skills of the two Québec men. One of the Québecois named Forestier had been with the regiment since the beginning. He had developed a love of the plains and was very talkative.

"The plains aren't actually flat, they roll. It's just the roll is so gradual it seems flat. All the trees are by rivers and the rest is bare, except for the grass. The grass is the most incredible thing. Sometimes its roots are two feet deep. It takes a man all day with a pickax to dig a hole. When it rains there is plenty of water but when it does not, there is none.

"West of here is the black water. We call it that. It is thick, dirty, and smells. It's as black as night. Nothing will grow around it and the animals avoid it at all costs. I don't know why God would curse a land with such a thing."

Toussaint asked, "What do the people eat?"

"Buffalo, oh my yes, buffalo. I won't tell you more, you must, and you will, see it for yourself."

On the fourth day they set off reaching Lake Manitoba. In two days the weather again turned bad. They camped in a snowstorm and in the morning the lake was clogged with ice. Nicolas* Reaume took one of the Indians to scout down the lake. They returned several hours later with bad news, "It's frozen as far as we could see. We must make a winter camp and wait for a thaw. There is a stand of trees at the bank a few miles down. Probably our best bet."

Winter camps were easy to make in the Québec woods because of the dense forest and many caves. Here there was only open plain and blowing snow. The few trees at the bank provided some protection as well as some fuel for fire. Fortunately these men knew how to survive in the frozen wilderness. On the third day Toussaint noted, "We should have brought the iceboat instead of the canoe."

On the fourth day Pierre Roy said. "I've had enough of pemmican," and he took his ax and a pack out onto the frozen lake. A few hours later he returned with a sack of fish. "At least we have something to eat that has not been dead longer than we have been alive."

Two weeks later it started to rain and within a few days the lake began to open. They were able to recommence and arrived at the south end of Lake Manitoba more than a month from the time of their departure. They started down a small stream that required frequent portage. Eventually they reached a real river Louis-Joseph called the Assiniboine. It was relatively clear of ice and the first real canoeing of the voyage. The days became warm and within a week the snow was gone, and it was actually hot.

François Gauthier explained that this was a typical weather pattern in the plains. "The hottest and coldest days of the year can occur in the same week. We will probably be more troubled by heat from now on."

The melting snow filled the river and portage was not a problem. The current, however, was, and François said it would remain upstream the entire way to the mountains. "At all points, the water comes from the mountains and from here it flows east to the Mississippi and out to *La Nouvelle Orléans.*"

If the water was a familiar sight, the land was not. As the snow disappeared, it was apparent how few trees there were, and there seemed to be fewer trees each mile. Several days later they came to a bend to the northwest. Louis-Joseph said, "This is now the *Souris* (or Mouse in English). It will take us to the portage to the Missouri."

A few days later, after making camp, Pierre* and Toussaint walked a short distance from the river. The occasional tree along the bank had shielded them from the sheer starkness of the landscape. They could see, well, as far as they could see. The boys had only experienced this on the great lakes. It became apparent to both of them that they had never in their lives been to a place that was not surrounded by forest.

The grass was a dull brown, but they could see small green shoots in its depth. Toussaint sat and took his knife to the ground. He cut down through several inches of grass that was almost a solid structure. At this point he encountered roots. The roots almost defied his knife and were like cutting into a maple tree. François Gauthier came by and joined them, "Why don't we try to find the soil?"

The boys rose to the challenge and began excavating a hole with their knives and axes. About an hour later they had reached a depth in excess of two feet when Toussaint yelled, "There it is!" and he brought up a handful of the darkest, richest soil he had ever seen.

Gauthier said, "The soil here is the richest ever known. Farming would be ideal when water is plentiful and if one could plow through the grass. I doubt, however, if this could ever be done."

The *Souris* River remained navigable with only occasional portage for the next few weeks. The landscape became barren and the voyageurs began to yearn for the backwoods. One night at camp, Louis-Joseph said, "The rivers in this country run primarily north to south. Very few go east and west. Indeed the Missouri goes north for hundreds of miles before turning west. It is because of this we will have a portage of note when we leave the *Souris*."

Michel Charbonneau asked, “How *notable* a portage?”

Gauthier responded, “It depends on the amount of water in the creeks that fill the Missouri and how soon we find one, but I would say under the worst circumstances, no more than one hundred miles.”

Pierre Roy added, “Damn, now my hearing’s going too. I thought I heard you say one hundred miles.”

Nicolas* Reaume interrupted, “I believe he did.”

Gauthier continued, “You must realize that it is not like Québec. The land is flat, we travel in a straight line, and the canoes can actually be pulled on the grass.”

Roy replied, “Can you pull a canoe with my ass sitting in it?”

Gauthier replied with a smile, “No, but we could use the lard from your ass to grease the canoe.”

Laughter broke out and Roy replied, “Well, thank God, Gauthier, I’ve been worried that you boys had no sense of humor.” At this point friendships began to form.

<u>The Northern Plains - July 1742:</u>

As the group was nearing the end of the *Souris,* they encountered a small Indian camp in the middle of the plain. Pierre* asked why they would be in this seemingly unlikely location, Louis-Joseph replied, “Hunting buffalo.”

Puzzled, Pierre* continued, “But they don’t seem to be hunting or doing anything for that matter.”

Louis-Joseph explained, “They wait for the buffalo to come to them. You will eventually understand.”

They went into the camp and their Sioux guide, Red Feather, spoke to some braves. He returned and told the men, "These are Sioux Indians of the Dakota tribe. They are usually friendly and have asked us to stay."

They set up at the side of the camp and waited. The welcome was quite subdued compared to those they had been accustomed to in the east. Red Feather, who spoke good French, explained. "These people have only seen white men once or twice. They see no reason to fear you but will remain aloof."

The camp seemed to be very organized, and the work seemed to be well organized as well. Pierre* and Toussaint were surprised a hunting party would include the whole village even the very old, the women, and the children including the infants. That night they ate roasted meat they were told was buffalo. It was surprisingly similar to beef.

The Indians wore clothing similar to the eastern Indians but more ornamented. One obvious adornment was objects made from snakes, including skin, heads and tails with large rattles. Pierre* and Toussaint had been warned that the rattlesnake of this country was much more dangerous than those found in the east.

Some trade occurred between the Indians and the Gauthiers. The brothers had brought trinkets and the Dakota traded with snake ornaments. Later François told them. "Trade here is symbolic. These people have yet to develop a concept of functional trade." There was dancing and singing that was more animated than the type seen in the east, and they smoked a strange tobacco that made the men very dizzy and caused them to have bizarre dreams that night.

In the morning they continued down the *Souris*. A few days later the terrain became hillier with a steeper roll than before. Red Feather sensed something in the air and spoke to Louis-Joseph who in turn instructed the men to stop and go ashore. As they landed their canoes, he told them, "Red Feather thinks if we hike to the west, we may see something worthwhile."

They began up a western slope and about an hour later came to a summit. Although there was no water in sight, this had once been the bed of the Missouri River and a large valley was all that remained. The grass, which had been briefly green, but was now turning a dull brown again. However, farther out in the valley it turned almost black. The men soon realized this was not grass, but animals. Even Pierre Roy was impressed, "My God, I have been told of this but never thought it could be so many."

The buffalo stretched as far as they could see and stood almost touching one another. Louis-Joseph said, "Let us go and get one."

They walked into the valley and eventually came to the edge of the herd, Louis-Joseph told the men, "We will find a small weak one and Red Feather will kill him with arrows."

Toussaint asked, "Why not shoot it?"

Louis-Joseph replied, "The shot may frighten the herd. If they start to move, it can be dangerous and if they start to move in our direction, it will be the end of our trip, and the end of us."

The Sioux scout quietly approached a small animal and shot it repeatedly until it eventually fell, but not without more than ten arrows. Red Feather then fell on it and began to skillfully skin and dissect it. While he worked, he explained, "The Indian uses every part of the animal, the skin for cover, the meat to eat, the bones for tools, the entrails for sacs."

In this case he took the hide and filled it with as much meat as the group could carry back to the canoes. Pierre* and Toussaint were amazed at the amount of meat from this comparatively small animal. They were still eating buffalo a week later when they came to a bend northward in the river, and Gauthier announced that they were at their portage to the Missouri River.

Gauthier had been correct. The portage was relatively flat and covered with grass. The bad news was that the July sun brought out midday temperatures over 100 degrees with no hope of shade. Also the only water available was that which was carried. Fortunately, Louis-Joseph knew how much to bring, but that did not make it any less heavy. They realized if Gauthier had been correct on the distance, at their current speed it would take them until the beginning of August to reach the Missouri River.

At the halfway point, Pierre Roy was making his daily complaint, "This is hotter than Louisiana ever thought about being."

Suddenly Red Feather ran to Louis-Joseph and began making wild gestures. Looking to the north, the men could see an enormous cloud heading their way. Gauthier told the men, "We must proceed as quickly as possible to the top of the hill to our left and bring everything with us."

Roy began to complain about carrying the canoes in the wrong direction when Louis-Joseph quickly silenced him and said, "Time is of the essence. Our lives may depend on it." When the men reached the hilltop, it was apparent that the cloud was not an ordinary cloud, but a brown one. They began to hear a constant roar of deafening thunder when Reaume realized what was happening and shouted, "Buffalo!"

François Gauthier looked down and hollered, "Thank God, they are going straight and away from us." And then he pointed and added, "They're heading for a 'drop'. They are being chased."

Indeed the herd was heading directly to a dry creek bed, which presented about a ten-foot drop. When the first animals came to the edge, they ran straight through and fell to their death. Others tried to stop but were pushed from those behind. The men could then see a band of Indians running behind and beside them, actually herding the stampede. During the time they watched, Pierre* saw two men fall under the hooves of the mob of animals.

Eventually the pile of dead buffalo caused the herd to turn, but unfortunately they turned to their left and headed up the hill toward the voyageurs. Gauthier shouted, "Bring the canoes to that rock!" and they carried their belongings to an outcropping of rock close by. He then instructed them to arrange the canoes like a wedge with the rock in the middle. He then instructed them to saturate a cloth in water and hold it over their faces. "Get together and huddle behind the rock and between the canoes. Stay down, this may take all day or longer."

As soon as they were in position, the herd arrived. The noise was deafening. The cloud not only made it impossible to see, but also impossible to breathe without the wet cloth. The sky turned as black as night and remained so for hours. After what seemed like days, the noise stopped. The air slowly cleared but the sky remained black. It took a while for the men to regain enough orientation to realize that it was now night! Eventually stars were seen and breathing became normal.

They realized that they had been saved by the rocks and the canoes, which caused the animals to part around them. Louis-Joseph said, "There are few men who have witnessed a buffalo stampede from their canoes." Then to the surprise of the others he added, "Of course, this was a very small stampede."

Fires burned brightly in the valley where pandemonium rang. François told the men, "The Indians are celebrating and harvesting the kill. The Indians wait for a buffalo herd to wander by, they surround it on three sides and start making enormous noise. They then drive the herd in a predetermined direction toward a 'buffalo drop'. These short cliffs are old dry riverbeds that are common in the area. As you have seen, it is difficult to kill a small buffalo with arrows and almost impossible to kill a large one. This method kills the animals as they stampede over the cliff."

Red Feather had gone down to the action at the buffalo kill and returned, "These are the same Dakota tribe we visited earlier. They have invited us; I believe you will find this interesting."

The activity was incredible. Although the young men had 'herded' the stampede, the entire village was now involved in processing the kill. Everyone had a job and as Red Feather had told them earlier, every part of the buffalo was harvested. The number killed on this drive, however, was more than the tribe could manage. After they had all the meat they could use, they merely skinned the rest and left the carcasses to the coyotes.

Red Feather said, "It is unfortunate that more animals than needed were killed, but as you see, this is difficult to control. In any case, there are more buffalo than could ever be killed."

After the work was done the tribe gathered about the central fire to eat and celebrate. Everyone ate until they could eat no more. They encouraged the Frenchmen to do the same and young women came, encouraging them to eat. Their guide explained, "The tribe will eat as much as possible tonight and for many days to come. All will grow fat so that they may survive until the next hunt."

The celebration was considerably different than they had seen some nights before. The level of enthusiasm grew as time passed and reached a level of savagery. It lasted until morning. Red Feather tried to explain as much as possible, "Now they are commemorating the two young braves who were killed in the stampede. This is not a sad mourning as these men will enjoy a privileged place among their ancestors."

In the morning the men returned to their canoes and the long struggle for the Missouri.

The Missouri River - August 1742:

Soon after leaving the Dakota tribe, the men found a dry creek bed heading in the correct direction. It eventually became wet enough for the canoes, and the long walk came to an end. The following day they came to the big river. The Missouri was the largest river they had seen since Québec. It was, however, much more variable than the eastern rivers. It went from deep to shallow, wide to narrow and rapid to slow quickly and frequently for no reason apparent to these men who had spent their lives on rivers.

In spite of its peculiarities this was the easiest part of the voyage so far. They made good time with occasional portages and ate well. Once they had finished their buffalo, they found trout and other river fish abundant. Eventually the river narrowed and became relatively wild, rapids became common requiring portage and the terrain became hillier, the slope of the voyage more upgrade. They came to a fork about the middle of August.

Louis-Joseph announced, "No one but Red Feather has been beyond this point. This is the Yellowstone River."

A few days later Pierre* Allard asked Red Feather, "Why is this river called 'Yellowstone'?"

The guide replied, "Because this water comes out of yellow stones. You shall see for yourself."

This river was narrower than the wide Missouri. At first it was easier going, although the current was always against them. Soon they came to considerable variation, sometimes very narrow and fast with rapids, and sometimes very wide and shallow, and occasionally nothing more than a bed of mud. Portage was common although easy in the flat barren terrain. Louis-Joseph said, "As we approach the beginning of the mountains, I suspect the water will be better but with more uphill portaging."

Pierre Roy laughed, "We have canoed to the very top of the Laurentian at Sainte-Anne. This cannot be any more difficult."

Gauthier replied, "I hope you are correct, my friend. I hope you are correct."

At one point while portaging a long, wide and dry stretch of riverbed, they heard thunder, which they now knew did not come from the sky. Red Feather spoke, "Quickly follow me!"

He led them to the top of a small rise. They could see the buffalo coming en masse and very fast. Unfortunately, the men were still in the path of the stampede. They raced with their loads to a higher place more on the anticipated periphery. Red Feather told the men to load their guns and wait. At the right time he instructed them to shoot at the leading corner of the herd. A few animals fell and the noise along with the carcasses in the path turned the herd just enough to avoid the men.

They sat and waited in fear that the buffalo would readjust their course. They waited for two entire days. Eventually the herd had passed. At the end Michel Charbonneau said to Louis-Joseph, "I see what you mean when you say they could never all be killed, I had no idea there were that many animals of any sort in all of the Americas."

They harvested enough from the fallen animals to make their diet for the next few weeks and then continued their portage.

August turned to September, and the weather became more tolerable. There was no change in color, as they would have seen in Québec. The terrain retained its flat, dull brown monotony, and what few trees there were merely turned the same dull brown. Roy complained, "I believe we have walked farther than we have paddled. We may have done better to leave the canoes." At that point it began to rain.

The rain continued without stop for two weeks. The canoes became more useful but the current became stronger as well. Fortunately it remained warm, as there was no means of becoming dry. Visibility was severely limited and when the rain did slow for a short period, it was replaced by fog. They continued to sleep under covers at night although they could not possibly be any wetter.

In the middle of the night more than two weeks after it started, the rain abruptly stopped. Each night the men took turns keeping watch. This night Pierre* Allard held the final watch. As the sun appeared on the eastern horizon making its first appearance in many days, Pierre* sat and watched. Once it had broken the horizon he rose to wake the others. As he turned to the west, he suddenly shouted, "*Sainte-Marie et Joseph!*" As the others awoke they looked to the west and for more than an hour no one moved or spoke.

Finally Toussaint broke the silence, "My father often quoted Jean* Gauthier who said the Kaskaskian had told him there were mountains no white man had seen and no man who had not seen them could comprehend. This was an understatement."

Their long obstructed view was now clear. The plain ran for a long distance and stopped abruptly to rise as mountains beyond belief. The peaks were without trees and still capped with snow at the end of the hot summer. In places the peaks disappeared into the clouds. The men continued with renewed vigor as anticipation of the spectacle before them removed the burden of overwhelming boredom.

Chapter 16

The Rocky Mountains - October 1742:

As they entered the foothills, Red Feather explained, "We follow the Yellowstone River up to the mountains which will lead us to a large lake. From there we find the pass which is well hidden but will lead us to the other side of the mountains."

The voyage became typical mountain canoeing, short periods of stream with portages at the falls and rapids, and always going up. The terrain was steeper and more rocky than the Laurentian. Trees began to reappear and became dense. At lower elevations they were a type of birch, called aspen by the natives, with gray-brown bark. Their leaves were turning bright yellow. Higher up they became conifers with enormously tall pines, spruce and fir.

Game was plentiful. Red Feather explained that animals went very high in the summer and were now coming down for the winter. Deer were everywhere including some extremely large species. Wild goats and sheep abounded as well and were the most sure-footed creatures the men had ever seen. Dinner was never a problem.

Although the Laurentian were filled with granite and limestone, the ground was generally soil. Here rocks predominated and portage became even more difficult. Eventually they began to notice that the stone was taking on a definite yellow hue. The view above was always spectacular but the view behind was becoming equally so.

The view of the plains from above was unbelievable. At one point Nicolas* Reaume said, "I believe I can see Montréal from here."

The going was very slow and occasionally they would be required to backtrack as they had taken the wrong branch of the stream. As the weather turned cold, it began to snow. That night at camp Nicolas* Reaume asked the obvious of Louis-Joseph Gauthier, "Unless we find a quick way out at this pass, we shall have full winter with which to contend. What are your plans?"

Louis-Joseph replied, "The trip has taken longer than I had anticipated. We will make a winter camp when necessary. With the fuel and game in the area, it should not be too difficult."

Pierre* Allard wondered how this would play with his fiancé.

The following morning they saw a high column of steam in the distance. Red Feather explained there were hot springs in the area that spouted periodically into the air. At the end of the day they came to a clearing in a pass they were portaging that overlooked a large spectacular mountain lake.

Red Feather exclaimed, "It is here that we will find our pass!"

The group descended and made camp for the night.

In the morning the men arose to find Red Feather missing. Louis-Joseph said, "He had the final watch. I wonder what could have happened?"

Soon their guide came quickly through the trees. "There is an Indian band advancing, they are about two hours away."

Louis-Joseph said, "Probably Pawnee, we'll be all right."

The guide countered, "I am afraid not, they are Arapahoe. They will not want us here, and there are many."

Nicolas* Reaume asked, "What do you suggest?"

"It is likely that these men do not know rifles. This is our only advantage. They are downwind and will soon know we are here. We should hide our canoes and equipment and take cover from where we can attack. Shoot only when you have a clear target. They may be frightened away."

Toussaint asked, "Can we try to reason with them?"

Red Feather said sternly, "Arapahoe do not reason."

They hid their things and found cover in the rocks. With the five men, two Indians from Québec, the Gauthier brothers, and the guide, they were ten in all, all armed with a gun and a bow. Red Feather had estimated forty Arapahoe, who eventually came stealthily through the pass. It was apparent they knew someone was here. Pierre* noted that they were different both in dress and physical appearance from the Sioux. If he needed a word to describe them, it would be 'ferocious'.

As they came into better view, Reaume took the first shot and the lead man fell. The others did not react other than to look confused. Three more shots were taken and three more fell. The Arapahoe began to advance quickly, but three more were killed. Seeing this the group turned and quickly disappeared through the pass. Red Feather carefully followed in pursuit but soon returned.

"They are regrouping at the pass. They seem confused but are not planning on leaving."

Nicolas* Reaume said, "Why don't we go over to the falls," indicating a falls above a stream that flowed to the lake from the north. "Some of us will make a stand there and some can stay below and perhaps get behind them."

Red Feather replied, "The Arapahoe invented the ambush, but it could work. We should move quickly as they may be back."

They broke in two groups with Red Feather, Charbonneau, Pierre Roy and the Iroquois brave staying below. Reaume ran to the hiding place of the canoes and returned with his pack and the men began to advance to the falls. The falls were long and impressive but the climb was not difficult. They got to the top and took positions where they could watch below.

It was not long before they could hear shots and shouting below. Reaume said, "It sounds as though our ruse is not working."

They then saw the Arapahoe advancing, quickly and skillfully coming up the grade. It was soon evident there were more than forty. Reaume called the men close, "We are not going to shoot this many, but I have an idea." He gave Pierre* Allard his gun, "Here you will have an extra shot. Stay at the top and give me a sign when they are no more than three minutes away. The rest of you take your cover. Don't shoot until you see me again."

Pierre was mystified, but he had decided years ago never to question the ability of Nicolas* Reaume. Pierre* watched carefully and Reaume went a short way up stream and went behind trees just remaining slightly visible to Pierre*. When the men were just below, Pierre gave him the sign and he disappeared toward the stream.

The Indians began to pour over the pass and soon twenty were in the clearing and looking about. Just at this point there was a shout and they turned to see Nicolas* Reaume stand up on the water, shouting loudly. The Arapahoe were terrified at the sight of the man walking on the water and the Frenchmen began shooting, first with their guns, then with arrows. There was total confusion, and the Arapahoe retreated in terror even dropping their weapons as they ran.

The men shot as many as possible as they retreated and heard more shots as they reached the bottom of the falls. Reaume pulled himself to shore with his rope. When he crawled onto the bank, he gasped, "That is one cold stream!" The men other than the Gauthier brothers quickly realized that he had taken his rope, which he had retrieved from the canoe and tied it to a tree. At the right moment, he jumped in and used the rope to 'walk the falls'. He was correct in assuming that seeing a screaming white man walking on the water would have the desired effect on the Indians.

The men quickly made their way to the bottom. Their joy was ended when they saw that both Pierre Roy and Red Feather had been shot. Roy had an arrow in his chest and was having difficulty breathing. Red Feather had been shot directly in the heart. They attended to Roy and he became stable, the Iroquois had followed the fleeing Arapahoe. He eventually returned. This man did not speak much French and rarely had spoken on the trip, but he was able to communicate, "They gone. They not come back. Too scared." As they took stock of the situation, they realized that they had lost the only man who knew where they were headed.

That night they discussed the plan. They had buried Red Feather, and Roy was stable. His lung had appeared to seal but he was in no condition to travel. François Gauthier suggested, "We will camp in good cover and have no large fires as not to attract any more natives. Hopefully the Arapahoe are too afraid of 'walks on water' to return. We should break into groups of three or four each day and search for the pass. Red Feather said that it was at the lake."

Pierre Roy said, "If there is one thing I can't be it's useless. Before you boys go, get me plenty of branches from these brown birch or pine saplings. I'll cut some of this buffalo hide into strips, and I'll make us some Indian Slippers." Looking up at the sky he continued, "I think we're going to need them soon."

They decided to go in groups of four until Roy healed enough to come and make groups of three. François Gauthier took charge. "We shall mark this rock wall to the south as the 'zero point'. Today my group will try all possibilities between there and this point. Indicating a point with a stake. The second group will do all between this point and the next, and he placed another stake moving in a clockwise direction. This way we will eventually cover all possibilities without the chance of missing one. Remember, Red Feather said it was hidden, so look carefully. Be back or send someone back by dusk."

Pierre* could see that François Gauthier had experience in organized exploration. Pierre*'s group included Louis-Joseph, Reaume and the Iroquois who had finally talked enough to tell them his name was Falling Star. Toussaint was with François Gauthier, Charbonneau, and the Huron, Jagged Rock. The Gauthier brothers would be leaders and keep maps and logs.

That evening all eight men returned and both groups had the same story. All paths eventually led to an impenetrable wall of rock. Pierre Roy was in good spirits and clearly on the mend. He had made three pair of 'Indian Slippers', which served to walk in deep snow and had prepared a buffalo stew for dinner. He was certain that he would be fit to search with the others by the week's end.

By the end of the week Roy was indeed fit. The reports at the end of the day had been the same, always a dead end. He had finished nine pair of slippers just in time as winter descended with three feet of new snow. In the first week of December, they had covered about one half of François Gauthier's 'clock' map without any hint of success. During the second week the trips became longer as they came to flatland and had more possibilities to cover.

The group split in three. Nicolas* Reaume led the new group which included Pierre* Allard and Falling Star. In mid December they had some luck. They had happened on a narrow opening in a wall of rock that opened to a second pasture, which led in the distance to an obvious pass. They decided to return to camp to report before proceeding. Back at the lake the group had begun to build a winter camp in the event no pass was discovered. Reaume entered camp with enthusiasm. "I believe we may have found it. The opening is definitely hidden and once on the other side the pass seems apparent. We will return and investigate tomorrow but will likely not see it through for several days."

They retraced their steps through the 'hidden path', then on toward the mountain pass. On the third night out, their Iroquois companion, Falling Star seemed anxious to talk. Either his French had improved during the voyage or he had lost his reticence. It was probably some of both.

"My father was chief of band of Oneida tribe. He was always wary of English. His first encounters led him to believe they were not to be trusted. He was torn between this and his allegiance to the tribe and to the Five Nations. I wanted to come with the French. I have always suspected they were more honorable and now I find it so.

"I confess that my emotions were mixed at Arapahoe battle. In my father's country I see English coming in great numbers. I believe French view they can hold their land. This is, how do you say?… naïve. These Arapahoe, and Sioux and others may be fierce, but will be no match for the English numbers. I am content I was given the chance to see this land, but I fear I return to a disappearing life. I feel you too are returning to a similar fate at the hands of these English."

Pierre* asked him if he had heard of Pontiac. Falling Star replied, "I met this man two years ago at the forks of the Ohio. He sees an alliance between the French and all Indians. He is a persuasive man and I wish he was correct, but again I fear he is naïve."

Two days later they began the ascent to the pass. After three days of climbing and twisting through the rocks they believed they could see it, and it was within an easy day's hike. They awoke the next morning with enthusiasm and proceeded. At midday they reached it, but were met by something unexpected. The path had been covered by an enormous rockslide. Reaume said, "By the look of it can't be more than a few days old. After approaching from every possible angle, they realized that this was, and would forever remain, impassible.

As they began their slow and sad descent to the camp, it began to snow. This snow was not like Québec snow, it was light and powdery, but it obtained great depths in a short time. It stopped two days later and the men realized that another foot would make it impossible for them to move even in their Indian slippers. Fortunately they were able to make the camp two days later.

Yellowstone Camp - January 1, 1743:

Their other comrades were all present. Reaume reported their finding, "I am certain this was Red Feather's pass, but it is no more and will never again be a pass."

The other groups had finished the rest of the area and on this side were always stopped by a giant canyon with sheer cliffs. The following morning another several feet of snow had fallen and meaningful travel was out of the question. The men settled into their winter camp and François Gauthier declared the voyage to the sea over.

Yellowstone Camp - March 1743:

Winter in the mountains had been an adventure but less difficult than expected. The men had built a series of lean-tos against a cave. There was plenty of wood, and game was easy to find. Ice fishing in the big lake was simple, and the sun shone most days. They also had periods of warm winds that would melt the snow. Red Feather had told them of these winds, which he called 'Chinook winds' which meant 'snow eater' in his language.

Spring came early and fine. The river started to run and melted quickly to the point where the men felt they could depart. Pierre Roy had occasional problems with his breathing but seemed fit enough. As they had anticipated, the return trip was much easier due to the downhill grade and the downhill current of high spring water.

The Gauthier brothers wanted to bury survey plates along the way to claim the area for France. They had brought a number of lead plates but as François explained, "We need to place more detailed information on them but do not have the means to do so."

Toussaint spoke up, "I believe I can do it," and the job of engraver was given to the skilled wood carver.

Nights were cool but the days generally sunny and warm. Snow fell occasionally but disappeared rapidly. When they reached the plains it was spring and the grass started to show its brief period of green. As they approached the Missouri, Pierre Roy took a bad turn. He began to cough and breathing became more difficult. Fortunately there were almost no portages, but the men knew that there was trouble when he said he could no longer paddle.

The next day he began to cough blood and in the morning he was dead. The men buried their old friend at the junction of the Yellowstone and the Missouri. Pierre* Allard spoke, "We shall never see another man that will so completely define the word 'voyageur'. He said he wished to see the west before he died, and I suspect he died without regrets. Although I would have preferred he be buried in the woods of the great north, this wilderness frontier has a certain appeal as well."

After they filled his grave, Toussaint buried their last lead plate. To this one he had added his initials TdB.

Chapter 17

The Missouri River - April 1743:

The Gauthier brothers left the group at the portage to the *Souris* River, "We have decided to return to report and hopefully stay with Commander Dandonneau and continue the search for the passage to the sea."

Nicolas* Reaume said that he was going home and proposed that the men continue on the Missouri, "It is more than 1000 miles to the Mississippi at Saint-Louis, but the travel will be fast and easy with little if any portage. At Saint-Louis we can make for *Lac Michigauma* or Erie depending on the circumstances." He heard no objection and in the morning the Gauthier brothers began to take the creek, which was now filled with water that should greatly shorten the portage to the *Souris*. The others continued on the Missouri.

The Missouri was indeed wonderful. Areas that had been dry creek beds in the autumn were now small lakes. Even the falls and rapids were frequently passable without portage. They continued through the plains, which continued flat and empty but at least at this point were green. Halfway to the Mississippi, the river headed more southerly and the terrain changed rapidly. Soon the men began to feel at home. Trees, shrubs and real grass were everywhere. By mid-April they arrived at the mission at Saint-Louis.

The mission had been founded at the intersection of the Mississippi and Missouri Rivers by Marquette and

Jolliet in the seventeenth century but abandoned for some time. Now it was again a small mission. Due to its position, it was frequented by voyageurs who could usually find supplies, information and old friends. The name Saint-Louis was taken from the name once used by the missionaries although now it had no official name.

The men went for the evening to a small building that served as a tavern and met with other voyageurs also passing through. There was considerable toasting to the memory of Pierre Roy. A man named Marchand told the group, "The old feud with the English is heating up. The militias are training in earnest. The army is burying survey plates along the Allegheny claiming it all for France, but the British settlers are coming from Pennsylvania and Virginia every day."

The following day the men departed. They had decided to take the Wabash River up to the Maumee and on to Détroit directly. Again the spring rivers were ideal and the travel rapid. They made Détroit in early May.

<u>Détroit - May 1743;</u>

It had been almost ten years since Pierre* and Toussaint had visited the city in the wilderness with their fathers. The fort had been enlarged and improved. There were more farms and most of the farmers now lived on their land rather than inside the fort. They were met by Jean* Saint-Aubin, who although he was now in his eighties, was as spry as ever. He invited them to dinner and they accepted. As it was still early, they went to the small tavern that had been recently opened inside the fort.

Word travels fast in a town such as this and within the hour all their old acquaintances had assembled. The news of Pierre Roy had been disclosed requiring many stories and many toasts. A few men had been planning a voyage to Montréal and decided they would advance their plans to travel with the group.

That night at Saint-Aubin's they met the new commander of the fort, Pierre-Jacques de Noyan. Saint-Aubin explained, "We had a dispute between the Ottawa and the Huron in '38. The Huron abandoned their fortified camp and have moved to the shore of Lake Erie. Monsieur de Noyan has directed much repair and improvement of the village. The Church of the Assumption on the south shore has been expanded and that side is growing too, but slowly. Although we have grown, we have only 100 citizens at this time."

De Noyan added, "And only half of these are farmers. The rest are traders and gone a good part of the year. In addition, our farmers have no market, so they grow what they need and spend the rest of their time in the woods or the lake. They have no compelling reason to expand. We still need people more than anything.

"Unfortunately, traditional hostilities with England are re-emerging. There is a war in Europe on the question of Austrian Succession. The daughter of the Czar of the Austrian Empire, a headstrong woman named Marie-Theresa, is taking the crown, and of course, there are always conflicting issues. I fear this will spread to the colonies, and we will be isolated at Détroit. In addition, the

English settlement of the Ohio Valley continues unchecked."

In the morning, they met at the dock. Pierre* Saint-Aubin and Nicolas* Reaume's brother, Pierre, were coming. Like Nicolas* and Michel Charbonneau, although they were in Détroit frequently, they continued to keep their families in Montréal. Nicolas* explained, "Détroit is still too distant and isolated for me and my family. If more people would come to Détroit, I would move in a minute."

Falling Star came by and said that he and Jagged knife had decided to stay at Pontiac's camp where they had spent the night.

Chapter 18

<u>Bourg-Royal - June 1743:</u>

The voyage was swift in the spring current, and the men had hardly enough time to recount their adventure before they were in Montréal. Pierre* and Toussaint landed at the Beauport livery late in the evening of June 1, 1743. They were greeted enthusiastically and sat up into the night sharing the adventure with their families. Pierre* was also pleased to hear that de la Vérendrye had brought word of their change in plans and the family realized that they would be greatly delayed. He had been worrying since Winnipeg about Marie-Angélique*, but he knew it was too late in the evening to call on her.

The next day was Sunday and the family went to mass at the Charlesbourg Chapel. Pierre* caught a glimpse of Marie-Angélique* but this only served to raise his level of nervousness. At last mass was over and the congregation adjourned to the square. He made his way to her as quickly as possible. She was talking to another young lady when he came into view. As he approached her, she looked up at him and said, "*Bonjour Monsieur,* you look curiously like a boy I once knew. I don't recall his name. I wonder whatever happened to him?"

Pierre* stepped up and began to sputter a combination greeting, explanation, and plea for forgiveness when she leapt up and put her arms around his neck almost knocking him to the ground. She gave him the sort of kiss one never gives in the square. "Thank God, you are home. I have prayed every night for your return." Then taking his arm and pulling him away, "Come tell me everything about your adventure. I want to hear every word. If only women were allowed on such journeys, what a life we could have."

They had a seat on the grass as she continued, "Commander de la Vérendrye came personally from Montréal to give me your message. He actually gave it directly to me. He was all dressed in his uniform and accompanied by other soldiers. He spoke directly with my father. Father has been bragging how important you are to everyone."

As quickly as that, all the fear left Pierre*. He said, "I was very worried that you would not wait for me."

"And give up the iceboat rides? Not on your life." And they both had a laugh that erased all the stress of the past year. Pierre* knew that he owed a good deal of work to his father, so they decided to marry as soon as the harvest was over.

The next day Pierre* and Toussaint jumped in with the final aspects of planting. Pierre*'s two younger brothers had been the primary workforce in his absence. More news from the home front was Pierre*'s youngest sister Marie-Charlotte had married one of Marie-Angélique* Bergevin's brothers, Germain, in January. Another surprise was that Franny, now age 24, had married the sister of Marie-Angélique*, Barbe-Louise Bergevin during Pierre*s absence. She was two years younger than Marie-Angélique* and had just delivered their first daughter. They had a small house just south of Jean-Baptiste*.

Franny told Pierre*, "We hope to have you and Marie-Angélique* build directly to our south. We have everything planned, or should I say Marie-Angélique* does."

Their youngest brother, Jacques, was now 22 but still single. At the end of the day, the three brothers and Toussaint made plans. Franny said, "If we start now, between the four of us and some help from Papa, we could easily have your house finished by autumn." In this manner, Pierre*'s life went from highly uncertain in a few days to planned down to the last detail.

The summer was a whirlwind of activity as the group worked three farms and built a house. As the Bergevin family lived a few houses down the square, Marie-Angélique* was ever present She was a very capable woman in a country of capable women. She particularly liked the carpentry jobs and was not opposed to any activity no matter how strenuous. Although she was at least a head shorter than Pierre*, she was almost as strong.

The project become more complicated when Toussaint announced he was to marry Monique Thomas, the daughter of their English friend Jacob* Thomas and the granddaughter of Pierre Roy. As both parties were *métis*, it was supposed that they would marry at the mission church in Beauport, but the current priest in Saint-Charles de Boromée, Père Morisseaux, would not hear of it. "Christians are Christians and it's about time we decided we are all the same Christians."

So they planned a wedding for the same day and the same church as Pierre* and Marie-Angélique*, and began work on another new house.

On November 5, 1743, Father Morisseaux married both couples and spoke eloquently on the future of the new world and a church with no prejudice. The harvest having finished, the couples fell to maintaining and improving their properties and when the ice was safe, they resurrected the iceboat. The winter was perfect for the sport and hardly a week passed without a day on the bay. More adventuresome than her younger sister, Marie-Angélique* frequently demanded to steer, and rides with her at the helm were always the most exciting.

In December, Marie-Madeleine Allard married Pierre*'s good friend Pierre Bergevin making the fourth union between the two families. By the end of the winter, plans for the upcoming planting were made and Pierre* and Toussaint believed that their life of marital tranquility was starting and their life of travel and adventure was over.

Chapter 19

Kensington Palace, London, England - Late Winter 1745:

Sir Robert Walpole sat patiently awaiting the King. Walpole was now well into his seventies but still had the zeal for his office. George II, now 62, had proved a superior king to his father, but he still needed guidance. He was quick to decide, sometimes too quick, and brave to a fault. He had led his men on the field of battle just two years ago to defeat the French at Dettinger. (History would show him to be the last king to do such a thing).

And the French, after all the years of peace and prosperity following the treaty of Utrecht, which Walpole had worked out to the last detail, they had to get involved in this Austrian thing. It mattered little to either country who ruled Austria but here they were back at each other's throats.

The door opened abruptly and the king entered as dapper as ever. Sitting, he opened, "Well, Sir Robert, what have we today?"

"Your Majesty, we continue to struggle with the question of the need for land in the American colonies."

The king replied, "It seems as this never goes away. I recall, it is problems with the French, the Indians and the mountains."

"That is correct, your Majesty."

Rising, King George II continued, "As for the Indians, tell them what they want to hear. They're savages and we can deal with them as and when we wish. As for the mountains, cross them. These people are pioneers, for God's sake. If they wanted the comfortable life, they should have stayed in England. And the French, Sir Robert? Help me here again. How many colonists do we have?"

"Something over one million, Majesty."

"And slaves?"

"Another quarter of a million, Sire."

"The French then are how many?"

"Something over fifty thousand, Sire."

"And slaves?"

"Well, Majesty, the French don't exactly have slaves..."

With a theatrical turn George II continued, "Good God, man! These are the French! Deal with them! What about this fort at the head of the Saint-Laurent?"

"Louisbourg, Majesty, on Cape Breton Island. Heavily fortified. Our colonists tried to take it some years ago with no success."

"Well, put more energy into it. Bottle them up. They have no port other than *La Nouvelle-Orléans.* And what about forts in this 'Ohio" place?"

"We have a few small posts, but we only have so many soldiers and so many officers, Sire."

"Use militia; train officers. We have many gentlemen colonists who have been educated back home. Make some of them officers, but for God's sake, Sir Robert, if we need the land, take it!"

The Palace of Versailles - Late Autumn, 1745:

Cardinal Fleury hurried across the courtyard to his meeting in the king's salon. Every year it was harder to get around the palace. With new additions and refinements, the former hunting lodge had taken on a life of its own. He could almost hear the sucking sound of money leaving the national treasury to finance this opulent place. As he entered the salon, he was not surprised that the king was not present. Louis XV was never on time. He heard grunts and squealing in the antechamber and felt that this meant that his Majesty would soon appear.

As suspected, the door swung open and a tall man with long black hair walked out, pulling up and fastening his trousers. "Sorry to keep you waiting, Eminence. I had a project that took longer than expected." Then sitting, he said, "What is it today?"

"Your North American colonies, Majesty."

"Again with the colonies. Don't I have enough to do with this war about Austria and the palace construction? Why the decisions on this place alone are enough for two kings."

Rising, the old Cardinal said, "The British have taken your fort at Louisbourg, Sire."

"And Louisbourg is where?"

"At the entrance to the Saint-Laurent, Majesty. It is the most strategic fort in New France, and we have spent an immense amount of time and money fortifying it. Now it seems British colonists have marched up from New England and taken it."

"Well, who needs it anyway."

"Well, Majesty, in fact we do. Not only is it vital to entering and leaving the colonies, but it is key to our Atlantic fisheries. If I may be so bold, they are the only French enterprise that currently shows a profit."

"Well, take the damn thing back then. Get the Indians or someone to help."

"Well, I'm not so certain it will be this simple, Sire."

"Alright, then declare war on England!"

"War? Sire?"

"Yes, war. Seems we're already at war over this Austrian thing. We just haven't declared it."

"Well is that is what you want, Sire."

"Of course, it's what I want. Go do it. I have another project awaiting me down the hall."

Chapter 20

Bourg-Royal - June 1746:

Pierre*, Toussaint, Franny, and Marie-Angélique* pulled the rock with all their collective might to get enough room to slip the sling around it. Eventually they had it. Pierre* slipped the old canvas around the rock so they could use the horses to pull it the rest of the way. After a brief rest, they hooked the ropes to the team of three horses and pulled it just to the position they desired. They still had much work to do to excavate a subterranean cave, but this was a start.

Construction of new caveaux was a common project in 1746. The Allards had depended on the one at Pierre*'s father's house as a potential hiding place in the event of an Iroquois raid. However the long peace had rendered such possibilities remote. Now with the recent hostilities in Europe and a formal declaration of war with England, the colony began to fear the resurgence of such attacks. The old caveau would no longer hold all the extended family so a new one was in order. There was a collection of boulders behind Pierre*'s house that it lent well to this project. They would excavate a large subterranean cave and cover it with a door, camouflaged with brush, and make it large enough to hold all three families.

As the church at Charlesbourg Square rang the midday Angelus, the foursome returned to the house. Franny's wife, Barbe-Louise, and Toussaint's wife, Monique, sat on the porch with four small children,

Franny's two girls, Toussaint's daughter, and Pierre*'s new son, Pierre Jr. now one year old. Marie-Angélique* preferred hard labor to domestic duties. Although she was petite, she was one of the strongest women in Québec, and she could work with the best of men, even now when she was four months pregnant.

It was an uncertain time for the colony. Although it was mid June, no ships had arrived from France. The Fort at Louisbourg had been captured by the British, and there was fear that Québec would be cut off from the old world. Unlike the British colonies that lay near the sea, Québec was many hundred miles inland and dependent on ships coming down the Saint-Laurent. Although New France had become quite self-sufficient, the colonists relied on the ships from France for certain items as well as news of the outside world. They also depended on it for the delivery of more troops should the need arise.

As they climbed the porch, Barbe-Louise said, "Your father stopped by. He said there will be a meeting of the militia tonight."

As Pierre* sank into a chair, he said, "Just what we need to do after today's work." He knew, however, that the militia might take on a level of great importance, especially if no help could arrive from France.

Bourg Royal - October 13, 1746:

Fire could travel quickly through the colony. The only thing faster was news. The men had hardly left for the fields when it arrived in the way of Pierre* and Franny's father-in-law, Ignatius* Bergevin. "A ship has arrived from

France! Your father and Joseph have already gone to get the story. There will be a meeting at the tavern tonight."

The men stopped work early that afternoon. When Pierre* returned home, he found his wife in the early stages of labor. He told her he would skip the meeting.

She responded, "My God, man, I have Barbe-Louise and Monique, and as soon as word gets out, both of our mothers as well. Help is the last thing I shall need from you. Go to the meeting, we're all dying for the news."

<u>Charlesbourg, The Blue Goose Tavern and Inn - Later That Night:</u>

The tavern was packed to capacity, business was brisk and François Fortin, the proprietor, was hopeful that he would have enough liquid nourishment to get through the night. Jean-Baptiste* Allard was the town representative of the Citizen's Council and was to speak. He had brought with him one of the Guyon brothers who had been in France and had returned on this very ship.

"It is true that a ship has come from France. It is stocked with provisions and has allayed many of the fears for the upcoming winter. Other good news is there appears to be some softening of relations with the British. Monsieur Guyon has been kind enough to explain what he has learned first hand."

The older man arose, "I have been in France this year on business for my family. I had hoped to return in the spring, but ships have been turned away at Cape Breton. It is true that the British now hold Fort Louisbourg, but their hold is precarious and they know they cannot hold it much longer. In addition, the war in Europe is calming down and the British have agreed to let some French boats pass. I hope next season will be more normal."

He was now required to wait as a new round of shots and beers was served to celebrate the news. He then continued, "On a more cautious note, I am told that the flow of British colonists into the French and Indian land of the Ohio River continues unimpeded. I fear this is a situation that will not remain unresolved for long. I encourage you to continue your vigilance and the maintenance of your militias." With this, he excused himself. Another round was ordered in order to help digest the report.

When Pierre* returned home, long after midnight, he was greeted by a new son. Two days later the boy was baptized Jacques* Allard, and two weeks later as he matured from a newborn, his grandfather made a discovery. "He has my father's eyes! I had hoped that this would occur someday in the new world." Indeed, the infant had the unusual circumstance of eyes of different colors. One brown like the rest of the family and one green like his own father's eyes.

Two months later, Toussaint's wife, Monique, delivered their first son. Jean-Baptiste* and Joseph were among the first visitors. Jean-Baptiste* said, "We had to be first to see the first man to carry the blood of both old Henri and Pierre Roy. This will be a man to contend with." Two days later he was baptized Henri-Pierre de Baptiste.

The following spring, ships arrived from France, the colony breathed a collective sigh of relief, and the new world returned to normal, at least for a while.

Chapter 21

Aix-la-Chapelle, The Holy Roman Empire, 1748:

Cardinal André Hercule de Fleury was exhausted. He was simply too old and weak for this type duty, but it was his sense of duty that drove him to do it one more time. In addition, there was the opportunity to visit the ancient seat of the government of Charles* I, or Charlemagne*, as he was better known. Both France and the Holy Roman Empire claimed Charles* as their first and greatest King. As he had conquered most of the western world in his day, this was probably appropriate on both sides.

De Fleury had been sent to negotiate France's position on the peace ending the War of Austrian Succession. In the Cardinal's mind, it was a foolish war, as were most, and there would be little to negotiate. There would be some minor changes in borders and some concessions but not enough to justify the lives and gold that had been wasted.

He would miss his old friendly nemesis, Sir Robert Walpole, who had died two years ago. Over the years the two men met many times to settle the differences of their two countries and their two headstrong monarchs. During their lives they had come to realize they could do a much better job managing the nations than these two 'great kings', but they were realistic in realizing they could only influence them with rarely heeded advice and by settling these terrible conflicts.

Fleury had been born and raised on the divine right of kings, but it had become more and more apparent to him that men chosen by ability would do better than those chosen by birth. He would never vocalize this heresy publicly, but he believed that if God did indeed ordain these men, God had a strange sense of humor.

This negotiation should be simple. In addition to the lack of any serious issues between France and England, Walpole's replacement was an inexperienced man. His name was William Pitt and he had served inauspiciously in a few posts. His presence here probably reflected the lack of interest George II had in this treaty.

The next day various representatives of the interested nations met for endless discussions of issues and demands. Over the next few weeks they agreed on various terms. A border moved here, something else ceded there, most of little interest to France. Toward the end of the deliberations de Fleury realized some additional token would be owed France by England. He chose this time to meet privately with William Pitt.

The language of these European peace conferences had always been French, the diplomatic language of the day. William Pitt was an educated man, and as all educated Englishmen, he spoke French. However he stumbled frequently with the nuances such as genders and verb tense, and his accent was dreadful.

Cardinal de Fleury, on the other hand, was educated as a boy in England and spoke the King's English with a perfect British accent. Robert Walpole had been equally skilled in French and as part of their constant friendly sparring, when the two men met privately, Walpole would speak French and de Fleury would speak English.

De Fleury saw that he could play this to his advantage by allowing Pitt to struggle for a while in French and then de Fleury would simply slip into his perfect English. To bring the stuttering Pitt to a disadvantage, the Cardinal casually asked for a strategic piece of British territory. Pitt was dumbstruck and said he would consider it but felt certain King George would not agree. They agreed to convene in a few days and de Fleury went to his chambers with a new spring in his step.

When they reconvened, Pitt commenced, "My dear Cardinal, the King will not agree to your proposal, perhaps we can settle on something else."

De Fleury sat pensively. Finally he spoke, "My dear Mister Pitt," sounding more British than Pitt himself, "there may be one thing, a trifle actually, but I may be able to convince his Majesty to accept return of the little fort at Louisbourg."

Trying not to look too stupid, Pitt was forced to ask, "What is Louisbourg?"

The Cardinal returned, "Oh, almost nothing really. I'm not surprised you have not heard of it. It is a small fort in the northern French colonies in the Americas. It overlooks nothing but frozen tundra. It was taken a short while ago by some colonial hoodlums. Nothing has come of it, shipping continues unimpeded along its watch.

"You see, the King has a cousin or something who is governor of this God-forsaken place, and it might please

His majesty if it would be returned. I can't think of a better circumstance for your side."

William Pitt looked bewildered, "Well, I suppose I can agree to that."

The men shook hands and several days later the Treaty of Aix-la-Chapelle was signed and delivered. It would be several years before a more mature William Pitt would realize the consequences of this action as well as the true meaning of the very French term, *finesse.*

Chapter 22

Bourg-Royal - December 1748:

The peace of Aix-la-Chapelle had returned tranquility to Québec. Shipping had returned to normal without the threat of blockade, and trade was brisk. The farming season had been fine. The militias did continue to meet, however, due to the ongoing English settlement in the Ohio Country.

Jean-Baptiste* and Anne-Elizabeth* were greatly enjoying their roles as grandparents. They had developed a special relationship with Pierre*'s two boys, Pierre, age 4, and Jacques*, now age 2. A few days before Christmas they invited the two to spend the night. Anne-Elizabeth* said, "And tomorrow we will take a ride into the woods by the Laurentian and cut a special tree for Noël." That evening was special as they played games and spoiled the boys terribly.

In the morning Jean-Baptiste* hitched the horse to the sleigh and they took the boys down the path that now led to the new farms to the east and then up to the mountains. Jean-Baptiste* had taken both boys on short excursions into the woods before. They were strong and withstood the cold well. They also showed no fear of the wilderness. They stopped by a small stream-fed lake where the two boys selected a tree. Jean-Baptiste* cut the tree, with some 'help' from his grandsons, and they placed it on the sleigh. They started back with promises from Mimi of a hot drink and treats when they reached home.

A short way down the path, the horse stopped suddenly and started to rear. Jean-Baptiste* was unable to calm him. He soon saw the reason as a great brown bear entered the path from the woods. The horse became hysterical and broke his reins and ran to the woods. Jean-Baptiste* grabbed his rifle and took careful aim. His shot was true and hit the bear near its chest but the animal proceeded as though nothing had happened.

Having no time to reload, he grabbed his ever-present bow and was able to land two arrows before the great beast was upon him. The bear lifted him like a doll and threw him into a tree where he fell limp. The bear then took the hysterical Anne-Elizabeth* and treated her the same. He then regarded the two little boys.

Pierre was screaming hysterically, but Jacques* remained silent. The bear started toward the older lad, but his brother toddled through the snow to stand between the bear and his older brother.

Bears sense fear better than they sense anything else. Large bears have a good deal of opportunity to do this. This was only one of many human encounters for this magnificent beast. He always sensed great fear and proceeded to maim and usually dine on his victims. But something here was wrong. This tiny creature before him showed no fear, or as the bear knew, this little boy had no fear of him. He starred with his odd eyes of different colors directly into the red eyes of the bear. Old Henri would have said that he looked into the very soul of the beast.

They stood regarding each other for a good long time. The bear rose to standing at his full and terrible height. Eventually the small boy toddled forward and hit the bear on the leg. The bear came back to all fours and simply turned and walked back into the forest.

Several hours later, Pierre* and Marie-Angélique* began to worry. Pierre* went to get Toussaint and they took their sleigh into the woods. The trail of the senior Allard's sleigh was easy to follow and they soon came to the terrible sight. Pierre*'s heart raced as he ran to the scene. The horse had returned and stood silently. Pierre* found his parents mauled and dead on the ground. He heard whimpering and discovered young Pierre crying, inside his grandmother's coat, and being comforted by his younger brother.

On December 23, 1748, Jean-Baptiste* Allard, the Iroquois slayer of Charlesbourg and his wife, Anne-Elizabeth* Pageot-Allard, the most beautiful girl in Québec, were buried together in the cemetery of Saint-Charles de Boromée next to their three sons who had also died tragically twenty years ago. He was 72 years old and she was 62.

Chapter 23

Charlesbourg, The Blue Goose Tavern and Inn - May 1750:

The Allard men sat having a beer and discussing the new season when the doors burst open. The doors had never burst open as they had in the days of Pierre Roy, but burst open they did. Four familiar men entered and joined the table. They were Nicolas* Reaume, Charles* Saint-Aubin, old Joseph Parent and his son Gilbert.

The men sat down and ordered the obligatory shots and beers. Joseph Parent was now in his eighties. He limped badly from an old broken leg but was still agile enough. They toasted the memory of their old friend Pierre Roy and talked about how there would never be another. The conversation eventually turned to business.

Nicolas* Reaume started, "My brother Pierre and I have now both moved our families to Détroit. The city is beginning to grow and Jean* Saint-Aubin has finally convinced France to help. The King is providing land, a plow, an ax, a spade and two augers as well as a cow, a sow, seed, and food for the first year to any man who comes to Détroit."

Charles* Saint-Aubin added, "The need for a first class mill is growing. Between our mill and that of Meloche we cannot even do the necessary work now. We have come to recruit mill workers and hope that Pierre* and Toussaint could help us recruit."

"We could go to Montmorency tomorrow," Pierre* said, then adding, "It might be worthwhile to spend two more days in the canoes and go all the way to Baie Saint-Paul. Millwork is slow this time of year and most of the workers live and farm up there. I think I know people who would be interested." Pierre Roy was toasted several more times and the men tried to find their way home.

They met the following morning at the Beauport livery and made the quick trip to the Montmorency Falls. Although it was not Niagara, or even the falls on the Yellowstone River, Montmorency had a certain majesty. It was relatively narrow but fell four hundred feet. Offshoots of the falls allowed a number of mills to be built with varying capacities to do certain jobs.

After the men toured the falls, they talked with the supervisor. "At this time we are only milling the lumber left over from the autumn tree clearing. Our real work begins at the start of the harvest and is full speed until the falls freeze. The boys you want will all be up in Baie Saint-Paul."

They left immediately for the northeast. *L'Ile d'Orléans* was beginning to look as settled as the Beauport Coast. Thirty miles long and five miles wide, the northern coast was lined with farms that ran like ribbons to the center of the island. The southern side was less populated but more was being settled each year. The population of the entire colony of Québec was approaching sixty thousand.

On the north mainland was the church of Sainte-Anne de Beaupré. It had been rebuilt several times and was beginning to take on the appearance of a cathedral. It had acquired a reputation for healings and miracles and was becoming a pilgrimage for people from old France as well as New France. Past the island, the river became very wide. The opposite shore was scarcely visible on a hazy day. Farms continued on the north shore with regularity.

On the second day they came to a greater widening of the river. Toussaint explained, "This is the Baie Saint-Paul, as you can see, the village is a bit of a hike."

The town sat on the top of a great limestone cliff. The men landed at the livery and walked the several miles up to the village. The view from the village was spectacular. On a clear day one could see all the way the most northern part of New England.

Reaching the village, Pierre* said, "I think I know where to start." And they entered a tavern with a rough sign that read 'Tremblay's'. In fact most establishments in the town said, 'Tremblay'. Entering, Pierre* saw someone he recognized and went to talk to him. He returned a short while later with an older gentleman, "May I present, Jean* Laforest. He traveled to Louisiana with my father and then went to Détroit."

The old man said, "I went to Détroit for two years to start a mill." Motioning to Joseph Parent, "Monsieur Parent was along. We were only able to make a crude mill, as there were few people and not much material. We set it on the *Grosse Pointe* in the *Grand Marais.*"

Charles* Saint-Aubin said, "That is where our mill stands today."

Laforest continued, "Yes, that is the place. There is wonderful wind at the end of the point, particularly a wild wind which comes frequently from the northeast. We were unable to use it to its best advantage as we could not get to the end of the point due to the swamp which was as bad as that of Louisiana."

Saint-Aubin continued, "We have the same problem now but are ready to make improvements and hope to find willing hands to help us."

The old man rose and said, "Son, you may have come to the right place," and he called to an even older man in the corner. When the man limped over, he was introduced, "This is Michel* Tremblay. His father was Pierre* Tremblay who cut wood in the area for many years. He eventually settled on a farm here next to my father, Pierre* Laforest. The two families became very active in the mill business."

Old Tremblay spoke, "We were just discussing Détroit the other day. Word of the King's offer of land, equipment and stock has been heard and my sons have some interest."

Charles* Saint-Aubin said, "It would be wonderful if we could get two men."

Tremblay chuckled, "There may be more. You see, we have large families here. Laforest's son Guillaume* is interested. His wife would come as well. She is the daughter of my older son Antoine*, who would not come. My three younger sons, Pierre, Ambroise, and Augustine* would come with their wives. Augustine*, he's married to Jean* Laforest's daughter who is, of course, Guillaume*'s sister. Then there are all the children."

Charles* Saint-Aubin took a quill and paper and asked, “Could you go over that again? I think I shall need a map.”

Tremblay repeated the story. At the end, Saint-Aubin discarded his ‘map’ and pulled out another paper. “One more time please.”

At the end of the third telling, he thought he had it basically straight.

1) Guillaume* Laforest age 25: son of Jean* Laforest.
2) His wife, Marie-Marguerite* Tremblay age 25: daughter of #9 below.

3) Marie-Judith* Laforest age 27: daughter of Jean* and sister of #1.
4) Augustine* Tremblay age 40: her husband and son of Michel* Tremblay and brother of #5,7,9.

5) Pierre Tremblay age 42: son of Michel* and brother of #4, 7, 9.
6) Marie-Magdeline Simard age 37: his wife and sister of #8.

7) Ambroise Tremblay age 41: son of Michel* and brother of #4,5,9.
8) Marie-Maguerite Simard age 24 his wife and sister of #6.

9) Antoine* Tremblay, who is not coming to Detroit but is a son of Michel* and brother of #4,5,7 and father of #2.

Along with this group there will be sixteen children, 11 of whom are under the age of five!

Charles* Saint-Aubin shook his hand in triumph, "This is much better than we had anticipated, where can we meet this group?"

Tremblay replied, "Well, you'll have to paddle on up to Tadoussac. All the boys are up fishing."

Pierre* Allard asked, "How will we ever find them on the Saguenay River? The trout are far upstream at this time of year."

Tremblay continued, "They are not on the Saguenay, they're in the Saint-Laurent, and they aren't after trout. They're after *baleine.*"

The men born in Québec and Montréal were not aware that the large whales came as far up the Saint-Laurent as the Baie Saint-Catherine by the trading post at Tadoussac. Pierre* exclaimed, "*Baleine?*"

Tremblay continued, "Mill work is slow now and there's good money in it. Not just for the oil, but the skins and bones as well. You boys paddle up to Tadoussac. You'll find them easily."

Tadoussac, Québec - May 1750:

Pierre* and Toussaint had only been this far north in the Saint-Laurent twice, when they had come fishing with their fathers for trout on the large Saguenay River, which went northwest to the great Lac Saint-Jean. The coast took on a much more wilderness appearance as they progressed until they could see the small town at the post of Tadoussac at the mouth of the Saguenay on the north coast. Old

Michel* Tremblay was correct. His boys were not hard to spot. They were in the center of the big river with three large canoes.

They came close and hailed the fishermen. Pierre* and Toussaint knew all the men from the mill but knew Augustine* Tremblay the best as he was closer their age. As they came closer, they explained the purpose of their visit. The fishermen agreed they were most interested and would meet at the post when they finished with the whales. In the meantime the men from Québec decided to watch the spectacle.

The men had large barbed spears, each tied on a long rope to one of several large wide logs. As a whale surfaced, they would try to spear it. If they were successful, the whale would swim away and eventually tire because of the log. Once they had used all the spears, they would round up the logs and eventually kill the whales. They would then take the whales to a central place where they were tied together.

Most of the logs were already out on whales. The men witnessed a few more spearing. The whales were not as big as those in the deep ocean, but they were large nonetheless. They ranked from twenty to nearly forty feet in length. As the whale was hit, it would dive frantically and the log would disappear. Eventually it would reappear and again return below the surface. Eventually the log would come to the surface for good, and it was then that the men knew the whale was vulnerable.

As they collected the rest of the whales, they began to drag them into shore. At the beach by the post, a few Indians had a small camp where they processed the whales. They would skin and de-bone them and then process their flesh into the valuable whale oil used in lamps. The area reeked of ripe whale.

The men went to the small tavern *La Baleine Blanche* and ordered a round of drinks. The tavern also reeked of ripe whale. Charles* Saint-Aubin introduced himself and explained his need. Pierre Tremblay spoke for the group. "We have been giving thought to this Détroit proposition; the prospects of ready jobs along with free land makes it only more tempting. We will finish here in a week and can be ready to go in two. And as simply as that, an arrangement that would affect the long-term future of Détroit was sealed.

Pierre* and Toussaint returned to the planting while the others remained in Québec to await the arrival of the Tremblay-Laforest entourage.

<u>Lake Ontario - June 1750:</u>

Up to this point the voyage had been not quite as difficult as Charles* Saint-Aubin had expected. Beside Nicolas* Reaume and Joseph and Gilbert Parent, he had managed to hire three Algonquin to accompany them. Of the sixteen children, three of Pierre Tremblay's were twelve years or older. Marie-Therese was sixteen and good help. Aside from them, the other thirteen youngsters were quite small with four of them one year of age or younger. Assigning them to canoes was a logistical nightmare. The eight adults were strong and willing, but did not come with much voyageur experience.

The group became rather friendly, beginning to address the women by first name when it became apparent that calling out 'Madame Tremblay' would be of little use in this group. The nature of the group caused them to move slowly. On the third week of the voyage they were along the south shore of Lake Ontario. Two days before they had spent the night at Fort Frontenac and were now rested. It was a lovely late spring day, the air was warm and the lake was calm.

Suddenly an enormous sturgeon rolled on the water at the canoe of Nicolas* Reaume. In his canoe was an Indian, Marie-Judith* Laforest-Tremblay, and her three youngest children. Two of the children, Marie-Reine-Chretienne* age six, and Jean, age four, rushed to the side to look. Their mother instinctively jumped to restrain them and before Reaume could react the canoe capsized.

Fortunately, young Augustine, age one, was papoosed to his mother. Reaume and the Indian reacted to get the mother and young Jean to another canoe. Marie-Reine* was managing to tread water. They righted the canoe and suddenly Marie-Reine* had vanished. Panic spread and many of the men carefully went into the water to search, being cautious not to overturn another canoe.

Reaume dove deep, and after more time than is possible for a man to stay under water, he had not returned. The panic mounted as another three minutes passed. Just as Saint-Aubin was to give up hope, a gasping Nicolas* Reaume broke water with the limp body of Marie-Reine*.

He quickly passed the girl to his Indian companion and skillfully reentered the canoe. He held the girl inverted and squeezed her chest, then pushed on her chest without effect. She remained still, blue and lifeless. He then knelt and began to blow into her mouth. After several more minutes, the girl gave a gasp and vomited water into the canoe.

Reaume struck her a few more times, and she began to cry. Her mother also began to cry and soon all the mothers and most of the children were sobbing. They retrieved all belongings possible and headed for shore where they made an early camp.

The next morning, Saint-Aubin tied a log to each of the small children to serve as a marker. "It seemed to work with the whales." he said.

Fort Pontchartrain du Détroit - June 30, 1750:

The group landed at Cadillac's old docks early in the day, and they were met by most of the city. The residents had been praying for more neighbors for several years and now it seemed to be happening. By the end of the year, the population would grow almost 50%, still not a great number of people, but a start nonetheless.

Among the first greeters was old Jean* Saint-Aubin. Although now 91 years old, he was still spry and still a patriarch of the city in the wilderness. They were treated to a brief service at the new Sainte-Anne church and a brief tour of the town. Then they were taken to the Saint-Aubin farm where they would have dinner and spend the night. As the Saint-Aubin family had great interest in the mill, they had agreed to accommodate the group on their several farms for a while.

Détroit was not much larger than Baie Saint-Paul, but it was a city. It had two churches (counting Assumption across the river), a fort, and stores. It was also filled with all manner of Indians, which excited the children greatly, although it gave their mothers pause. They dined and were housed in what the Tremblays regarded as splendor. By the next morning it was clear no one in this group would ever want to return to Baie Saint-Paul.

The following morning, Charles*, Jacques*, and Gabriel Saint-Aubin took the men on a tour of their new home. The Grand Marais lived up to its name as the great swamp. The land was low, wet, and almost impassable. The point was very large, and the Saint-Aubins said they could arrange land claims for the group to control the entire point. Other than the swamp issue, the property was spectacular. A large portion had been cleared to make the log road that led to the current mill. They toured the mill. Although the Montmorency mill was water-powered, the men had experience with windmills as well. Guillaume* Laforest said, "The differences are actually small. Except for the fact that wind only works when there is indeed wind."

Charles* Saint-Aubin said, "If we can access the end of the point, there is almost always wind."

As they returned outside, Laforest continued, "My grandfather came from the Bordeaux region of France. Where he lived there was much low ground. He used to tell us how they controlled that issue and I believe we can do the same thing here."

It was becoming apparent to the Saint-Aubins that Laforest, although he was youngest, was the 'brains' of the group. Charles* said, "Well, we can start at the beginning of the week."

Pierre Tremblay said, "Why not today?"

As Saint-Aubin would learn, if there was one thing this group was not, it was lazy.

Laforest said, "We will need implements with which to dig and move earth."

Saint-Aubin responded, "Much of the items promised by the king are at the storehouse at the fort. I can supply you with more shovels and a wagon and horse"

Hearing of the horse, Laforest's face lit up. "What about a plow"

"Of course," Charles* responded, and the group left to round up the needed items.

That night the families stayed on the two Saint-Aubin farms just to the south of the point. By dawn the men were hard at work. When Jean*, Charles*, and Gabriel Saint-Aubin came to visit in the afternoon they were shocked at the progress made. Guillaume* Laforest took them on a tour. "The problem is not just that the land is flat and low. It is mainly that it is poorly drained. Although it seems the same level, there are variations in the elevation of the land.

"We will build the land up on the high areas where we will set buildings. We will plow land to do this but also fill with soil we take when we dig this series of ditches, which are constructed to drain to the lake." By the end of the week, the soil was already more firm and dry.

Once the canals or 'ditches', as the Tremblays preferred to call them, were completed they began to cut trees. The Saint-Aubins had never seen anyone clear trees as fast and effectively as this group. Jean* Saint-Aubin said, "I never had the pleasure to meet old Pierre* Tremblay, but I was told that he was the strongest man to live in Québec. These acorns did not fall far from that tree."

They used the trees to complete the log road to the end of the point so large loads could be transported to the very end even in the wettest of times. Then they made pointed logs to be sunk into the ground at the beach as 'pilings' to protect the shore from erosion. When this was completed, they began construction of the first mill. In the evening they worked on their four new houses. The women worked on the grounds and in spite of the lateness of the season were able to grow staples and vegetables for the winter.

By the first of November, the largest and finest mill in Détroit was in operation. It was high powered and cut wood much better than the Meloche mill on the south shore. Laforest told Charles*, "Next year we will make this mill capable of turning the wind vanes to maximize the wind efficiency. We will then put in two gristmills. We will give you the lumber to build your city and the flour to feed it." As he walked off, Charles* Saint-Aubin realized that the *Grand Marais* was no longer a swamp.

Pierre* Meloche became a frequent visitor and had arranged to hire the men to help him improve his mill.

PART TWO

THE WAR

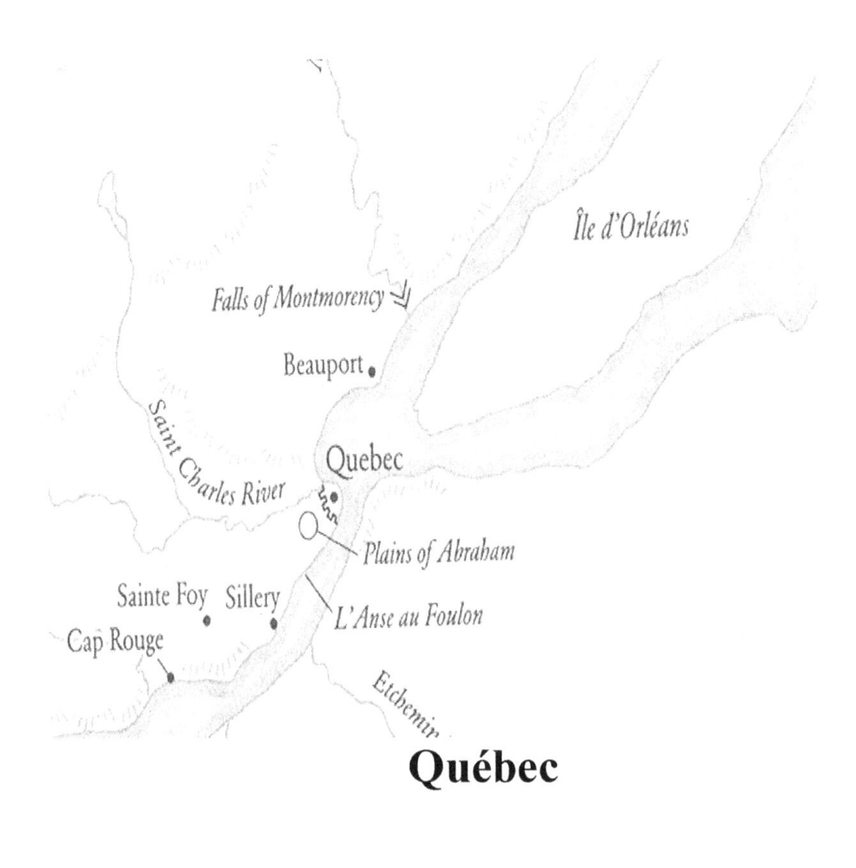
Île d'Orléans
Falls of Montmorency
Beauport
Saint Charles River
Quebec
Plains of Abraham
Sainte Foy
Sillery
L'Anse au Foulon
Cap Rouge

Québec

Chapter 1

The Saint-Laurent River - July 3, 1608:

The billowing sails blended with the billows of clouds in the glorious north wind. It was perfect weather to sail into the great wilderness. Samuel thought this was one of those days which made sailors return to the sea. He had spent most of his life aboard ships, his early years in the Spanish colonies of Mexico, Panama, and the Islands. The last five had been in this great land called Canada. He was beginning to realize he would spend the rest of his life exploring this endless place, although he would never know that someday he would be regarded as 'the Father of Canada'.

A young voice aroused him from his thoughts. "Captain Champlain, is that it?"

Looking upstream to the narrows Samuel replied, "Yes, Etienne, that is it. Indeed that is *Kebek.*" He used the Algonquin term for a narrow place in the river. He would soon give it a French spelling, Québec.

Young Etienne climbed on the rail, "It looks as though the river ends."

Samuel replied, "Yes, it does, and that is part of its beauty."

Young Etienne Brûlé had been found stowed-away in the hold at the beginning of the voyage. He was unsure of his age but seemed about fourteen years old. He told Champlain that he had been born in Champigny-sur-Marne near Paris. Orphaned at a young age, he had heard tales of Champlain and yearned to travel, so he had walked to the port at Honfleur where he was able to hide himself on the ship. Champlain found him intelligent, strong and resourceful, and decided to make him cabin boy.

Jacques Cartier, who had sailed for King François I, had claimed this country in 1535. During the past 73 years, little had been done other than develop the fishing ports in Acadie and a few fur trading posts. The most remote at this time was Tadoussac about one hundred miles downstream to the northeast of Québec. Champlain had been to Québec and beyond in 1603 and had recognized this narrows as the best place for a settlement. He had finally been sent by King Henri IV to build this settlement.

Along with his crew, and now Brûlé, he carried twenty-eight brave French souls to remain in the new settlement. Among the group were five missionaries and twenty-two men, some from France and some from Acadie, some seeking adventure, others fleeing earlier adventures. It was hoped these men would breed with the Indian women and populate the settlement. They were also accompanied by six Abenaki from the east to serve as guides and interpreters.

Just one year earlier, a group of English explorers had started a similar venture along a river named for King James of England. Jamestown and Québec were to become the first two permanent European settlements in North America.

The geography of this place was unique. As one approached it from the northeast, the wide river split into two channels around a great island, each channel one-mile wide. The island, which Champlain had named "*L'Ile d'Orléans*", was thirty miles long and five miles wide. If one sailed straight down the northern channel, he would enter a bay and perfect natural harbor. At the end of the bay was a smaller but respectable river, which Champlain had named 'Saint-Charles'. The northern shore of the bay was the north coast of the river and would later be named Beauport.

The southern shore of the bay was an incredible peninsula ringed on the north, south and east by sheer, high granite cliffs. At the foot of the northern cliff was a low piece of land that would serve as the town for some years and be named Place Royal, so well placed that Champlain could almost land his boat aside it. Eventually a dock would be constructed to make a perfect mooring.

Upon landing, the group made the difficult climb up the promontory to the plateau atop the peninsula. From here one had a long view up and down the river including both channels around *L'Ile d'Orléans.* Champlain exclaimed, "This is protected on three sides by cliffs no one can climb and even cannon cannot reach. The fourth side is protected by hard terrain and endless wilderness. It is here we shall eventually build our fort." He planted the *fleur de lis* flag of France and christened his place Québec. They spent the next two months exploring and making contact with the local Indians. In August, Champlain and his crew returned to France.

The following year when Champlain returned with a few more men, he was greeted by a group of only eight, all that remained from the previous year. Of the others, some had died of disease or cold, and some had run off with the Indians. Two of the men had taken Indian wives and one infant had been produced. The group had built their small village in the harbor in what would later be called the 'lower town'. The only structure on the cliffs was Champlain's flag.

During the following years, he brought more and more settlers. Names like Hebert, Langlois, Martin, Desportes and others came and began to prosper. However, Québec remained only a small outpost. It was overtaken for a short while by three English seafaring brothers, the Kirks. However, soon it returned to France and in 1633 Champlain came to stay with the wherewithal to build a true city. Almost all of the early settlers lived on the north shore or in the city. There was very little on the south shore. When people in Beauport said they 'crossed the river' it meant that they crossed the bay but actually stayed on the north shore of the Saint-Laurent.

Work began on the fortress, which became known as the Citadel. Eventually the great granite boulders of the region would replace the foundation. By spring of 1759, the Citadel of Québec was certainly the most impregnable fortress in the North America, if not in all the world.

Chapter 2

Bourg-Royal - May 1753:

As the warm spring sun came from beneath the clouds Pierre* and Toussaint along with their three boys were busy planting. The wheat would be finished today and the corn would go in next week once all fear of frost was past. Their three sons were beginning to be an asset to the procedure. Pierre Allard Jr. was now nine years old and his younger brother, Jacques* seven, the same age as Henri-Pierre, the son of Toussaint. Pierre* had a daughter, Marie-Angélique now four. A third son, Joseph had been born last year but died soon after. Toussaint had a three-year-old daughter as well.

Although the colony had been at peace since the treaty of Aix-la-Chapelle five years previously, tensions were on the rise. The continued struggle for the land of the Ohio Valley was always present. Although this place was far away from Charlesbourg, the colonists realized their well being was tied to the well being of New-France as a whole.

That night at dinner, Pierre* announced, "Toussaint and I are going to the tavern tonight to see what news there is." Marie-Angélique* replied, "I would guess the same news as last week, worries about things we cannot change."

Young Jacques* asked, "May I go with you, Papa?"

Pierre* replied, "Not yet, *Petit*, but some day soon."

He could never look into the youngster's different colored eyes without a fond remembrance of his own grandfather who shared the same trait. "Once you are twelve, you may come, sometimes."

The Blue Goose Tavern and Inn was busier than usual for a weeknight. This was becoming more common as worries about the safety of the colonies arose. Although there had been several years of peace with only a few minor breaks over the past few years, many of the older citizens remembered the old days with the constant fear of Indian raids. The three men took a table toward the center and were soon joined by a few friends. Pierre*'s brother-in-law, Pierre Bergevin, came in with Louis Jacques. Jacques was a few years older than Pierre* Allard and had never married. This is probably why he had been chosen as the head of the local militia. Normally the militia had a leader with military ties but most of the true soldiers were on duty in the Ohio Valley.

They were happy to see Louis Jacques as he generally had the latest news. After ordering a shot and a beer, Louis began, "News is not good. If only France would allow us to conduct our own affairs." Looking over his shoulder to make certain no strangers were in the house that night, he continued, "As we know, Jonquière (referring to the late Governor of Canada) had an expedition through the Ohio region. These men returned to report the English are trading in increased numbers with the Indians, and not just the Iroquois and Mingo. They trade with Delaware and Shawnee as well as Miami.

"Unfortunately Jonquière died soon after their return. The new Governor, Marquis de Duquesne, has been here less than a year. He has heard that the English have built a few small forts near the frontier, and his solution is to put all our efforts and resources into building our own forts. We have tried to convince him that greater trade with the Indians will work better all around. These men believe they are fighting in Europe. If the Algonquin all remain our friends, we could hold the area. However, if they lose interest in their French friends, we are lost."

Pierre* Renaud spoke up, "They believe they are going to fight with soldiers trained in France. I would sooner have three colonialists, or even two voyageurs, than ten French infantry."

Pierre* Allard replied, "Or one Indian with a bow."

Louis Jacques continued. "I am afraid they are going to alienate our best allies and start a war they can never win in this country. Unfortunately, we have no options on our own. I am calling for militia training twice a week. I fear we are our own best hope."

On the way home the men rehashed the evening. Toussaint said, "If we are called to fight in this Ohio country, we will be very far from our homes and families. Then who would they have to protect them?"

Chapter 3

Williamsburg, Virginia - October 1753:

Young George paced anxiously in the anteroom. He hoped today he would receive a real assignment. One year ago, at the age of 20, he had joined the colonial militia, and he now held the rank of major, but his biggest role had been in training recruits. George had been born and raised on his father's small Virginia plantation. His father had died when the boy was eleven and George had worked as a surveyor in his teenage years. He had some schooling and felt he was capable of rising to a high level in the military. It had become apparent to him he must excel in the colonial militia and hopefully be promoted to an office in the British army itself.

The door opened and a servant asked him to enter, "Governor Dinwiddie will see you now."

Robert Dinwiddie was the acting Governor of Virginia. He had summoned George for some sort of mission, and the young man hoped it would be important.

As he entered the older man rose and greeted him, "Good afternoon, Major Washington, I have an assignment for you, and I shall be brief. I want you to take a few men to the French Commander at Fort le Boeuf in the Ohio River Valley. You are to give him this order," as he handed Washington a letter, "demanding he withdraw his forces from that territory." He motioned to a rough looking man who sat in the corner, "This is Christopher Gist, who will serve as guide and interpreter. He has a group of four frontiersmen, and you will be joined by a few of his savage friends."

George looked at the letter and asked, "You want me to simply deliver the letter?"

"That is correct, put the riff-raff on notice. If they want more, we'll just go clean them out. The very idea of half-breed lumberjacks standing in the way of the British Empire. Well, be off with you and report when you return."

One month later, the group stood in sight of the small fort in the Pennsylvania countryside. Growing up in the country, George had hunted and camped since he was a boy, His surveying jobs had often taken him into the frontier. This, however, had been a different trip altogether. It had taken one month to forge through the wilderness and the mountains. Had it not been for Gist and his companions, who knew how to find and travel on 'Indian roads', he would have never made it.

The frontiersmen were strong, rugged men of few words. They had picked up three Iroquois braves at a camp enroute. The savages seemed to communicate but never actually spoke and looked at George in a way that made him want to sleep lightly at night. George had no idea how he would gain entry to this enemy fort, but Gist merely went to the gate and called out in French. The gate opened and two similar rough sorts greeted them, shook hands with Gist, and bade them enter.

They were taken to the commander who was dressed in uniform and appeared to be from a different planet than the men who had greeted them at the gate. George started to tell Gist what to say, but the frontiersman took the lead and held a short conversation in French with the older man. The officer went to his desk, quickly wrote and sealed a letter, handed it to Washington and said something in French to Gist who turned to Washington and said, "We can go now."

George started to protest but Gist took him by the arm and ushered him out. Once outside the walls Washington blurted, "What was that all about?"

Gist replied, "He said no."

George exclaimed, "And that was it?"

Gist began to look aggravated and said, "We must get back beyond the mountains before the big snow comes. I suggest we start now. We can discuss this at camp tonight."

Western Allegheny Mountains - November 1753:

The men made camp, and as had become the custom, ate quickly and began to smoke. Gist began, "Major, I fear there are a few things you did not learn on the plantation or when they gave you the fancy coat. First of all, the British are fools. Second of all, the French military are almost as stupid. These are men who insist on fighting battles of the old world in a land they do not begin to understand."

Washington protested, "There were no more than five men in that fort. We should have protested. Why we could have taken it."

Gist shook his head. He then motioned to one of the Iroquois, "Dark Cloud, you waited outside the fort. How many men were in the forest?"

The Indian, who had not spoken during the entire trip began in reasonable English, "Fifty, maybe one-hundred.

Most Indian, Algonquin, Delaware. And some Voyageurs as well."

Gist returned to George, "We would have been scalped and hung out to dry within thirty seconds. This is the frontier, Major, these people don't think like you do, and they don't fight like you do. They don't line up in bright red suits and shoot at each other. The British couldn't win Queen Anne's war like that and they won't win this one. If you want to succeed here, Major, look about you and learn something."

Still processing the conversation, Washington inquired, "Why has the Indian not spoken before now?"

Gist laughed, "You never asked him anything."

In late December 1753, after a deadly trek though the mountains in early winter, Major George Washington of the colonial militia delivered the French commander's letter to Governor Dinwiddie. The Governor read the letter, set it on his desk, and looking at George, said, "Unlike the French to be so brief and to the point. What did you make of this country, Major?"

Thrilled at being solicited for an opinion, George rose to his feet. "It is certainly a wild place, Excellency."

"And what of the men in the fort?"

Washington replied, "There were only a few. The commander appeared to be the only real military man. However, there were many French and Indians in the woods, hiding. Not a very honorable lot if I may say so."

The Governor continued, "What would you suggest, Major?"

"Well, Your Excellency, I believe we need a strategic fort in the area. The frontiersmen and the Indians suggested a place. I drew some maps, sir."

"You take the advice of these savages?"

"Well, they do live there, sir."

"Highly irregular. Let me see your 'map'."

Washington handed him some maps. The older man looked them over then replied, "These are quite good. Where did you get them."

"Actually I drew them, sir. You see, I worked some years as a young man as a surveyor."

"And what is this place with the star?"

George replied, "This is called 'the forks'. It seems three major rivers join at this point. I see it as the most important point in the region from a military standpoint."

"Well, I will have to look into this and discuss it with the military council. Thank you, Major, I believe I may have need of you in the future."

Major Washington left the Governor's Palace with a better attitude than that with which he had entered.

Forks of the Ohio River - Spring 1754:

It had not been long until Major Washington was again called to Williamsburg. This time he was sent with a group of 159 men to build the fort he had suggested to Dinwiddie. During the construction, they encountered French forces that chased them back to Virginia and then proceeded themselves to build a French fort at the forks called Fort Duquesne.

Undaunted, Washington's men were ordered immediately back to the Ohio Valley to construct a road from Wills Creek (now Cumberland, Maryland) to the Ohio Valley. While waiting for reinforcements in the Great

Meadow of Pennsylvania, they encountered a group of friendly Iroquois from the Seneca tribe, a group called Mingo. Washington welcomed them to help with their task. The leader of the Indians was the chief Tanaghrisson, also called 'Half-King'.

They were occupying themselves by exploring the local water routes when they were met by Christopher Gist. Gist had been at a local trading post when he spotted a group of French soldiers headed in their direction. Later that day, Washington and his men came upon the French near a clearing at the meadows.

<u>Bourg Royal - Summer 1754:</u>

Planting had gone well and the habitants were trying to live as normally as possible in spite of the constant threat of war. The Allard compound was using the labors of Pierre*, Toussaint, Joseph, and Pierre*'s two younger brothers Franny and Jacques. Pierre*'s boys Pierre Jr., age eleven, and Jacques*, age nine, along with Toussaint's Henri-Pierre and Franny's nine year old son made up the rest of the males. Of course, Marie-Angélique* could always be counted on to pitch in.

As the group was returning to the barn at the end of the day, they were met by Louis Jacques. "There's big news from the Ohio Country. We can hear about it tonight at the tavern."

After dinner the men quickly excused themselves to the tavern. The women waited on the porch with the children to hear the report of the news when the men would return.

At the tavern they were surprised to see their friends from Détroit, Pierre* Saint-Aubin and Nicolas* Reaume. After drinks were served, Saint-Aubin arose. "We had been scouting for trade in late May around the forks of the Ohio. We stopped at Fort Duquesne when we were asked to guide a group of soldiers on a diplomatic mission. It seems that the Governor had sent a group under a man named Jumonville under a flag of truce to meet with a group of English soldiers and ask them to vacate the French land.

"By an area called the Great Meadows, we were surprised by a group of English and Iroquois who attacked in spite of our flag of truce. Most of us escaped to the woods, but they captured Jumonville and a few of his men. We were able to watch from the cover of the forest while Jumonville tried to deliver his message to a young British militiaman. During their discussion, the Iroquois jumped on the French soldier and their chief killed Jumonville and a few others. He was the Mingo chief they call 'The Half-King'.

"We returned to Fort Duquesne for reinforcements and went after them. The new leader was the older brother of Jumonville. We discovered their bodies unburied which sent the elder Jumonville into a rage. The British had built a simple fort at the meadows, which they called Fort Necessity. We had little difficulty. The fort was exposed enough that we could fire into it from behind the trees on a hill. In addition, it began to rain a deluge and their trenches flooded. They were forced to surrender on July 4th. The young officer was a man named George Washington. He signed a surrender admitting to the murder of Jumonville.

"I fear that there can be no conclusion other than we are now most definitely at war."

Chapter 4

Charlesbourg Square - April 1755:

Militia training had become very serious. It began to take precedence over hunting, family, church and even farming. Louis Jacques held regular marching and target practice and occasionally an officer from the fort would come to discuss military tactics and fighting from formation. Much of the 'wisdom' here was lost on the *habitants* and particularly on the Indians who felt that fighting in formation was the most counter-intuitive thing they had ever seen.

Toussaint said privately, "When we form formations, the first thing I'm going to do is form behind a tree. It's better for me, and worse for the English. If I have a choice between an officer and a common man, I will take the officer."

As good weather approached, energies were divided between getting ready to plant and getting ready for war. Rumors of battles at the many forts in the Ohio region were rampant. The tranquility the region had experienced since the treaty of Utrecht, now forty-one years ago, had totally disappeared.

In April, the long feared news arrived. A group of soldiers from the fort were being called to Ohio and the Beauport and Charlesbourg militias called to supply some men to accompany them. Each neighborhood decided who would go and who would stay to try to grow enough food to feed the community through the winter.

Pierre* and Toussaint had been chosen to go, leaving Joseph, Pierre*'s two boys, ages twelve and ten, and Henri-Pierre, also ten. Pierre*'s brother, Franny, would stay with his ten-year-old son, and Pierre*s other brother, Jacques. Jacques had only two small girls. Many of Pierre*'s cousins as well as many men from the other families were also called to what was the first occasion for the local militia to leave the area for an indefinite period.

How the community would manage without many of its most productive farmers was a constant source of discussion at all the venues from the church to the tavern. The rugged Québecois, however, knew that they would manage. Dinnertime discussion became a twofold discussion about the problems in Ohio and the anticipated problems in Québec. At this point the Québecois regarded their problems as being agricultural, as they felt that the Blessed Mother would never forsake the city to a band of Protestants. In addition, everyone knew the Citadel was impregnable.

Obviously, the children had also been discussing the issues. Jacques*, always the more talkative of the two boys, said, "I could go with you, Papa, I could kill English with my bow or even better if you would give me Pipi's rifle."

Taken by surprise, Marie-Angélique* said, "Jacques*! No one is going to kill anyone. Your father and Toussaint are going to make a peace with these men."

The youngster continued with his different colored eyes ablaze, "That's not what Louis* Renaud said." Louis* was about five years older than Jacques* and was one of the leaders of the local boys. "Louis* said his Papa is going with mine and they are going to kill all the English because they worship the devil."

Pierre* stepped in, "Don't believe everything Louis* tells you, *petit*, It is true that the English are different from the French, and they worship God differently. However, they are people just like us and they have children just like you. We only want to find a way that we can all live together. Besides, you must stay and help Joseph and your mother with the farm."

Two weeks later, the Charlesbourg and Beauport men met at the canoe livery and paddled to the fort to join with the soldiers.

Chapter 5

Alexandria, Virginia - May 1755:

Braddock surveyed the room with his characteristic blend of confidence and arrogance. These men would help him lead the invasion that would finally break the French hold on Ohio. Various British officers and colonial militia officers, they were not the finest but certainly good enough to do the job under his direction.

Major General Edward Braddock had been selected to go to the colonies to lead the battle for the Ohio country and west. He was a seasoned veteran of European wars. As most British officers were gentlemen who had purchased their commissions with family fortunes so as to have a respectable occupation, Braddock was born to be a soldier. He had successfully led the 'cleansing' of the Scottish Highlands ten years before. He had been given the nickname 'the Butcher' because of his brutal tactics. If the Scots hid in their caves and forests, he merely burned them out. In fact he burned so much of that country, few forests remained.

The nickname was meant to be pejorative, but he regarded it well. After all, wasn't this what war was about? He had now been assigned 1400 regular British Army troops, which he felt would be more than adequate if by nothing more than sheer numbers. He had also been given a thousand troops from the provincial soldiers. In addition many Iroquois braves, and a few hundred colonial civilians would serve as workers along the way. However, he regarded the three later groups with nothing short of disdain.

As the group had assembled. Braddock arose to his imposing height. No longer a young man, he was nonetheless as fit as a much younger man. His level of authority would give younger soldiers nightmares.

"Gentlemen, the king has given me the task of taking this western land from the French once and for all. I plan to conduct this campaign in a proper military fashion. Instead of proceeding like savages, as has been done previously and without success I might add. We shall proceed in two groups. I shall lead the first group, which will begin to clear the way and remove any hostiles we may encounter.

"The second group will be the work party which will do a more thorough clearing of the route and build bridges and roads as necessary. We shall build a proper road all the way from Alexandria to here." With a flourish he pointed to the forks of the Ohio and the position now labeled, 'Fort Duquesne'. "This location is clearly the military key to the area and will be the first step in our removal of the French from all these other forts. Once we have a secure fort and a good road, we may bring supplies easily to our future staging area.

"We shall travel heavy. We will bring cannon, supplies and armaments to supply an excellent fort at this place. I expect the trip to take two months. I suspect that, due to our obvious superiority, the battle at the fort shall take less than two or three days. After we vacate the French, we shall build a formidable fortification from which we may stage future campaigns. Chains of command have all been assigned and you all have your orders. We will prepare to depart in one week. Dismissed."

George stood as the rest of the men filed out. This was the time for a bold move, he came forward and approached Braddock. "Excuse me sir, could I have a word?" Braddock rose from the chair he just occupied. George was pleased, as although Braddock was an imposing figure, young George Washington was even taller. "I am Major George Washington of the Virginia Regulars. I have been twice to this place and, if I may say so, have had more personal experience there than anyone else here."

Braddock replied, "Yes, I heard of you when I met with the colonial leaders. It seems you do have some friends in that group."

Washington continued, "Thank you, sir, I am certain they are too kind. I did, however, wonder if you could find some post here for me?"

Braddock regarded this brash youngster who reminded him of himself at this age, someone more interested in the battle than going to balls in dress uniform. "Well, Major, the commands have all been assigned to British officers; however, you could serve as my civilian aide-de-camp and ride with me. I could give you some rank, should we say Captain?"

This was less than George had hoped, but he could see this would be an opportunity, so he agreed. As they shook hands, one of Braddock's officers approached. "Excuse me sir, but there is an Indian chief, a rather savage looking fellow, who wishes a word with you."

Braddock replied, “Very well, I suppose I must. The colonial governors warned me of this.”

Actually the governors had tried to convince Braddock of the value of the Iroquois to the mission. The British had even signed a treaty with them agreeing there would be no more English settlers in the Ohio country after the war. Braddock had simply nodded and personally dismissed all these ideas out of hand.

He went to the hallway where the savage stood. The Indian began, “I am Scarouady. I am chief of the Oneida people and speak for the Iroquois nations on the matters of this battle. I seek an assurance from you that the British will support the sanctity of the Indian lands after the French are gone.”

Braddock regarded him with arrogance and replied. “As far as I am concerned, anyone who fights to make these lands British will be allowed to live on them.”

Scarouady returned, “But will they will remain Indian lands?”

The old general looked into the man’s black eyes and said, “The Indian can live on the land, but no savage will inherit the land.” With this the Indian left and the general returned to his business.

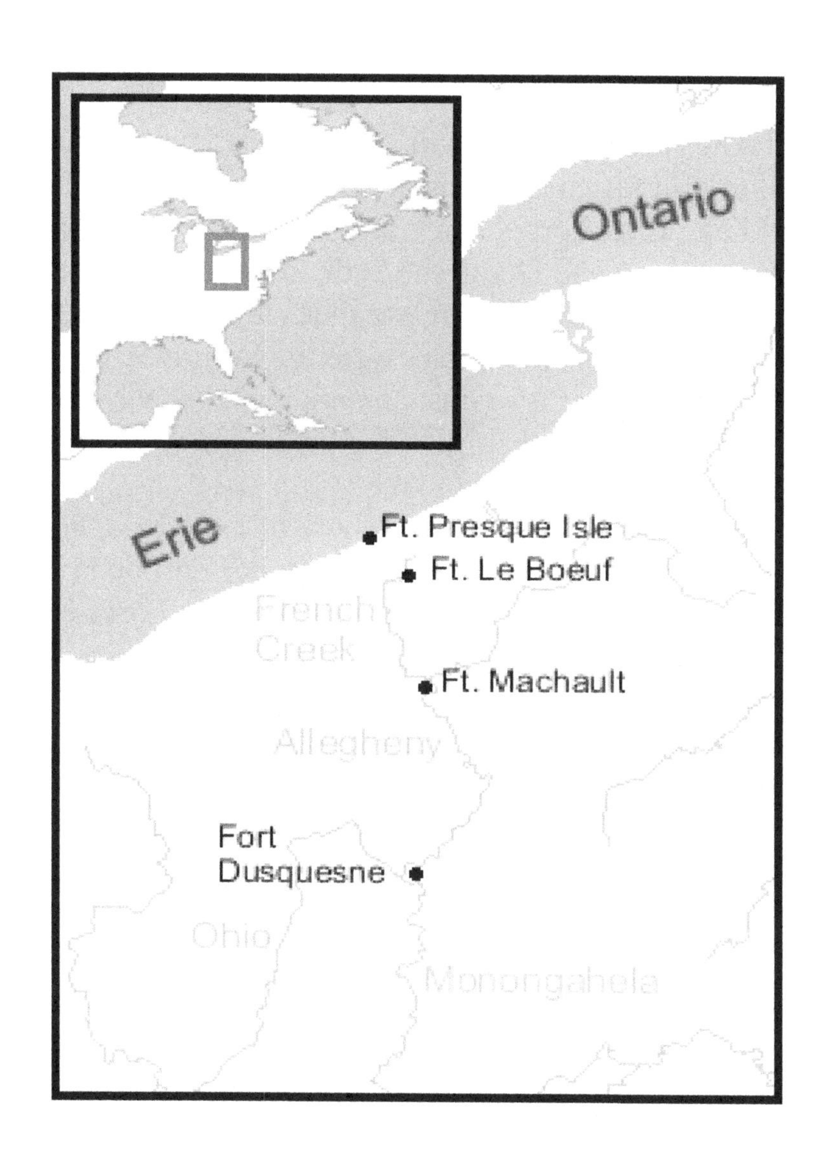

Fort Duquesne, at the Forks of the Ohio River

Chapter 6

<u>Fort Niagara - May 1755:</u>

After portaging Niagara, the Charlesbourg and Beauport militias came to the prominent fort on the eastern end of Lake Erie. Fort Niagara along with Fort Frontenac on Lake Ontario and Duquesne at the forks of the Ohio River was among the biggest and most strategic to the region. Later that evening they were told to travel to Fort Duquesne to protect it against an anticipated attack from the British. They left the following morning.

Traveling along the south shore of Lake Erie, they landed a few days later at the much smaller Fort de Presque Ile. From here they went inland to the south to Fort Le Boeuf at the headwaters of the Allegheny River. Henceforth the trip south was easy, even pleasant. The water was readily passable and the countryside idyllic. They saw a surprising amount of civilization in the way of a few French farms, but more English. In addition they encountered several Indian camps, both Algonquin and Iroquois.

A few days later the river widened and they came to the famous forks. The men from Bourg-Royal who included Pierre* Allard, Toussaint, Louis Jacques, and Pierre Bergevin (Pierre* Allard's boyhood friend and now brother-in-law), had never seen this place. Its strategic nature was at once evident. The Allegheny River flowed southwest as the Ohio River flowed southeast. These formed a triangle and met at the apex of the triangle to form the Monongahela River, which continued south. The tip of the triangle pointed due south and on its promontory sat Fort Duquesne. It was reminiscent of the triangle formed by the Saint-Laurent and the Saint Charles River, continuing on as the Saint-Laurent.

The men landed and entered the fort. It was considerably more secure than the forts of Presque Ile and Le Boeuf but not as substantial as Frontenac. However, it had a strong stockade, a battlement with a few cannon, and a formidable location. The men were invited to dine, drink, smoke and tell tales off their voyage. In typical French-Canadian style, business could wait until tomorrow.

In the morning they met with the commandant. Who began, "Our scouts and spies report that the British are beginning a large raid starting at Alexandria in Virginia. They apparently are bringing a modern army with them and plan to build a road as they proceed. Reports are of a great number of British regulars as well as colonials and Iroquois. Even with the reinforcements you have brought, we cannot hope to withstand them by traditional European means.

"I propose we send small bands of scouts made of men with wilderness experience and a few Indian runners who will return to the fort with information as is necessary. We will plan accordingly for the battle. I suspect our only hope will be using 'Canadian means' along with our Indian allies."

The four men from Bourg-Royal formed a squad and with four Indian runners departed the next day to make their way toward Alexandria.

Alexandria, Virginia:

Two days latter, Braddock's army began its march in the opposite direction. His men were ready, dressed in battle gear and having been drilled to a fine edge. They appeared the most disciplined army in the world. As Braddock and Washington surveyed them from horseback, the old general was obviously pleased. "Two or three days, did I say? This group will be finished with the French in a matter of hours."

The colonial militia and workers made a less impressive showing but were impressive nonetheless by their sheer numbers. The Indian contingent was much less impressive. Only seven of the several hundred braves expected showed. Washington was alarmed by this turn, but Braddock was indifferent at best.

Three hundred miles separated Alexandria from the forks. Pierre* and Toussaint's squad made rapid progress as they traveled Indian style, in single file. In addition, their Indian runners were familiar with the terrain and the fastest Indian roads. Ten days later as they approached Alexandria, they saw Braddock's first column.

Hacking their way through the forest, they made a spectacle. Led by frontiersmen, leveling the occasional tree and beginning to clear the way, more than one thousand soldiers in full uniform, both on foot and horseback followed. Their passing alone made a respectable road. As the French squad watched carefully from the cover of the forest, Pierre* commented, "Not a difficult trail to follow."

After the marchers passed, the squad moved east to encounter the second or work brigade column. They were clearing trees and using the logs to pave muddy areas and build rudimentary bridges over streams and creeks and even a few small rivers. Behind this group was the most impressive part of the army. An endless string of wagons and horses pulling carts, covered and open, filled with supplies and armament, and then cannon, both on carts and on their own trolleys made slow progress into the wilderness.

Following last came more work crews, women to cook, do laundry and other necessary camp maintenance. Louis Jacques said in awe, "They are indeed moving an army. There are as many people here as live on the north coast of Québec!"

The men followed the army as it progressed. The progress slowed some as they crossed the mountains but regained its speed on the other side. Once they had a good grasp of the size, equipment and speed of the group, they dispatched their first runner back to Fort Duquesne.

At night the men discussed the battle plan. Pierre* noted, "There are barely two hundred soldiers at Duquesne, even with the colonials and Indians, the odds will be overwhelming."

Louis Jacques replied, "We will have to abandon all thoughts of 'traditional European battle'."

Toussaint added, "Particularly things such as not targeting officers, what sort of idiocy is that. Why not kill those responsible instead of the ordinary men?"

For the next few weeks, as Braddock's army slowly made its way toward the forks of the Ohio, the French squad followed them along, carefully observing, to obtain as much intelligence as possible. They could not fail to be impressed by the sheer mass of the group and the meticulous fashion with which they fashioned their road. They were also surprised by the lack of Indians in the group.

Six weeks after their departure from Fort Duquesne, two French soldiers traveling with two Indian guides met them. As they greeted, one of the soldiers announced, "We have been sent to return you to the fort to report to the commandant."

They quickly started along toward the fort, this time at a much faster pace than that of Braddock. They camped on the first night. After eating, one of the soldiers observed, "It is odd that you followed these men for five weeks closely and without ever being noticed. However, these two Indians found you immediately with no difficulty."

Toussaint replied, "I believe you observed the only advantage that we shall have in this encounter."

The following afternoon after arriving at the fort, they were taken immediately to see the commandant. Arising to greet the men he began, "What can you men tell me about this army of Braddock?"

Louis Jacques stood to respond, "It is an enormous group and an enormous effort. Their leader, an older officer named Braddock runs his men with precision military technique. They are leveling every anthill and bridging every creek. They are clearing a road to hold the largest wagon."

The commandant asked, "What of their numbers?"

Pierre* Allard replied, "Beyond belief. We estimated 1500 regular British soldiers, many on horseback. Another 1000 English militia and several hundred frontiersmen and women to do work."

The commandant continued, "And armaments?"

Pierre* answered, "Many, more than fifty cannon."

With a dazed look the commandant said, "Dear God, we are expecting reinforcements in the next two days but that will bring us to barely 200 regular army and 150 militia."

Toussaint stood, "What may be more important is what they do not have."

"What else could there be?" asked the commandant.

Toussaint continued, "Indians, Monsieur. They have almost no Indians. We counted seven braves at best."

The commandant looked puzzled, "Our intelligence indicated they were to have several hundred. What could have happened?"

One of the Indian guides named Diving Eagle, who knew the commandant well, stood, "The British promised the Iroquois that no more English will settle this land of Ohio after the war. This Braddock made it clear that he had no intention of holding to such a guarantee. The chief brought only these few to save face, but I am confident that they too will disappear at the first sign of battle."

Looking more perplexed, the commandant asked, “And how did you learn this?”

Diving Eagle gave as much of a chuckle as Indians ever give and replied, “We had dinner with them in the British camp. They told us.”

“In their camp? How could this be?”

The Indian replied, "The British have neither respect for nor understanding of the Indian. To them we are all the same. Just as the beaver are all the same to you, Monsieur.”

At this point Pierre* reentered the discussion, “If I may say, sir, we have nowhere to return but our homes in Québec. We cannot return to France as you will, or to England as this man Braddock will. The outcome of this fight, if I may be so bold, is more important to us than to you. Toussaint and I have a plan…”

Chapter 7

Fort Duquesne - July 1, 1755;

The next evening the men joined a campfire outside the walls of the fort. Several colonists had arrived a few days ago from Détroit. Among them were Pierre* Saint-Aubin, Nicolas* Reaume, Niagara Campau, Antoine* Tremblay, and two new settlers they had not met, Julian* Fréton who had recently immigrated from France and an odd German man named Michel* Yax.

Pierre* Saint-Aubin did most of the talking. "Détroit continues to grow, but slowly. We now have a good mill thanks to Monsieur Tremblay and his family. We hope the fighting will not reach us, and we have become a staging area for travel to the Ohio battle."

Toussaint inquired into the health of the senior Saint-Aubin. Pierre* Saint-Aubin replied, "Still the same. Although he is now 96 years old, he is as active as ever."

Allard asked, "How does he view the war?"

Saint-Aubin replied, "He supports our efforts but is as ever a realist. He and the Campau brothers believe we cannot hold off the British Empire forever. Because of numbers alone, if we do not fall in this war we will in the next or the next. He agrees with others that our real salvation will be an alliance with the British colonialists after the fall of France in the New World. He believes it is that alliance that will remove the British Empire and allow us to be free. He and the Campau brothers have even begun an English school to learn the language. Monsieur Yax here speaks English and is helping with the effort. My father strongly believes that a knowledge of the language will assure success in the future. We are all compelled by him to study it."

Toussaint inquired after Joseph Parent, Niagara Campau answered, "Three years ago he was trading along the Miami with his son, Gilbert, and some others when they were ambushed by a group of British and Iroquois. Gilbert was killed and they buried him there. Last year, Joseph returned and exhumed his son's body and brought it back to be buried at Sainte-Anne in Détroit. Joseph died several days later."

Fortunately, Campau had brought corn whiskey and the men toasted the old voyageur. This brought on stories of Parent and his old colleague, Pierre Roy. This required considerable additional toasting. As day broke, the men awoke around the dead fire still holding their glasses.

During the ensuing week, they became acquainted with the two new men from Détroit. Julian* Fréton was in his late twenties and had come in 1750 from a small town near the city of Nantes, the great seaport of the Loire River. "My town is Moisdon-la-Riviere in the south of Bretagne. My father was a weaver. Having no interest in his trade, I joined a military group as a worker and was sent to Québec. We were sent immediately to Détroit. My home in France is located on the confluence of two rivers. As a boy I loved fishing. Upon seeing Détroit, I quit my job and took advantage of the King's offer to new settlers.

"My father had given me enough money that I was able to get a nice farm south of the Grosse Pointe where Monsieur Tremblay has his windmill. A wonderful river with cloudy water but many fish borders it. We call it the Milk River due to the cloudy water. I am searching for a wife but was asked to accompany this group, so I am now back with the army for the present."

Michel* Yax was a strange man with an even stranger story. He spoke German and English and now had acquired a reasonable grasp of French with a strange accent. "I come from da region of da Rhineland. Here da people are speaking German and English. Because George, da King of England, he is from dis place too. My vife, her family is coming too from da Rhineland and ve meet in da Pennsylvania. Ve get married der, but her fater, he not like me so much. He tink I don't have so much money. So me and my new vife, we are thinking to leave this Pennsylvania. And we are not so much liking da English anyways.

"So ve are hearing about dis place Pointe Coupée where der are deese German peoples lifing by da French. It's at Mississippi near da Louisiana. I'm getting a map and ve leave, but ve doesn't know is so much da vilderness. Ve are to dis place here, da Ohio, when ve are captured by da Ottawa Indians.

"At dis time ve are not speaking da French so dey are thinking ve are English. Ve are being prisoners and go to Détroit. Here dey takes us to da chief Indian called Pontiac. He is knowing we not English and take us to a man called Longueuil who is being head of Détroit army. He says to me, you stay and be farmer and I'm saying, 'Vhy not?' So here ve are. Ve are being Lutheran and he say ve are here Catholic. My grandmother is being Catholic, so I say 'Vhy not?' So now ve 'av four childrens and I am Michel* not Michael* like in English colony.

"Monsieur Saint-Aubin says, 'You go vit militia because you are speaking good English.' So I am saying, 'Vhy not?'"

Scouts returned in the early morning reporting that Braddock had assembled his forces and was camped less than one day from Fort Duquesne. The commandant ordered one half of the regular soldiers and almost all the militia and Indians to assemble outside the fort and march slowly to make contact. The remaining 100 soldiers remained inside the fortifications.

The Forks of the Ohio River - July 9, 1755:

Braddock made his formation and began to march to the fort. In the early afternoon the two groups caught sight of each other. Braddock surveyed the numbers, "My God, this will take a mere hour. It's almost an insult." The British shot their first volley and a few French fell. The militia and Indians retreated to the woods. In his glee, Braddock did not even notice that his Indians had already departed.

The French volley took a few British troops. The British prepared their next volley, but suddenly their men began to fall silently all around them. By the time they had taken their second shot, confusion reigned. For every shot they heard fired, ten men fell dead. For every musket ball, there were twenty arrows. The front ranks tried to regroup to take on the invisible enemy that surrounded them. The

French regulars were now able to began to bring down the front ranks of the British who had turned their focus.

Toussaint had been shooting arrows when he saw a grand opportunity. The great British General was no more than fifty feet from the tree that shielded Toussaint. He took his loaded musket and landed a ball squarely in the chest of the ornate red coat. The now mortally wounded Braddock fell limp from his horse. George Washington and the other aides dismounted and rushed to his aid as their confusion turned to panic.

Seeing no other option, the British began to retreat, but their way was impeded by the wagons, canon, and groups of workers that they had labored to bring this far. At this point the Indians descended. The British soldiers had never seen the potential of the various Indian hatchets or tomahawks. The English colonists had seen them and this raised their level of terror even higher. As the British tried to retreat, the Indians cleaved, dismembered and beheaded them ruthlessly.

The retreat turned into an eastward stampede. They dropped all weapons and other articles and fled for their lives. After a while, the French gave up the chase and sent a light squad to follow them and report back. The Indians began to take prizes. They scalped countless bodies, took uniforms, guns and whatever articles they could carry including 200 gallons of rum and disappeared into the forest.

The French collected arms and other items and returned them to the fort along with almost fifty new cannon. The area was heaped with bodies. Over two-thirds of the entire British contingent of 3000 had been either killed or wounded. Including sixty of Braddock's 86 officers and Braddock himself. Of the entire French contingency of soldiers, militia and Indians, there were 23 dead and 16 wounded. Braddock had, however, been correct. It took less than one hour. Fort Duquesne was now as well fortified as Fort Saint-Louis at the Citadelle of Québec.

The scouting squad returned three days later. Nicolas* Reaume who had led the group reported. "They ran like rabbits into the night. They stopped and buried their general who had died along the way. The next day they were met by a large supporting group under a Colonel Dunbar. He had nearly 2000 men ready to resume the attack, but the others were so panicked that they persuaded him to destroy all the remaining heavy arms and cannon and march back to Pennsylvania. They were well on their way as we left them. It's good they didn't realize that the Indians would return home after taking prizes. They would have fared better on a second try."

A few days later, the men from Québec and Détroit left to return home and try to make something of the remaining growing season. In his long planned and expensive march and short battle, Edward Braddock had achieved many things:

He had lost a large portion of the men and officers from one of the largest British forces ever assembled in North America. Those who did survive were rendered disabled by fear to fight again in such a battle.

He had left the French with enough armaments, light and heavy, to turn Fort Duquesne into the most formidable fort in the Ohio region.

He had destroyed the Iroquois trust in the British.

He had strengthened the French ties to their Indian allies.

He had constructed a road, which would now be a convenient route for staging raids on the British, which caused a veritable evacuation of the British settlers from the area.

He had taught George Washington that the British army could be defeated and demonstrated to him how it was to be done.

Chapter 8

<u>Québec - August 1755:</u>

A jubilant community greeted the men as they returned home. The news of their spectacular victory had preceded them by a few days. A high mass and great celebration occurred at the cathedral on Sunday and a picnic reminiscent of earlier days took place on the green of the upper town. The colony had made do during their absence, but some hardships were apparent in the economy of the food and the tattered nature of the clothes of even the more wealthy residents. Worse yet was the fact that the weather did not bode for a good harvest.

The men gathered to discuss issues and make the militiamen current on other affairs. Pierre*'s uncle George was becoming frail at 75 but remained up to date on every thing. "News from the Ohio country and west continues to be good. There have been failed British attempts on several of the forts in the area. Although none so overwhelming as yours," he said referring to Pierre*, Toussaint and the others. "News from the east is not so good. The strong Fort Louisbourg stands and attempts on it have failed. As a result many ships still pass to the Saint-Laurent but not all.

"The British have managed to seize much land in Acadie and have deported a large number of the *habitants,* to New England. Many have moved on to the Louisiana Territory and are forming a large part of the population there. I hear they are called by the strange term, *Cajun.* I hear the news from France is also not encouraging. Is that correct Monsieur Juchereau?"

Philippe Juchereau traveled frequently to France on business and had recently returned. "That is correct, Monsieur Allard, The crown has considerably more interest in its colonies in Africa and India, as well as in its battles in Europe with the British Empire. I met briefly with his majesty and it is clear that he has little regard for our prospects. In fact I believe he has more interest in continually pouring the national treasure into his palace at Versailles." Turning to Pierre* he asked, "Having just return from a first hand view, how do you view the British, young Allard?"

Starting slowly, Pierre* responded, "We were able to defeat them because they were stupid and arrogant. In addition they have angered their Iroquois allies. They fail to see the value of Indian fighting. This being said, I fear though they may remain arrogant they will not remain stupid. Their sheer numbers alone are a problem."

Shifting his weight, Pierre* decided to pose a more controversial issue, "There is considerable unhappiness among the British colonists with the attitude of their mother country. The colonists feel this is their land and they are given little say in its government. Some even feel an eventual alliance with the French colonists is possible,"

With a pained look on his face, Juchereau responded. "I think it unlikely either colony could exist on its own, even joined with the other. No, I fear our best hope is with our own people." The discussion led to more mundane topics and eventually the families headed home.

The Allard farms had done better than most. Franny, Joseph, and Marie-Angélique*, had worked double time, and Jacques*, Pierre, and Henri-Pierre were becoming quite valuable in spite of their youth. The crops would be acceptable and there had been several births in the livestock, which served as a safety valve for food in case of local hostilities. In addition, the three boys were becoming accomplished hunters and fisherman, and had learned a great deal that summer under the capable tutelage of Joseph. Young Louis Allard, who had been born in February, was becoming very robust and it appeared another able lad would soon be available.

<u>The Blue Goose Tavern and Inn - September 1755:</u>

The Allard men sat enjoying a shot and beer and discussing the harvest. Louis Jacques had become a fixture in the group. His small farm was just across the square, and as he lived alone, he was always available to help the Allards. As head of the militia, he also had early access to all the news from the outside. "Word is that there have been attempts on forts in the Ohio. Fortunately they are stalled and it is doubtful that the British can withstand the winter and they will likely be forced to retreat. In addition, Indian raids in the British settlements have been greatly facilitated by Braddock's road. I hear that by the end of the month, virtually all British colonists will have abandoned the Ohio Valley."

Pierre* finished his beer and replied, "I keep thinking of the great numbers in Braddock's forces. Had they the nerve to return with their reinforcements, we may not have prevailed. I don't see how we can hold on forever. We can't leave every summer to fight a war. What will we do when they come to Québec?"

Franny responded, "Everyone knows that the Citadelle is impregnable."

His brother countered, "And what about your farm? Everyone in Québec can't hide in the fort. And they certainly can't farm from the fort. What do we do? Hide in the caveau? These won't be random Iroquois raids. They will burn the farms and stay. What will we do with our families?"

Pierre Bergevin rose, "On this cheery note, I'm off to bed. If my farm is still here in the morning I plan to harvest it." And the group made its way back to Bourg-Royal.

Winter of 1755-1756 was good. Just enough snow for good hunting, and cold enough for good ice on the bay. For the first time in a few years, the iceboats reappeared. Pierre* and Toussaint took the boys out whenever possible. Jacques* and Pierre even fashioned their own simple boat. Although it was not up to the standards of their father's, it did work surprisingly well. Marie-Angélique* even made it away from the family a few times to go for a ride with her husband. It reminded both of them of the early, exciting, and carefree times of their youth.

Jacques* and Henri-Pierre went as often as possible to the woods to hunt. They also took to trapping. Joseph had patiently instructed them in this art and they actually began to supply a large amount of needed winter food for the families.

The season of 1756 was easier as all the men were home. The weather, however, was not as good and poor rainfall resulted in a second poor crop. The militia continued to meet and train regularly and the colony was always anxious to hear news from the outside. Although British raids continued, the Québecois continued to hold their own. In November of 1756, Pierre* and Marie-Angélique*'s fourth son was born and baptized Michel Allard. He appeared as active and healthy as his older brothers.

Québec - June 1757:

Planting was just finished and the weather remained favorable. It appeared that a successful crop was in the making when the long dreaded news arrived. Louis Jacques appeared on the Allard porch one evening early in June. "There is new difficulty to our south. We are being called up and I'm afraid this will involve even more men. There is to be a meeting of the leaders tomorrow morning at the fort. I have been asked to bring you and Toussaint."

The sun broke over the men pushing from the bank at Beauport to cross the bay to Québec. Landing at Place Royal they made their way to the upper town then farther up to the gates of the Citadelle. Fort Saint-Louis was an imposing place. Large granite stones made the bottom walls, topped with high pointed stockades with high turrets for guards. The inside revealed ramparts all along the walls, which held cannon to cover all 360 degrees. Three of the four walls ended at sheer granite cliffs 100 feet high or more. The fourth wall faced the Plains of Abraham, the former farm of the old ship builder and pilot, Abraham Martin. These held no cover for an enemy and ended at cliffs and other impassable terrain.

The men were taken to the great hall where they met with officers of the army and other militia leaders. Two men stood conversing and examining maps at the front of the hall. They all recognized Pierre de Rigaud, Marquis de Vaudreuil, the immensely popular Governor General of Québec. Pierre de Vaudreuil's father, Philippe, had been born in Carcassonne in France where he had been commandant at the famous fort of the same name that dated back to the early middle ages. Called to Québec to serve as interim governor of New France, Philippe de Vaudreuil stayed to live and raise a family.

His son, Pierre, and other children were born and raised in Québec, and although Pierre de Vaudreuil had spent time in France for education, the fact that he was a native-born Québecois was a source of great pride in the colony. He had become head of the military forces of the colony and in 1755 was promoted to Governor General. Not only was he a true Québecois, but he also related well to the citizens and held in high regard the importance of the Indians to the colony and particularly to the military.

The younger man with him was unknown, but the men soon learned that he was Marquis Louis-Joseph de Montcalm, who recently had arrived from France to serve as the head of military operations. He was young but came with great respect and credentials. He was fit and appeared younger than his 43 years.

As the men had assembled, Vaudreuil brought the meeting to order. "Men, it seems that our old friends, the British, are again on the prowl in search of French lands.

We are embarking on a campaign to enhance our control of Lake Champlain and the water route to Montréal. In 1755 after our victory at Fort Duquesne with the defeat of Braddock's army, the British made an attempt to take Fort Carillon at the southern end of the lake. They were repelled and withdrew to Lake George, south of Champlain. Here they built a small fort. Over the last two years they have been enlarging and fortifying this location and now plan to use it to stage a series of attacks on Carillon. Then they plan to go on to Fort Chambly at the Richelieu River and thereby gain access to Montréal. As some of you know, the Marquis de Montcalm has been sent to continue my old job as General of the Army. He will lead the campaign. Monsieur le Marquis."

Montcalm rose. He was not very tall and spoke with a soft southern French accent. He appeared capable but kind. The men took an immediate liking to him. "*Bonjour Messieurs,* the geography of the problem is simple and I suspect most of you are familiar with it. Along the Saint-Laurent, halfway between *Trois-Rivieres* and Montréal, the river narrows at the town of Sorel, which has been home to voyageur families for many years. There is a large island, *Ile Dupas,* where a few families live today. At this point a branch of the river heads due south, now called the Richelieu River but earlier known as the River of the Iroquois as those savage people used it as access from their winter camps at Lake Champlain to raid the French colonies.

"Some years ago, the French built Fort Chambly twenty miles down the Richelieu which has served to cut off the Iroquois both by land or the river. More recently we have added smaller forts, Saint-Jean and Ile-Aux-Noix along the river; the last being at the entrance to Lake Champlain. Even more recently we have added Fort Saint-Frédéric at Crown Point at the southern end of Champlain. Just south we have Fort Carillon that seals off access from Lake George through *la Chute* River .

"This new British fort at the end of Lake George as it enters the Hudson River has been slowly made into the best British fort in the region. It and Fort Edward to the east form a staging area to attack our forts and gradually gain access to Montréal and Québec. We shall follow this route south and take this British fort, which is now called William Henry after two sons of the British King.

"This will be a slow voyage as we must bring heavy arms and cannon if we are to breech the fortifications and lay siege. As a result much of the travel will be by land with carts and horses to transport the armaments. As a result we must leave soon so as to complete the mission by winter. Upon arrival we will lay siege to the fort, which may take some time. I wish to leave in two weeks' time. That is all."

As the group broke, Pierre* said to his friends, "I think I would like to talk to this man." Louis Jacques gave a look that showed that he found this a bad idea but knew that he was unlikely to discourage Pierre*. They worked their way forward to where Montcalm and Vaudreuil were speaking to another officer. Pierre* waited patiently and when the opportunity arose he spoke. "I beg your pardon, Monsieur, my name is Pierre* Allard. I am an *habitant* from Charlesbourg. My friends and I were with the militia at the battle of Fort Duquesne."

Montcalm quickly interrupted, "Yes, well, congratulations, I hope we can again do so well."

As Montcalm tried to leave, Pierre* said, "If I could be so bold, sir, I believe there is a much easier way to deliver your cannon to Lake George."

Montcalm looked irritated, "And how might that be, by canoe?"

"Well, sir, in a way, actually, yes."

Montcalm was now losing his patience, "Sir, even a large canoe cannot move a cannon."

Pierre* persisted, "If Monsieur le Marquis would care to come to the ship works in the lower town, I believe I can show you a way."

The Marquis studied this young man a few years younger than himself. He had a simple confidence that was not quite arrogance. He decided to play along. "Very well Monsieur Allard, but I must warn you I am pressed for time."

Pierre* couldn't resist replying, "Monsieur, I believe I can save you several weeks."

Vaudreuil, who had been listening, entered the conversation, "I will give le Marquis a ride in my carriage and meet you men at the shipyard."

Pierre*, Louis Jacques, and Toussaint hurried out and down to the lower town and off to the shipyard so as to arrive first. Once in the carriage, Vaudreuil spoke, "This man Allard has somewhat of a reputation as an inventor. He has made a sled that sails on the ice. Fast as lighting, quite remarkable. He may have something."

When the carriage arrived at Place Royal, the men were already digging through a pile of Pierre* and Toussaint's old projects. Old Louis Langlois greeted the two Marquis at the entrance. After the exchange of pleasantries, they entered the warehouse. Pierre* and Toussaint had put the basic parts in place. Pierre* began, "We connect the two canoe hulls and can carry heavy loads in a stable fashion in the bridge. We can even attach a sail if you want speed, but for these purposes we will be safer paddling. We can even adjust the width as we go to get better maneuverability in the narrows and better stability on the lakes."

Montcalm studied the craft, then looking to Langlois, "Does this actually work?"

Old Louis replied, "It always has."

Montcalm continued, "How long to make enough for fifty cannon."

"Depends on the size of the cannon, two to four weeks."

Montcalm thought out loud, "The time we save in travel would more than make up for it. Monsieur Langlois, could you began immediately?"

"If it's to fight the British, we shall began this evening."

Then turning to Pierre* Montcalm said. "Monsieur Allard, I'm promoting you to Captain of Transport. If this works as you say, I may make you General."

Chapter 9

Ile Dupas - June 1757:

Pierre*, Louis Jacques, and Toussaint had been transferred to the island to prepare the cannon boats. The materials were made at the ship works and sent by sailing vessel to the island with the cannon. The men would assemble and ready them for the departure down the Richelieu River.

The island lent itself perfectly to their purposes. It was actually three long thin islands, as it was cut by two narrow channels parallel to the mainland. The downstream end of the island was marshy, but the upstream half was dry and beautiful. The main channel of the river was to the south. If they used the northernmost part of the island, they could unload materials by the inner channel and avoid being seen from the main channel. It would be very simple to launch the pontoon canoes loaded with cannon, paddle the half-mile to the south shore by the small village of Sorel and enter the Richelieu River.

The men were spared some of the worry of their farms as they were being well paid for this work. In addition the island was idyllic. About five by three miles in size, it was surrounded by enough water to protect them from an enemy ambush. Only two families lived in this quiet place. Louis Jacques remarked, "It seems that one could come and farm here and leave the rest of the problems of the world behind."

Work proceeded rapidly and by the end of June, the men had assembled enough boats to carry 30 cannon as well as heavy supplies and even horses if the need arose. The British fortunes had remained poor in 1756. Fort Oswego, their stronghold on the southern shore of Lake Ontario had fallen to Vaudreuil. This allowed the French to pass freely down the Richelieu River all the way to Lake George. The British attempts on the French forts in the region had all ended in failure, in large part due to the use of Indians.

The war between France and Britain had worsened in Europe, and the British were having difficulties with both their Iroquois allies and their own colonists. The Iroquois had lost faith after the defeat of Braddock and were allowing and sometimes even aiding the French as they raided the frontier. The British colonists were unhappy with the uncertainty of their eventual control of the Ohio Valley as well as the new taxes imposed by the Mother country to fund the war.

On July 1, 1757, Montcalm's army departed Ile Dupas. As usual, Pierre* had devised a way to load and launch the boats easily, and by the day's end, the entire flotilla of 8000 men, including soldiers, colonists and Indians were on their way south. Montcalm was amazed at the sight. Instead of the difficult march he had anticipated, they would float his army to Lake George. Accompanying the men on this trip was Michel Charbonneau who had traveled to the Rocky Mountains with Vérendrye. He had brought his thirty-year-old son, Jean-Baptiste Charbonneau, also a voyageur.

They remarked on the irony of using what had been the traditional path of attack for the British and Iroquois on the French to turn the tables with their own attack. There was no resistance as they made their way south. They encountered two bands of Iroquois and were surprised to find they wished to join in their attack on the British.

At the end of July, they arrived at Fort Carillon, a short distance from their target at Fort William Henry. Here they met a contingent from Détroit that included their usual friends as well as Julian* Fréton and Michel* Yax. That evening Montcalm met with the leaders. "We will leave part of our group here at Carillon. We will proceed with 6500 men. I am told William Henry is well defended. New reinforcements have swelled their ranks to over 2000. They have many cannon and a well supplied and fortified fort. We plan to lay a traditional siege. We will advance as close as possible to the fort then dig trenches for our cannon. We will began to shell them and continue to advance until they are easy targets. At that point without help from the outside, they cannot stand. This may take many weeks or only a few days. We will send a squad east to Fort Edward. This is their only hope of reinforcements. These squads will try to stop any such effort and relay intelligence to our front."

They arrived outside the fort on August 3. Montcalm ordered, "Monsieur Allard, please form squads consisting of militia and Indians each with two soldiers. They are to surround the fort to prevent travel in or out. Monsieur, do you think these savages can be trusted?"

Pierre* replied, "Monsieur le Marquis, I would trust the savages above all other men here."

Montcalm proceeded to dig in and set the 30 cannon. They worked through night and by daybreak they were ready. At this point, Montcalm took a white flag of truce and asked Pierre* to accompany him as they rode to the fort. Pierre* was not quite certain of what was happening, but they rode to the gates which were opened allowing them to enter. They were led to a room where an older man in full British uniform stood with a few soldiers and colonists by his side.

Pierre* thought one of the British colonists, a man about his age, seemed somehow familiar. He thought he saw the same thought in that man's eyes as well. Montcalm spoke to the General in rapid English, and Pierre* understood only a little. "General Munro, as you know, I am about to lay siege to your fort. You are hopelessly outnumbered and I ask you to surrender now and avoid terrible bloodshed. I am ready to hear your terms."

General Munro replied more slowly and was easier for Pierre* to understand, "Monsieur le Marquis, I am grateful for your concern, but I am unable to give up my fort. I wish you luck and may the best win."

With a salute, Montcalm turned and left as they had arrived.

Back at the camp, Pierre* learned that this was typical protocol for 'civilized warfare' something he found to be a true contradiction of terms. The shelling commenced. The British had moved a number of men out to the perimeter where they hid behind brush and such barriers as they had been able to construct while they shot at the French lines with little success. As the French moved them back with the cannon fire, they advanced toward the fort.

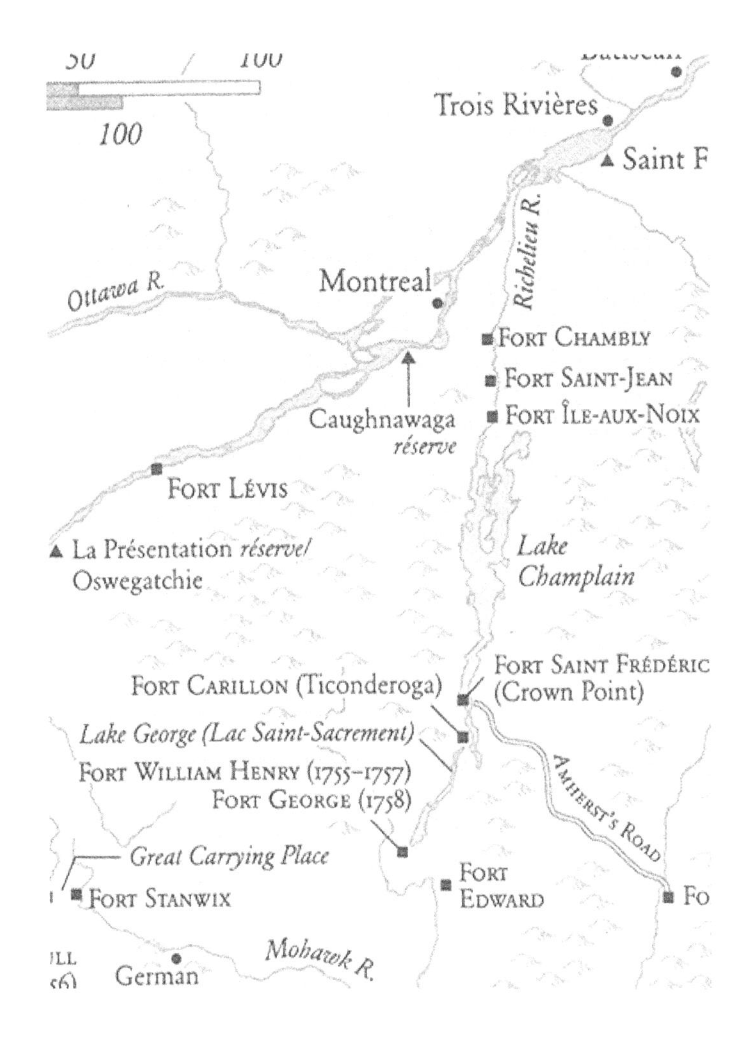

Fort William Henry

Chapter 10

Lake George - August 6, 1757:

Montcalm called Pierre*, "Monsieur Allard, we must get someone inside the fort to gain information. I understand that there are a few French prisoners there who may have intelligence as to the state of the defense and the possibility of aid from the outside. I am asking you to meet with Monsieur Charbonneau from the Détroit militia to select four men of talent. One must have knowledge of English."

Pierre* found Michel Charbonneau. He suggested that Pierre* go with Jean-Baptiste Charbonneau, Julian* Fréton, and Michel Yax. "Jean-Baptiste is the strongest man here, Yax knows English, and Fréton has a skill you may need."

"And what is that? If I may ask."

Charbonneau replied, "Apparently fishing with lines is very popular in his old home in France. He can throw a line like no man you have ever seen. Including a rope!"

With considerable trepidation the men left the camp late that night. Their scouts had indicated that the west wall was the least guarded. The sentries changed every four hours and they decided that about three hours after the change would be best. "I know that's when I start to lose interest," Pierre* noted.

When they reached the wall of the stockade, Fréton put a large knot in the end of the rope and threw it with great skill indeed. The wall was twenty feet high, and the knot fell precisely behind it and in between two sharp posts. He pulled it and it held firm. They waited a few minutes and hearing nothing, Jean-Baptiste Charbonneau as the strongest man, went up and was over the wall in less than two minutes. Almost immediately, a body in red came over the side. The men rushed to tie the guard, but when they saw that he had broken his neck in the fall, or that Charbonneau had done the deed for him. He was in no need of restraint.

Pierre* went next, then Fréton, and last came Yax. As he was older and not quite so fit, Yax came slowly. The others aided him by pulling up the rope. Once all four were on the ramparts, they surveyed the situation. Pierre* had spoken with a man who knew a little of the fort. While pointing he said, "I believe the cells for prisoners will be in there. Julian* and Jean-Baptiste, go to the corner and start a fire for diversion. Michel* and I will slip into the building. If we are not out soon, go back over the wall. Good luck"

Soon the two men had a small fire going. When it started to grow, Charbonneau yelled, "Fire!" in his best English. The ruse worked and all those awake responded leaving the men a clear shot into the building. It worked perfectly, except there were no prisoners. When they tried to exit, they were seen. A man ordered, "Halt!" Pierre* tried to avert him but the man shot and Pierre* felt a searing pain in the side of his chest and the world went black.

He awoke a short time later. Michel* Yax was sponging his face while holding pressure on his chest. The small cell now held two prisoners. Michel* went to the door and shouted. “I am needing help vith this man. He is bad shot. I am needing bandages and vater.”

The guard at the door ignored him, but another British colonist came up and said to the guard. “You watch the outer door, I’ll see to this.”

He came and knelt over Pierre*. Michel* had removed Pierre*’s shirt and the man pulled his wampum and medallion to the side to get a better look. The man jumped and quickly withdrew his hand. He was the man Pierre* had vaguely recognized with the general a few days before. “It stung me!” Then he looked closer at it. “My Aunt Elizabeth was said to have a medallion such as this.” What was amazing is that he said this in French.

He started to clean and dress Pierre*’s wound, “She was given it by an Indian who had kidnapped her and my father to Montréal.”

Pierre* looked though bleary eyes, “Monsieur Price, from Pontiac’s camp, of course.”

Price then had his memory jogged, “Of course, Monsieur Allard from Québec.”

Pierre* had a rush of energy. “This was my grandfather’s. He gave it to the Indian who gave it to your aunt who returned it to my grandfather. What a small world in this great country.”

Samuel Price continued to dress the wound while he spoke softly and quickly in French. “The colonists are becoming very unhappy with this war. All we get from Britain is more taxes. We expect they will vanquish the French, but then we will vanquish the British. Monsieur, you and I are soon to become allies. Munro has sent for reinforcements from Fort Edward, but they do not seem to be forthcoming. Without them we can only stand a few more days. Do you think you can stand?”

"Pierre* rose slowly, "Yes, thank you, I think I will be alright."

Then Price looked about and said, "The guard will be back any second. I will leave the door unlocked. When he goes to the other side, go quickly and quietly. There is no guard on the south turret."

Pierre* asked weakly, "How will we get over the wall?"

Before Price could reply, the guard came back, "Price, what are you doing? Playing cards? Get out here!"

Price turned quickly and began to talk to Michel* in English, loud enough for the guard to easily hear him. He went out, shut the door and feigned locking it. When they left, Pierre* asked Michel*, "What did he say to you?"

The German looked puzzled, "He is saying something about valking on the vater at da falls by da Niagara."

Pierre* smiled weakly, "He told you how we will get over the wall." When Michel* started to ask him something, he quickly replied, "Not now, I'll explain it back at camp."

The guard went to the other end of the hall as predicted, and the men slipped quietly out. Pierre* was having difficulty breathing and felt very weak. They made it slowly up to the south turret without drawing attention. As predicted there was no sentry and as Pierre* had guessed, there was a large coil of rope. He told Yax, "I don't think I can climb down, can you lower me?"

The older man looked up and said, "Vhy not?" and he tied it under Pierre*s arms and lowered him down. A few minutes later he was down, and as they headed toward the woods, they met their two friends.

Julian* said, "As soon as you entered the building they were on us. We fought our way though, or should I say Jean-Baptiste did, and made it back to our rope and out. Looks as though you did not fare so well."

Michel* Yax replied, "Pierre* here is being shot. But now he is patched by some English guy vhat speak French and good. Vee got vhat vee vanted doe. Now vee should be running. And how !"

They made it back to camp and to Montcalm's tent. Pierre* struggled to get out his report, "They can only hold out a day or two without reinforcements but they are hoping for help from Fort Edward."

Montcalm smiled. "We just intercepted their runner form Fort Edward saying that they have no men to send. I shall order advance of the cannon tonight. By morning we can blow down their turrets. I think you gentlemen should get Monsieur Allard to the doctor's tent."

The doctor noted that his wound had been expertly dressed, put him in a bed and found a bottle of brandy, which helped immensely. Soon the men were all being treated, and Pierre* finished the story about Samuel Price. The men found his observation about the eventual outcome of the war was interesting and even a little optimistic for everyone. Then Michel* Yax asked, "And vhat is dis about valking on vater?"

Pierre* laughed, which made his chest hurt and said, "When we were at Pontiac's camp many years ago, Niagara Campau told Price how we used to hold a rope and rise up on the fast current of the falls. Price knew that would tell me there was a rope, but the guard would not understand what he meant."

As Montcalm had predicted, the next two days were horrific for inhabitants of William Henry. The Frenchmen began to wonder just how much the British were willing to take, but on the ninth of August, the flag of surrender went up. Montcalm and the officers rode to the fort and discussed the terms with Munro and his men. Then to the astonishment of the *habitants* and the Indians, they put out a long table and dined together at a veritable banquet.

Michel* Yax remarked from afar, "Ees also like dis in German countries. One day dey kill you, nex day you friends. Ees crazy I'm tinking."

When Montcalm returned he reported to the men, "I have agreed to let them leave the fort with their belongings including the weapons they can carry. They in turn have promised to leave directly for England."

Later, as the French were moving in and the British moving out, Toussaint came to Montcalm, "The Indians are upset, especially the Iroquois who joined us. Traditionally, they take spoils of war, the guns, ammunition, and other things. They feel they have fought for nothing."

Montcalm replied in a dismissive fashion, "They had the honor of fighting for France, if they want more, they should stay home."

Toussaint mentioned quietly, "But they are home."

Montcalm merely sighed and walked off.

Toussaint turned to Louis Jacques, "I am beginning to fear this man."

The Charlesbourg-Beauport contingent stayed at the fort waiting for Pierre* to be ready to travel. The battle had been good on this group and they lost none of their numbers.

Two days later, two voyageurs arrived at the gates. They entered hurriedly and insisted to see Montcalm. He met them in his office. "Monsieur le Marquis, it was terrible. They killed them all."

Montcalm replied calmly, "What do you mean?"

"All of them, the British. They were half a day from the fort when the Indians descended en masse. They butchered them, every man. They took everything, their guns, their horses, their clothes and their scalps. They took all the women and children and disappeared into the forest."

Toussaint lamented, "I feared this might happen."

Montcalm was less calm, "Blasted savages, so this is what we get for our kindness. And what are the British to think of us. It's so uncivilized. I shall not trust them again." And he left for his quarters. In the ensuing days, Montcalm moved everything of value to Fort Carillon at the south end of Lake Champlain. He then burned Fort William Henry to the ground. The French were again in full control of the frontier.

As soon as they were given their release, the men from the militia headed up Lake Champlain and then toward home. Pierre* Saint-Aubin went with the men from Québec and Montréal. Although he had been born in Détroit, and held property there, he had maintained his home in Montréal to facilitate his fur business. At an overnight camp on Lake Champlain, the men began to revel in their overwhelming victory. Saint-Aubin said, "I do not wish to dampen everyone's enthusiasm, but I know what my father will say about this. We have had our successes due to the arrogance of the British and the aid of our Indian allies. But the British are over one million and we are scarcely sixty thousand. Arrogance can deter them only so long."

Toussaint added, "I am afraid this man Montcalm may be a great general, but he does not see the importance of the Indians as Vaudreuil does. This may be his undoing."

Saint-Aubin continued, "I believe that I will move my family to Détroit after the harvest. I think it will be safer and maybe the English will not have much interest beyond the Ohio Valley. At the same time, I am taking my father's advice and studying English."

Still having some difficulties with his injury, Pierre* Allard remarked slowly, "This man Price said that the British colonists are going to turn against the British government. He believes we will join with them." He continued to tell the story of his medallion and Price's aunt.

At this point Pierre* Saint-Aubin had a bolt of realization, "This man's aunt was Elizabeth* Price?"

Pierre* Allard answered in the affirmative. Saint-Aubin continued, "I never made the connection until now. She is my mother-in-law! Or should I say was, she died when my wife was quite young. So the medallion on your neck is the famous medallion that I have been hearing about all my married life."

Pierre* Allard had met Madame Saint-Aubin on brief occasions. Puzzled, he said, "I thought your wife was named Brindamour. Elizabeth* Price married a man named Fourneau."

Saint-Aubin replied, "He was Jean* Fourneau dit Brindamour, and my wife is Marguerite* Fourneau dit Brindamour." He came over, felt the medallion, and jumped back. "It is true, it is alive."

After Fort Chambly, the men headed to Montréal. There they left some of their comrades and continued to Québec and the Beauport livery.

The men were greeted with joy. In addition to their safe return was the fact that they could help finish the harvest. Sparse rain had made for another mediocre crop. Marie-Angélique* told her husband, "Young Pierre and young Marie-Angélique have been very helpful with the farm, but had it not been for Jacques* and Henri-Pierre we would be going hungry this winter. They have brought home game every day, and the traps they and Joseph have been setting have given us a good deal of meat and many furs."

Pierre* congratulated his children, especially his odd son with the odd eyes. He thought to himself, "I only hope we have someone to trade with for the furs."

The Blue Goose Tavern and Inn - Early October 1757:

As the end of the harvest was near, the men met to discuss life in the colonies. There was considerable worry about poor crops, but the war was foremost on their minds. Ordering a second round, Pierre* Allard told the men, "Joseph is going to take young Jacques* and Henri-Pierre to the forest this winter to trap to try to supplement the farm. Their mothers are not in total agreement, but the boys are in paradise over the prospects. I don't know if the woods may not be safer than the farms these days."

As head of the militia, Louis Jacques was the bearer of news from the military and the government, "Currently all forts are secure, but the threat of a new barrage of attacks looms. Particularly in the east where, although we hold Fort Louisbourg, most of Acadie is in British hands. Governor Vaudreuil has always favored a strong alliance with the Indian, but the new General, Montcalm, is not in agreement. He believes all battles can be won with European means. He doesn't realize how lucky we were at William Henry this summer."

Toussaint added, "If he doesn't change his ways, I am considering moving my family to Détroit."

This news stopped the conversation. "When did this come to be?" Pierre* asked his best friend.

"Since William Henry. Jean* Saint-Aubin is correct. We cannot prevail forever against the enormous numbers of the English. I know Détroit and could do well there. The English have little interest in it. They want the Ohio and the passage through Québec. In addition, Détroit has a fine relationship with the Indian."

Pierre* remained silent for the remainder of the evening.

Chapter 11

The Palace of Saint-James, London, England - October 1757:

William Pitt sat quietly, pretending to listen but actually thinking ahead of the speakers. Pitt had risen slowly through the British bureaucracy. Two years before he was appointed Secretary of State in charge of the war with France. He was soon replaced due to lack of progress but recalled when the war proceeded even more poorly without him. He now believed he could turn the tide and had built enough influence in Parliament to sell his policies. He also continued to hold the respect of old George II whose health was failing.

Lord Roger Chauncy continued his endless speech, "Gentlemen, the war goes badly with no progress on the continent and now these disasters in the American colonies. First, we have had unbelievable defeats of our overwhelming forces by a handful of rabble, and now we hear the colonists are unhappy with the lack of progress and actually balking at paying their taxes. Mister Pitt, what do you propose?"

Pitt was happy to be called; at least he could rise and stretch his legs. "Lord Roger, I believe we need to busy the French on several fronts. I propose supporting King Frederick in Prussia to aid him in his problems with the French. I also propose increasing our efforts both in India as well as Africa. As for the Americans, unlike our other colonialists, they are all loyal British citizens, born in or descended from these Isles. I think we should ask them what to do."

Before Lord Roger could arise, sputtering, to his feet, Pitt turned to a balding gentleman sitting in the corner, examining a clock and seeming oblivious to the conversation. "Mr. Franklin, you can speak for the colonists. How do you advise us?"

At 51, Benjamin Franklin had recently arrived from the American colonies. The war with the French had forced him into a position of influence there, and he had become an eloquent spokesman for the colonies. He rose and began to speak. Much to their dismay, it was clear this man felt himself on an even plain with these lords of parliament. "Gentlemen, the American colonists are indeed loyal British subjects, but will remain so only if you treat them as such. I had the opportunity to supply General Braddock's ill-fated march. The colonists had worked long and hard to forge an alliance with our Iroquois neighbors. We advised the late General to use them. He, however, refused and paid the price. He took the largest and most expensive force seen in the new world and marched it for two months only to be annihilated in two hours by an enemy he never even saw.

"The colonists asked for help in settling the lands of the Ohio. Now they are told that after the war, there will be no more settling of this land. In addition, they are asked to pay for this war (for which they receive no land), with taxes in which they have no say and from which numerous wealthy landholders are immune. All they ask is that if you wish taxes, they want representation. If you want war, they want some of the spoils. Your lordships can fight this war with or without the cooperation of the colonists. It is your choice."

Franklin calmly took his seat leaving everyone but Pitt speechless. Pitt rose and concluded, "I propose sending Colonels Amherst and Wolfe to lead the battle in the Americas. I am charging them to first take the Fortress at Louisbourg in Acadia. This will give us control of the Saint-Lawrence River and the route to Québec and Montréal. From this vantage we can remove the French from the Americas for good."

At long last William Pitt was about to have his revenge.

Boston, Massachusetts - March 9, 1758:

John Campbell, the Earl of Loudon, paced angrily facing a group of colonial gentlemen appearing equally displeased. Loudon had served the past two years as commander of British forces in the American colonies. He now had a detailed plan that would vanquish the French once and for all, but he could not secure the approval of the riff-raff before him. "Gentlemen, if I am to conduct this fight for the lands of the Ohio and elsewhere, I must have your co-operation. I need men and they need to be equipped and trained."

Young Samuel Adams arose in the rear of the room. Recently chosen for the Massachusetts colonial legislature, he knew how it aggravated Loudon to have to address this group of colonial governors and, worse yet, colonial legislators as 'gentlemen'. "Lord Loudon, you must understand. Our people are viewing this as your war, not ours. If we are to fight, we need some say in decisions and some financial aid from the crown. We also want the land we conquer."

Loudon looked over to a friendlier face. John Pownall was the governor of Massachusetts and born in England as was Loudon. "Governor, can't you make this rabble stand to reason?"

Pownall replied, "Your Lordship, they do have somewhat of a point."

Loudon exploded, "Point? I'll show you a point. If we cannot move forward, we are going to discuss acts of treason. I have had enough for today." And he stormed from the room.

The next morning as the group reconvened, Samuel Adams sat with his rebellious friend, Samuel Price. Governor Pownall entered and called the meeting to order. Conspicuous in his absence was Lord Loudon. "Gentlemen, I have received this morning a communication from the Secretary of State that arrived on a ship from England just last evening. I have asked Mr. Adams to read it."

Trying to no avail to mask an obvious feeling of glee, Adams rose, "This information was accompanied by a letter from our friend from Pennsylvania, Benjamin Franklin.

London, November 1757
My Dear Countrymen,
I have been meeting with Secretary of State William Pitt and members of parliament. They have agreed to some changes, which I believe you shall approve. I must say we have found a willing ear in Mister Pitt.
Sincerely,
Franklin

"I shall summarize the documents from Pitt, and they will be posted for you all to read at your leisure. He is recalling Lord Loudon and replacing him with General James Abercrombie. He is sending Colonel Jeffery Amherst and Lieutenant Colonel James Wolfe to help lead a renewed conquest of the French. He is empowering the colonial governors to raise militia. These militia will have rank similar to that of British army and be paid in kind. The crown will finance their provisions, equipment and training. In closing Pitt says, '*Assure the colonies that I will neither bankrupt them nor destroy their liberties.*' Gentlemen, I believe this is what we have awaited."

By spring a large colonial militia was finishing training and awaiting orders to march west.

Chapter 12

<u>The Laurentian Foothills - Early Spring 1758:</u>

The colorful bird rose quickly from the meadow, stopping suddenly and falling silently to the ground. Two others rose behind him and suffered the same fate. Seeing no more, the boys went to retrieve their prey. Pheasant were uncommon this early in the spring, but the youngsters were pleased to find anything to eat. Jacques* removed his arrow and Henri-Pierre removed his two. Jacques congratulated his young friend. Hitting two birds from the same flight with a bow was a feat of great skill.

Normally they would be hard at work planting, but torrential spring rains had left the ground unworkable. Ironically the past two seasons had been badly hampered by drought. The end result was a Québec that had survived three years without its usual excellent supply of food. Now in early spring there were no remaining food stores. The boys had left to kill any game they could bring back to their hungry families. Their fathers and Jacques*'s older brother, Pierre, had gone fishing for the same purpose.

Crossing the meadowland, they headed into the great forest of the Laurentian hoping to find something that had not yet headed up for the summer. They followed an old Indian trail for a few miles when Henri-Pierre stopped short. He sniffed the air. Jacques* knew that his friend had inherited the Indian sense of smell. Henri-Pierre surveyed the forest. Then stopping, he motioned silently to a small clearing. Here was something better than the boys had dared to hope for, a bull caribou!

Fortunately, Jacques* had brought his rifle. They had hunted with bows as all the *habitants* had been asked to conserve ammunition for use in anticipated British raids. Jacques*'s father had allowed him to take the gun but told him to use it only on something valuable. He carefully leveled the weapon and took patient aim. His shot hit home and the great animal fell softly to the ground. The boys controlled their excitement and approached the beast cautiously, knowing that if it was only wounded it could be extremely dangerous.

Having determined that it was dead, they fell to the task of gutting the creature and preparing it for a difficult transfer back to their canoe. They noticed that the animal had a fresh wound on its hind leg. Realizing what this meant they both stood and looked about. They heard a faint rustle and then saw what had caused the wound. Jacques* had hoped it might be a wolf, but to his dismay, it was something much worse.

Jacques*'s different-colored eyes stared into the evil yellow eyes of the largest female mountain lion he had ever seen. Whereas a wolf was more cowardly and would be frightened off with an arrow wound, the mother cat would not leave this meal for any reason. They knew that they would not be likely to kill it with an arrow and Jacques* had used their only rifle shot. Unlike the wolf, an arrow wound would cause the cat to attack rather than flee.

Jacques* never took his eyes off those of the mountain lion. He casually dropped his bow to the ground and approached the cat slowly. Henri-Pierre stood motionlessly with his bow at the ready. Jacques* moved up to the cat and continued to stare. All animals in the forest, even the bear, will not challenge a cat, especially a female as large as this one. The mountain lion was confused and unsure how to consider this odd young creature. Jacques* slowly lowered his hand and touched the animal softly on the nose. The bewildered beast turned slowly and walked back into the forest.

Henri-Pierre stood with his mouth gaping. He had seen his friend "charm" animals before but never one like this. "How do you do that?"

"I just show it I'm not afraid."

"But how can you be so deceitful?"

"I'm not, I knew she would not hurt me," Jacques* replied.

"Well, who told the cat?"

"I don't know. But I knew she wouldn't."

Regaining his composure, Henri-Pierre continued, "We had better get going, she might reconsider." And the boys finished preparing the caribou, placed the pheasant and their other small game inside the caribou and tied it to a strong stake that would allow them to transport it.

Just before dusk they reached their canoe, loaded the game and proceeded south. They reached the Saint-Laurent within a few hours and went to the Beauport canoe livery where they left the boat and continued to haul their prize home. On their arrival they woke their parents to help process the meat. Everyone arose with some enthusiasm. They could not risk losing any of this to spoilage. Fortunately the fathers had been equally successful on the river and they had a great amount of fish. The families would eat well for a few weeks on today's bounty. The boys never mentioned the encounter with the mountain lion for fear of upsetting their mothers.

Dawn came upon a family again ready to farm. The past few dry days had rendered the higher ground workable and the planting recommenced in earnest. The Allard farms had changed greatly in the past few years and not for the better. The fields were sparse due to the poor conditions of the past two years and the constant threat of British raids. The houses were in poor repair and few animals remained. A few years previously, the Pierre* Allard farm boasted four horses, a dozen cows, and many pigs and goats as well as numerous chicken and other barn fowl.

They were now down to two cows, two pigs, one goat and a few scraggly birds. They had one remaining horse, a strong part-Perchon stallion related to the first Allard horse brought many years before from France. The others had died or been sold. Many of their neighbors had been forced to eat their older horses, as food was very scarce in the winter. This generation of Québecois had been often cold and tired, but the past two years was the first time many of them had been truly hungry.

<u>The Blue Goose Tavern and Inn - Late May 1758:</u>

The men ringed a large table to discuss local affairs, as well as those of the larger world. True to his word, Pierre* allowed the boys to attend now that they were over twelve years old. Pierre* lamented the poor season, "Even though the rains have now subsided, much of the seed rotted in the fields. If we have another dry summer, we shall have no crop at all. Even the drink is suffering,” Referring to the state of poor homemade beer and corn whiskey, which were the town’s only remaining libations.

The door opened with a flourish and three men entered. All known to the group, they joined the table. They were Pierre* Saint-Aubin, Jean-Baptiste Charbonneau, and Pierre Reaume, brother of Nicolas* Reaume. All three men farmed, but were primarily involved in the fur trade. All three traded out of Détroit although Charbonneau still kept his family in Montréal. Pierre* Saint-Aubin began, "We are off with a contingent of militia to help out Montcalm. We had business to conclude in Québec and thought we might find you boys here.

“The Marquis,” referring to Montcalm. “is over at Fort Carillon, north of Fort William Henry in Lake Champlain. It seems the British are planning another attempt to take the area. We’re going to help him out.”

Louis Jacques asked, “Does Montcalm still propose not using the Indian in battle?”

Charbonneau answered, “As far as we know, yes. He and Vaudreuil continue to be at odds on the subject.”

Toussaint spoke up, “Vaudreuil is Québecois, he knows that we cannot prevail without the Indian and the Indian method of fighting, why is Montcalm so stubborn?”

Saint-Aubin returned, “Hard to say, he has this thing about ‘honorable war’, a contradiction of terms if I ever heard one. They say that Bougainville has gone to France to ask the opinion of the King as to who should make the policy.”

Changing the topic, Toussaint asked, “And how goes Détroit?” Pierre* Allard knew that his life-long friend had thought to move there.

Saint-Aubin answered, “Much as always. Still not enough people, but we’re growing. There is a settlement now at the north of the Grosse Pointe at the Milk River. Pierre Reaume”, referring to his companion, “has a place there as well as our friends Michel* Yax and Julian* Fréton who you remember from Fort William Henry.”

Pierre* Allard asked cautiously, “And your father?”

Saint-Aubin laughed, “Still the same. Can you believe it? He will be one hundred years this winter, and I still can’t keep up with him. He continues to study English and forces it on the rest of us. He outlived both the Campau brothers”, quickly crossing himself, “And now Niagara Campau has gotten into it with him. They say that Détroit will not be part of France, or part of England; but it will be the real ‘new world’ the real *America.* Well, here we are, out to help Montcalm prove him wrong. God help us.” With that the group broke for the evening.

On their walk back to Bourg-Royal, Pierre* asked Toussaint, “Do you still have this thing about Détroit?”

His friend replied, “Yes, if Montcalm won’t use the Indian, he will not prevail. I agree with Jean* Saint-Aubin, I believe it is a place less tethered to the affairs of Europe.”

Pierre* continued, “My family has now lived three generations in Québec, four including Jacques*. I cannot bring myself to leave it.”

His friend replied, “Pierre*, my family has lived here a thousand generations. Sometimes it is just right to change.” They continued home in silence.

Chapter 13

Québec City - July 3, 1758:

Québec was in a festive mood as its citizens gathered throughout the town to celebrate the 150th anniversary of the founding of their city. New France now counted 60,000 residence and more than one-third lived in the area of greater Québec. Many of them were in town. The dress of the *habitants* was definitely more threadbare than usual. Even the wealthy citizens dressed in worn clothing. New items from France were now uncommon to non-existent. Fewer animal drawn vehicles lined the square as their desperate owners had eaten many of their former 'motors'.

Picnics and banquets abounded, but the fare was far less and more basic than in years past. The spirits however were good. News from the east was hopeful. No English attacks had been successful and France continued to control all of the western fortifications. Some help from France had been promised though not yet received, but the citizens remained cautiously optimistic. At mass the Archbishop had appealed to the Blessed Virgin to continue to aid her chosen people.

The square was lined with exhibits to Champlain, Cartier, Etienne Brulé, the beaver, the canoe, the friendship with the Indian, maple syrup, and, of course, snow. Pierre* and Marie-Angélique* walked hand in hand followed by their family. Jacques* and Pierre, now 12 and 14, were off with their friends but Marie-Angélique 9, Marie-Anne 5, Louis 3, and Michel 2 were all along for the festivities.

Marie-Angélique* squeezed her husband's hand, "It seems almost like the old days, before we were married, before the war. Do you remember?"

He replied, "Of course, though it seems so long ago."

"I hope our next child can see more peaceful times," referring to her enlarging abdomen.

They stopped and visited with friends, trying to talk of happier things, particularly the fact that the weather had improved along with the outlook for farming. They tried to avoid other things on everyone's mind including ongoing battles on Lake Champlain and at Fort Louisbourg in Acadie.

Bourg-Royal - July 15, 1758:

As a brutal sun baked his back, Pierre* Allard inspected the worst crop he had ever grown. Early rains had ruined much of the seed and now lack of the same rain was causing them to burn in the fields. He had planned to deal with weeds today, but in truth, even the weeds were dying. This winter they would rely more than ever on game from the woods, but even here things were sparse as all the *habitants* were relying more on the hunt, and the game close to home was scarce. His thoughts were suddenly broken by a friendly call.

His friend Louis Jacques was on his horse and appeared to be in a hurry. "Meeting tonight at the tavern, there is news from the Ohio." And without further adieu, he rode on to the next farm. By dinner time news of the meeting had already spread to the wives. Marie-Angélique* said, "We must pray that it is good news. With the poor crops we will need outside supplies more than ever."

Arising from the table, Pierre* said, "It shall be what it shall be. Boys, are you coming?"

Pierre Jr. and Jacques* arose quickly being thrilled at the invitation. Outside they met Toussaint, Joseph and young Henri-Pierre and headed to the Charlesbourg Square. Inside the Blue Goose, the neighbors were gathered. Louis Jacques arrived with a paper. "The news is good." Before he could continue, a second round of drinks was ordered. "It seems that the old Marquis de Montcalm had again prevailed. The new British general, Abercrombie, attacked with a larger force, but Montcalm was ready and had set traps of spikes and ditches about the perimeter of Fort Carillon.

"When the British became entangled he was able to attack. Apparently Pierre* Saint-Aubin and Pierre Reaume took the Indians outside the fort and met them from behind. In spite of the success Montcalm was critical of them as he had not ordered it."

Toussaint said, "Will this man never see the value of Canadian fighting?"

Jacques replied, "We will have to wait for the return of Bougainville from France with King's decision."

<u>Québec - August 12, 1758:</u>

The next bit of news was not good and it did not arrive by courier, rather by a more ominous source, Acadian refugees. The news spread fast and the Place

Royal was filled with *habitants* to greet and help the wretched hoard. They arrived by river in canoes, rafts, and anything else that floated. They had only the clothes on their backs and were both sickly and starving. Many were severely wounded. Québec had seen such refugees before, after the first fall of Louisbourg many years ago; but then they were healthy and traveled with their belongings. This group was near death and empty-handed.

The current Mother Superior of the Ursuline Convent, Marie de l'Assomption was organizing the women and the other nuns to run a makeshift hospital. Although she was very young, the convent and mission had prospered under her leadership in the past few years. She was more fearless than pious and would have reminded the original settlers of Marguerite Bourgeoys.

A man named LeClerc who came with a wife and five hungry children told the story. "The British have had a foothold in Acadie for several years, but we have continued to hold the Fort at Louisbourg. The British came several weeks ago with a great number of troops under a new leader named Wolfe. He laid siege to the fort for six weeks. When our General Drucour failed to yield, Wolfe began to burn the town and the farms and kill the *habitants.* Ultimately Drucour was forced to surrender. Wolf said that the French deserved no honor because of the Indian massacre at Fort William Henry.

"He made all French soldiers prisoners of war. He deported all *habitants* to France although most have lived here for generations. Those like me who were able to escape made our way with nothing but the clothes on our backs. The British took all our tools, weapons and animals. They massacred all of our Indians save the few who were able to flee with us, and some others who made their way to the Saint-Jean River Valley. There will be many more of us that follow, many on foot. Most of us have family in Louisiana due to the refugees from the first fall of Louisbourg. Once we are sound enough, we will make our way there. Most of our friends and neighbors have been slaughtered, all the farms have been burned and the property taken. These men have no shame or honor. We have had enough of war and certainly enough of the British."

Someone asked, "Are they likely to continue to allow traffic down the Saint-Laurent?"

He replied, "This man had no use for the French. It is clear that he will do anything in his power to ruin us. I would anticipate few ships."

Marie de l'Assomption called the men together, "We must help our brothers. They must be fed. I realize that the crops are barely enough to sustain the farmers, but we must provide. We will pray for rain, but I feel we must take more immediate action. Monsieur Allard, you and Monsieur de Baptiste and your boys are renowned hunters and fishers. You must form a group that will go to the wilderness to supply us game. Leave enough men here to tend the land. With our prayers, I know we shall prevail." It was not lost on Toussaint that for the first time, a mother superior had referred to an Indian by other than his first name.

That afternoon the men met and organized hunting parties. Joseph, Pierre Jr. and the other children would stay at the farm and Toussaint, Pierre*, Jacques* and Henri-Pierre would leave for the frontier. The men divided themselves into those that would fish the streams, those that would fish the Saint-Laurent, and those that would head to the woods. Pierre*'s group went with the latter.

<u>Québec - August 15, 1758:</u>

Marie-Angélique* and the other village women took turns helping at the convent hospital. The patient list grew daily, space, supplies and workers were scarce. The condition of the refugees was appalling. All were burned, injured or wounded and all were sick and hungry. Most of the patients died and body removal became a high priority. The enthusiasm of the young mother superior was all that kept their spirits alive.

Marie Dumas was a young mother several years younger than Marie-Angélique; however she appeared much older. She had arrived with her husband and four of their children. Two others had died in a fire and two others succumbed on route to Québec. "You cannot imagine the terror", she whispered weakly to Marie-Angélique*. "When the commandant would not surrender the fort, they began to burn the town and then the farms. They came one night and set us ablaze. It was a miracle any of us escaped, but my youngest daughter was caught in the house and my oldest son died trying to save her.

"When the surrender finally came they rounded up all the citizens like hogs into a fenced area. They stripped the soldiers of their weapons and uniforms and loaded them on a boat to France. They split the *habitants* into two groups, one to return to France on a slave ship, and the others to be taken as slaves to the British Colonies. We were allowed nothing but the clothes on our backs. We were selected for the second group but my husband and some others managed to break us free. We found canoes and parted upstream. We traveled at night and slept in the day. We were pursued and many were shot or captured and hung on the shore. My two youngest died of hunger. We buried them along the way. We never saw the remains of the two lost in the fire.

"When we recover we hope to go to the Cajun colony in Louisiana." She began to sob and finished, "These are evil people, Madame. Fear them, for they will come here. Their leader is a man named Wolfe who is the devil himself." And with that she sobbed herself to sleep. Marie-Angélique* had not the heart to tell her that the rest of the family had already died.

That night at dinner Marie-Angélique* told the story to Joseph who had stayed to help the farm. Although he was now in his eighties, he remained bright and capable. "I can scarcely bring myself to return to the hospital. The stories are filling me with fear. What if the British come before the other men return?"

Joseph responded, "We will manage. The British cannot advance so quickly and this represents only one lost fort. Besides, the Citadelle is impregnable."

The hunters did return a few days later with an abundance of fish and game. Sister de l'Assomption had it divided in thirds, one-third for the families of the hunters, one third for the population in general and one third for the refugees. The farmers returned to their parched fields and tried to eek out as much as possible from the worst growing season in memory, always keeping one eye on the farm and one to the east and l'Ile d'Orleans, always fearing what might be coming.

Charlesbourg - September 4, 1758:

Toward the end of mass, the priest noticed Louis Jacques entering silently. Jacques made a silent motion to the curé and sat in the back of the church. At the conclusion of the service, the priest announced, "It seems that Captain Jacques is here and wishes to address the congregation."

Jacques came slowly to the front and began quietly, "It is bad, this time it is Frontenac that has fallen. I will have details this evening at the tavern."

That evening the Blue Goose was packed to overflowing. Jacques arrived late and took the floor, "Frontenac fell quickly. It was a force of less than two hundred regular soldiers and seventy Iroquois, but the death knell was from five thousand colonist militia. The British have finally enlisted the enthusiasm of the colonials. What is more disturbing is that they were led by a colonist named Jean-Baptiste Bradstreet, the son of an Acadian mother and British father."

Later as the talk fell to smaller groups, Toussaint said, "Now we have vulnerability both from the east and the west. The attack of Québec is bound to come, and what is this of a British leader of French-Canadian heritage?"

Pierre* replied, "I feel this is a sign that our English colonial friend, Samuel Price is correct. This man represents a new breed, not French or British, but American. This is who will eventually prevail."

Pierre Bergevin entered, "I hope you are correct, but it will be little comfort when they begin to burn our homes."

The harvest was as poor as expected, and the *habitants* made plans to scrape things together and with good hunting they might survive the winter. In addition, the fear of invasion remained ever present. One bright spot was the birth of Louis Allard on October 12, 1758. However, due to the poor nutrition of his mother, he was not as robust as his siblings.

Just before Christmas, more bad news arrived; Fort Duquesne at the Forks of the Ohio River had fallen. Louis Jacques reported, "The British General Forbes had made a treaty with the Iroquois to forbid any additional British settlement in the Ohio Valley. The Iroquois went with his large force and built a road through the Pennsylvania woods. When they arrived at Duquesne, our captain realized it was futile, evacuated the fort, and then blew it to ashes. It is rumored that the British are rebuilding it as 'Fort Pitt' and have named the village about it Pittsburgh."

Pierre* added, "I can predict one thing, this treaty with the Iroquois will not be upheld by the British, and eventually this will fall to our advantage."

The men returned slowly to their farms and began to endure the worst winter in Québec memory.

Chapter 14

Détroit, Cathedral of Sainte Anne - February 12, 1759:

Simple Bocquet was lost in his thoughts as he recited the well-memorized lines he had come to know so well. A Franciscan priest in a nation of Jesuits, he had come to Détroit from France in 1750. He set at once to building the new edifice in which he now stood. He had great plans for his parish, but now, as it was for all the parishioners before him, things were in doubt.

At the end of the prayer his thoughts returned to the present, and as was tradition, he pronounced the young couple before him to be man and wife. The bell on the new church tolled loudly as the congregation exited onto a bright crisp winter morning. Although the Détroit winter was mild compared to that being endured by their Québecois cousins, the parishioners walked quickly to the warmth of the parish hall and rectory where a celebration would take place.

By the time the young priest reached the interior, the men of the parish had begun the celebration with their first round of drinks. After pleasantries with some of his flock, he worked his way to the new couple. Julien* Fréton had come from France at the same time as the priest; in fact they had traveled on the same ship. When Fréton ended his very short military career he stayed with Bocquet in Détroit. Gaining respect of the city as a strong, honest and energetic man who had served well in a few skirmishes with the British, he had obtained a farm east of town at the

Grosse Pointe at a place called the Milk River Settlement. He had taken for a bride the much younger daughter of his neighbor, François* Gatignon dit Duchesne.

Marie-Josephine* Gatignon dit Duchesne was only fifteen years old, but this was prime marriage age in the young colony. The oldest of six children she was mature and capable of running a household. She was short, but even in her wedding dress it was clear that she was very much a woman. Her family called her Josie*. They exchanged pleasantries with the priest and the conversation led to their new home.

The Milk River was a deep but murky river that emptied into Lake Sainte-Claire seven miles north of the Détroit River just at the north end of the broad Grosse Pointe. The river entered the lake parallel to the northern border of Julien*'s farm but quickly turned south and cut across his and all the other ribbon farms in the settlement. This was a wonderful source of water and transportation for the settlers but it posed a problem as it cut each farm in two. Julien* told Bocquet, "One of our first chores in the spring will be to bridge the river so we can cross with wagons."

Trying to keep the conversation alive, Bocquet asked, "How many farms are now in the settlement?"

To his surprise it was young Josie* who jumped with the response, "Six altogether. My father's, of course, he was the first settler when he arrived from Montréal in the 30's. Then Julien*'s best man, Hyacinthe Reaume and his family. He is here with his brother Nicolas*, the voyageur.

Then Michel* Yax and his family from the Rhineland. He and Julien* fought the British together."

Bocquet knew that young Josie* was lively but he did not know how talkative. She continued, "Then there are our two remaining bachelors, Louis* Greffard and Pierre* Huyet dit Champagne. Of course, all the others from Grosse Pointe are here, the Tremblays, Laforests, and of course all the Saint-Aubins. And did you see our other sponsor, Claude Meunier from the army? He is with Major Jean-Baptiste* Billiau dit Lesperance in the gorgeous uniform. And did you see how many of the Indians have come?"

Bocquet gently broke from the conversation to mingle with his flock. Always politically astute, he started with a group in uniform. The speaker was Major Jean-Baptiste* Billiau dit Lesperance, "I am telling you they will come. It is only a matter of time and if France will not send more men, we shall be at a loss."

The man next to him, also in uniform responded. He was François Bellestre, the new Commandant of Détroit. "I agree, Major. Don't forget, I was educated in France but born in Détroit. My family came with Cadillac himself, but I fear we may be on our own."

A third rugged looking man not in uniform spoke up. He was Nicolas* Reaume, the voyageur, "The major is correct. They will come and we will be few. The chances of help from France are as good as the beaver returning to *Belle Ile.* Our only strength is with our Indian allies, and we must use them."

Bocquet grunted a pleasantry and decided to leave this conversation to the military. He settled on another group of men nearby. The speaker was very old but quite lively and alert. He was Jean* Saint-Aubin who had just passed his 100th birthday, "The British are coming and we cannot stop them forever. We must decide how to best suit our needs to maintain our lives, commerce and society."

A younger man, Antoine Campau, answered, "They have finally gained the full support of their colonists. Why there were 5000 at the fall of Fort Duquesne."

A third man spoke. He was clearly an Indian, but dressed in European clothes and speaking perfect French. His hair was long and tied in back, but this was common for the day. His only Indian mark was a single long blue feather in his tied hair. He was the Ottawa chief, Pontiac. He had become active in all aspects of the community and was almost as well regarded as old Jean* Saint-Aubin, "The British promised the Iroquois full title to the Ohio Valley. We all know how well that will be honored in the end. At that time the Iroquois will again appear at my camp, and you, Monsieur Saint-Aubin, you will be there as well, seeking my assistance."

Seeking an end to the talk of war, Bocquet called the group to attention and proposed a toast as he signed the parish record book. He read the marriage document that he had prepared ahead of time and then added his signature. At the top he added the number 157 for the number of marriages performed in the parish. Although it had been 58 years since Antoine Cadillac laid the stone for the first Sainte-Anne, the parish had recorded on average only three marriages per year.

Sainte-Anne Cathedral, Détroit - Two Weeks Later:

The bell of the new church was ringing again but this time on a much colder and grayer day and for a much more somber reason. Father Simple Bocquet rose to what was definitely the largest assembly of his congregation he had seen. "Today we are gathered to say goodbye and to pray for the soul of one of the great men of our city in the wilderness. He has been here since the time of Antoine Cadillac. He has served as the advisor to many and was the very heart and soul of our community.

"Born one-hundred years ago in a small village in Bordeaux, he was baptized Jean* Casse but during his years he took the name of the village of his birth, Saint-Aubin-en-Blaye. You all knew him well, I dare say better than I. I have asked his son Pierre* to say a word."

As Pierre* Saint-Aubin rose to the altar, his fifty years were beginning to show. Although he was dressed in his finest, there was little doubt that this was a man who led a rugged life. "You all knew my father as a man who dedicated his life to Cadillac's 'city in the wilderness'. Everything he said and did was for the good of the community. Last week, when he knew the end was near, he asked me to relay a last wish to you. He believed that our community and this new world in which we live is more important than any of the far away places from which we or our ancestors came. He knew that bad times are ahead, but he strongly believed that if we reason together with all, we can prevail."

The silence was broken by a slight commotion in the rear of the church. Pierre* Saint-Aubin looked up to see a man exiting. The only thing that caught his eye was the bright blue feather tied to the back of his hair.

Chapter 15

Bourg-Royal - March 1759:

The bright sun on the snow made Pierre* wince as he left the house. It was the first time he had seen the sun in some weeks. It appeared that the end of the worst winter in memory was approaching. Now the snow would melt and the ice on the Saint-Laurent would begin to break. The animals had done poorly and many had died. This at least gave the family something to eat. The harvest of the weakest had become a regular ordeal. Pierre*, Toussaint and the boys had been able to kill enough game to make up the balance of their poor diet.

The Acadians had, for the most part, departed, many to Louisiana and even more to Eternity. The few remaining had planned to depart with the thaw. Although the colony was braced for the eventual attack of the British, these people had lost their taste for battle. Marie de l'Assomption and her nuns had labored beyond all expectations to keep the few survivors alive through the terrible winter.

Fatigued, as he now often was, Pierre* drew a deep breath. His old chest wound from Fort William Henry pained as he exhaled, his breath easily visible in the cold. The pain troubled him more and more, and he occasionally had coughing fits, which frequently produced blood. As he regarded the sun, he hoped that this year would produce a reasonable crop. At least there would be no stumps to pull this year. No wood had been cut save for that necessary to burning. For the first time since the founding of the colony, no one was expanding his farm. Such was the gloom of uncertainty that hung low on the community.

His friend, Louis Jacques, appeared on foot. Louis's old horse had become frail and became Louis's nourishment for the winter. What remained of the steed was given to Marie de l'Assomption at the Ursuline Convent to feed the Acadians. "Well, perhaps spring will come," Jacques began, "It is a shame that the British did not attack this year. This winter would have killed every Englishman in the New World."

"Perhaps this winter will be as bad," replied Pierre* as he coughed a blood streaked spittle on the ground.

"Well at least Bougainville should arrive on the first boat of spring that can run the blockade at Louisbourg and we shall at least have the King's answer as to whether or not we can use the Indians to battle the British."

Pierre* only nodded.

Louisbourg - May 1759:

James Wolfe, now General James Wolfe, viewed the training on the parade grounds. Acadie, or Acadia which the British now called it, was finally firmly in his hands. He had been training his men whom he called the Louisbourg Grenadiers for almost two months. They began as soon as the dreadful winter broke. Wolfe realized that they could not have survived the terrible season had they not held control of the shelter of the fort. Even so, his health, even at the young age of 33 was not good. His cough had become steadily worse.

"Good morning, General." Wolfe tuned to see Hopson, his first officer. "The men are progressing nicely. They will be ready for battle by the end of the month."

Wolfe replied, "We should be ready to sail at that time. General Amherst and the others will be staging attacks on the remaining French holdings in the West. Our holds on Fort Pitt at the Forks of the Ohio in the South and Fort Frontenac in the West will give us great advantage. Our job will be to lay siege to Québec, certainly the most important and most difficult part of the great plan.

"Champlain's old Citadel remains one of the most formidable fortifications in the world, and we must prevail before winter. I am told that the winters there are harsher than the one we have just endured. I find this hard to believe but terrifying if it is so." Quickly changing the topic, "How is our success in stopping the French fleet at the Gaspé?"

The young officer replied, "As well as can be expected. As you know, even the hold on Louisbourg does not guarantee anything. The area to be patrolled is enormous and there is no way to stop everything from entering the wide opening to the Saint-Laurent. Some boats slip by but I assure you that we stop most."

Stifling his chronic cough, Wolfe continued, "This will surely be the most important campaign of our careers. If we prevail, England will finally have total control of the continent. We sail the last day of this month. At this point you may tell the men our plans."

Québec - The Same Say:

The Place Royal was filled with an exuberance not seen for some time. Three French warships had arrived carrying much needed supplies as well as armaments and 800 fresh French troops. One also carried the Marquis de Bougainville who had been sent for instructions from the King. Governor Vaudreuil called a meeting of the military leaders for that afternoon.

Vaudreuil and General Montcalm stood in front of the assembly. Vaudreuil spoke, "Men, le Marquis de Bougainville has returned with his majesty's wishes. Briefly, he requests that Monsieur Montcalm take lead of our forces, Monsieur le General."

Montcalm rose, "Gentlemen, we must now prepare for the inevitable British attack. Our voyageur spies indicate that General Wolfe will soon sail for Québec. We anticipate his arrival around the end of June. We must make our final preparations. We must be ready for a long siege and hope that we can contain him until winter. If so, we will prevail. We cannot fortify our entire coastline so we will key on strategic areas. Monsieur Jacques," referring to Louis Jacques who stood in back with Toussaint and some other *habitant* militia, "Your men are to help fortify the north shore from Beauport to Montmorency.

"We cannot cover *l'Ile d'Orleans.* The *habitants* of the Ile may stay on their farms or take refuge at the fort as they wish. We cannot cover the south shore but will fortify Pointe Lévis so that we may prevent them from going south of the city. We will train once a week and work on fortifications the rest of the time. At night you can pray to the Virgin to continue to protect her people."

The Blue Goose Tavern and Inn - That Night:

Pierre* Allard had begun to hope for a good crop. The season had started well, weather was good and the crops were ahead of schedule. Today's news seemed, however, to bode poorly for the farms. Jacques had made his report to the men when Toussaint began, "It seems that the King and the General are prepared to make the impossible more difficult by not using the Indians appropriately. If it were not for the men in this room and their families, I would leave tonight with my family for Détroit.

"That not being the case, I volunteer to head a group of *métis*. The King and General both think we are actually French anyway, and we will form small Indian bands to act as independent agents in our own interest and do what we do best."

Louis Jacques replied, "I have no objection, but we must keep this plan in this room. Pierre* Allard and I have drawn plans for the north shore fortifications, I would like to start with assignments so we may begin in earnest tomorrow. We will work on an honor system. I realize you all have farms to run, but this must take precedence.

Beauport - June 15, 1759:

Pierre* drove his Perchon horse in a line parallel to the coast of the Saint-Laurent. His plow was expertly raising an earthen wall to serve as a barrier. He was fortunate the plowing was done at the farm and he was able to use the horse and plow to build the barricade. The weather had remained fair and crops were doing well. It was a shame that most of the men were building fortifications when they should have been tending their fields.

As Pierre* made the wall, his brother-in-law, Pierre Bergevin pulled in brush and other rubble to impede the invaders. Some others then placed sharp pikes to further discourage the enemy. Pierre pulled up by Louis Jacques who was distributing water. He drank a cup, then poured one on his head. “Do you actually think this will work?”

Louis replied, “One can only hope.”

A uniformed man on horseback approached. He dismounted and greeted the men. Jean-Louis Dandonneau was the official military head of the group. He had been born in Québec, but educated at military school in France. He had a Parisian wife and planned to return to Europe. However he understood the *habitants* better than the French natives, and the locals in turn trusted Dandonneau above most others.

With a friendly grin he said, “We won’t get this built by talking all day.” Pierre* laughed and coughed at the same time. His chest wound was becoming more painful and he was growing weaker. He was secretly glad to be driving the horse, as he feared he might not be able to do the heavier work.

Louis replied, “We were discussing the remote possibility of success.”

Smiling, the officer said, “I’m certain that General Montcalm would appreciate your confidence.”

Stifling his cough Pierre* said, "Seriously, we are going to be out-manned and greatly out-armed. We need something more than traditional tactics."

Having overheard the conversation, Toussaint joined them, "He's right you know, Jean-Louis."

"Well, perhaps you should advise the General."

Toussaint replied, "The General doesn't take well to Indian advice."

Pierre* spoke up, "He's correct. Maybe we should do some things ourselves."

Jean-Louis Dandonneau began to look worried, "Like what?"

Pierre* sat on the edge of his wagon to catch his breath, "The way I see it, we have one great ally, **winter**. We can't kill all the British, but if we can hold them until the snow, winter will do it for us."

"And how do you propose this?"

Pierre* coughed and continued, "First of all, you don't have to have been educated at a Parisian military school to know where they will land. *L'Ile d'Orleans* is made to order. They can't shell the city from there but it's perfect as a staging area to supply the ships."

Jean-Louis protested, "We can't fortify the entire perimeter of the island. It's almost 100 miles!"

Pierre* continued, "We can't and needn't. We let them land. Most of the farmers have left for the city or to stay with relatives on the north shore. We will send small bands to disrupt them."

Toussaint entered the discussion; "I will take my *métis* rangers with Indians in very small groups to cause mischief. We can't keep them from using the island but we can keep them busy and worried and disrupt their progress."

Looking more concerned, Dandonneau said, "Montcalm will never stand for it."

Toussaint replied, "He doesn't have to know," And with a sly grin, "Besides who would tell him?"

Pierre* continued, "Another thing is this fortification of the north shore. These walls will slow them down, but we don't have nearly enough men to watch every foot of it."

More exasperated, Dandonneau asked, "And how do you propose to remedy this?"

Pierre* returned, "Give them a good option. What is the most difficult section to fortify?"

"I suppose the falls at Montmorency."

Pierre continued, "Of course. We will do a very sparse job of fortifying the banks and it will be the obvious place to start their invasion by land. Our real defense will be farther inland. If we know where they will land, the watch becomes simple"

Dandonneau sat on the cart, "Maybe I should have stayed here instead of going to military school. You have some good ideas. I will communicate what is necessary to the General and you can proceed accordingly. I won't say anything about the Indian raids. But if Montcalm finds out, I know nothing. I have a wife in Paris."

Toussaint stood to return to his work. "Don't worry, Jean-Louis, you will still become a Marquis."

Baie Saint-Paul, Québec - June 24, 1759:

Antoine* Tremblay carefully hoed his new rows of corn; the small plants were better than they had been for the past three years. The crop was promising, if the weather held and if the war did not involve this area. The village of Baie Saint-Paul was sixty miles north of the city of Québec. His farm was at *Les Éboulements* three miles further north. The name was for the spectacular stone cliffs on which his farm set. From where he stood, he could see across the entire river, almost twenty miles wide. On a bright clear day such as today, he could see all the way to New England.

He hoped the war would not bother so remote a place as this. He thought of his three younger brothers and his oldest daughter who had moved nine years before to Détroit. He had not heard from them other than second-hand from trappers for almost three years. He hoped Détroit, too, would be too remote for the English who only wanted the Ohio Valley.

His solitude was broken by the cry of his six-year-old grandson Pierre who had been helping him pick up brush. The boy ran wildly toward Antoine. He was the fourth Pierre Tremblay to run in these fields, named for his great-grandfather Pierre* Tremblay who had come from France over one hundred years ago. "Pipi, look! A ship! A big ship!"

Antoine* looked up and indeed there was a large vessel under full sail on this glorious day in the wonderful cool northeast breeze. Ships had once been common, but since the fall of Louisbourg, they had become rare. "At last," he thought, "more needed men and supplies for the colony." As they continued to watch, it was apparent that the ship was not alone and soon many more appeared in the distance. Antoine* wondered why so many boats would come at once, but his question was soon answered and his hopes dashed when he saw the British Union Jack flying from the lead ship.

"The invasion," he said as he crossed himself. He then sat on a nearby boulder and they watched silently. In the next few hours they counted forty-nine warships with more small vessels than they could count. One ship was so large that he counted more than forty cannon to a side. Finally he said to his grandson, "I believe we need to go to the village." They loaded the wagon and departed.

HMS Harwood, the Saint-Laurent River - June 25, 1759:

General James Wolfe stood on the bridge of his lead ship. "I believe this is it, hand me the glass." He peered through the telescope. "Yes, this is *l'Ile d'Orleans*. Nothing else would be so large. We will stop here for the night and look tomorrow for a suitable landing." His heart raced, as he knew this was the beginning of the pinnacle of his career. He also knew that it would probably be the end.

His health continued to fail. He had frequent terrible bouts of kidney stones, and the cough and night sweats continued to worsen. His ship's physician had diagnosed consumption. He had barely survived the winter in Louisbourg. He knew that he could scarcely endure another

Québec winter and was certain that unless he could gain control of the fort and town, few of his men would survive it.

By evening, the entire city knew of their arrival. They had been alerted of the voyage and now the waiting was over. Montcalm dispersed his troops to cover the north coast at Beauport and the southern coast at Pointe Lévis. He did not realize that the colonists had also planned activities on the *Ile* itself.

The following day, Wolfe circumnavigated the island in a smaller gunboat. Even though the boat was fast, propelled both by sails and oars, the voyage lasted from dawn to dusk. That evening he met with his officers. "The Island is quite large and wooded, the terrain is rather flat. There are many farms, but they appear to be mostly deserted. There are no fortifications, as they must feel that is too large to defend.

"The north shore of the mainland is crudely fortified except at this point," motioning to his map, "by the long waterfall. I suspect the terrain was too difficult to fortify. The south shore is heavily guarded at this point called *Point-Levi.* If we could control this, we could shell the Citadel from the shore. As it is we can only reach it with cannons from the ship. The worst news is that the legendary Fort of Saint-Louis and its citadel are indeed impregnable by ordinary methods.

"We will land tomorrow at the northwest corner of the island. They know we are here and there will be no element of surprise. As we cannot reach them by cannon, they cannot reach us. We shall establish a base and began to stage the shelling of the city and the siege of Québec. Gentlemen, Godspeed!" And the weakened Wolfe limped off to his bed.

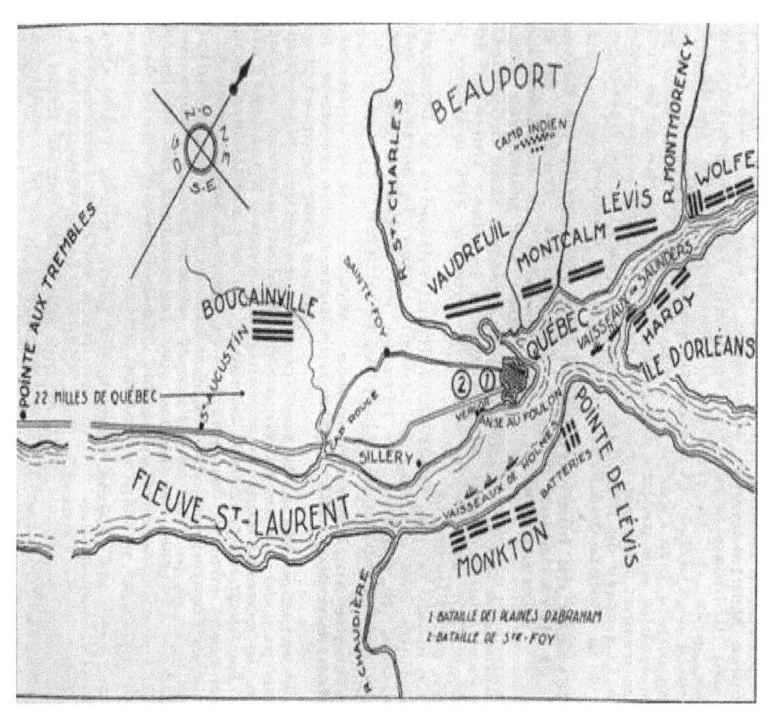

The Siege of Québec.

Chapter 16

L'Ile d'Orleans - June 27, 1759:

The scouting party having just returned from the island met with Wolfe. The head scout reported, "Most of the south end of the island is deserted. We saw no evidence of military or hostiles. At the tip there is a large deserted farm. Our scout with local knowledge said that it belonged to an aristocrat named Gourdeau who has left for France. It will be perfect for our purposes."

Wolfe replied, "Very well, begin to unload what we will need and we will set a camp of men. Most however will remain on their boats at night."

The first skiff arrived on shore with twenty men. They briefly examined the area; it was a lovely setting with a view of the fort. There were many trees but some areas of clearing in the yard or park as the British called it. The house was large and appeared to have been grand in the past. Now it was obviously deserted and all the furniture and other items had been removed. The Lieutenant said, "We will set out tents in the park and make an office in the house." Just as the men began to move their things, two of them fell silently with arrows in their chests.

The soldiers formed a circle and looked about. They saw nothing. Then as from nowhere, a loud group of screaming Indians appeared from the woods. No one saw from where they came or to where they disappeared, but it happened in a matter of seconds and when the commotion settled, another two soldiers had fallen dead to head wounds. The Lieutenant halted the move and formed squads to inspect the vicinity. They returned around noon having seen nothing.

Back on the ship, the lieutenant reported to Wolfe who ordered, "Continue as planned but post guards and keep a cautious watch at night." The rest of the day went without incident. That night they posted two guards. In the morning they were not at their posts. The lieutenant left to return to Wolfe, but as he arrived at the beach, he could see a commotion had started on the boat. He turned to his left and to his horror, the heads of his two guards sat on pikes.

Wolfe in turn called for many squads to search the island and posted some of the smaller boats around the island to intercept anyone coming or going. He had not expected this to go easily. He was not given as many ships as he had hoped and not as many troops. In spite of this he could not see how he could fail. The following morning he was informed that three of his scouts and several of his Iroquois scouts had disappeared. He was not certain if it was desertion or kidnapping. He was not certain which would be worse. The exploration of the island took four days and produced nothing but the delay of his plans.

The Citadel of Fort Saint-Louis, Québec - July 29, 1759:

Montcalm paced as he addressed his officers. "We must reinforce our position upstream. We have word of multiple attacks at the forts to the south and west. Marquis de Vaudreuil I am sending you with two regiments to go to

Batiscan and fortify the position to stop hostiles from the south and return when you are called."

This was not a bad plan, but in truth it was mainly to get Vaudreuil out of his way. He continued, "Monsieur Langlois has informed me that he has five old sailing vessels at the ship works that are no longer in use. The wind is shifting to the south and I believe we should try something daring."

He went with a group of men to the docks. They loaded the ships with a moderate amount of gunpowder and a few men set sail in them at dusk. The south wind brought them in direct line with the British fleet off the north side of the island. They approached under the veil of darkness and when in range, the set the ships on fire and left by canoes to the north shore. By the time the British saw them, they were on a collision course.

Montcalm watched through his glass from the wall of the fort. "They are on a direct course, this may work." The British were frantic. Wolfe gave the order to abandon the ships when an enormous explosion lit the evening sky. Montcalm was in despair, his boats exploded just feet short of the mark, causing only minor damage to the enemy.

The following day, the first British boats came into firing range and began to shell the city. Little actual damage was done, but the threat and constant bombardment took its toll on the colonists. The next day they began to shell Pointe Lévis. The ships were now also in French range and the Citadel began to return fire. The skies were lit all night and the peace constantly shattered by explosion.

Some occasional damage occurred on either side but there was no movement in the process.

On July 8th Wolfe's men managed to land on the Québec shore by the Saint-Charles River. They were making good progress toward the lower town when the Indians descended. They ran in panic, but only a few escaped to the ship. The rest lay dead and dismembered on the shore. Beginning to be beset with failure, Wolfe set fire to the lower town on July 16th.

Fire was commonplace in the colony, and the colonists knew how to contain it; but as the blaze smoldered into the night the people began to feel despair. The next many days were the same, constant shelling with occasional raids, generally foiled by the phantom Indians. By the end of July, he had set fire to the town four times. At one point in desperation, the British went north to Sainte-Anne and burned part of the village. This however had no strategic affect and afterward Wolfe realized that it was a sign of weakness on his part.

HMS Harwood - July 30, 1759:

Wolfe surveyed his officers. The frustration was palpable. His health was deteriorating by the day but he dare not mention it for fear of being replaced in disgrace. "We must break this battle if we are to succeed by winter. Tomorrow we will mount a full frontal assault on the north coast. We will obtain a foothold and march to the city to flank the Citadel from behind. We will enter at the low point of the fortifications here at Montmorency just south of the falls."

Montmorency - July 31, 1759:

The Beauport militia had gathered in force that evening, joined by a group of regulars with Jean-Louis Dandonneau and even a few cannon. Their sources had guessed that this would be the day. Pierre*, Louis Jacques and Toussaint sat smoking. Dandonneau began to again repeat the plan. "Timing is everything. No one is to move until I signal. They will be very close when I do so. When we fire the cannons, they will be confused. They would never expect them here. Toussaint, your moment is when they hesitate, no sooner."

Toussaint laughed, "Jean-Louis, for a thousand years, this is what Indians do best."

His friend replied, "Yes, but are you enough Indian?"

A sarcastic Toussaint answered, "Montcalm thinks so."

The British landed at dawn with 13 companies of Louisbourg Grenadiers supported by five thousand men. They were troubled by some small arms fire but continued inland. About a mile inland they encountered the real fortifications. The French let go the first volley when the British were almost on top of them. The British reacted and took formation. After a few returns, Dandonneau had two cannon fired. The surprise was obvious. He then fired two more to make them believe there were many cannon.

Wolfe hesitated considering a retreat when he heard the whooping behind him. General James Wolfe was only 33 years old, but he had been fighting wars for half of his life. He was a master tactician. He could not believe he had fallen for such an obvious trap. The British fled in full retreat. The Indians mowed them over like hay. By the time they reached the shore, insult had been added when Wolfe saw that they had burned his two ships. The British had to ferry back to the fleet in skiffs, allowing the Indians to do more damage.

The French were ecstatic at their success. That night they met at the tavern to celebrate. At the end Pierre* said, “This is fine, but it may not work again and we still have three more months until winter. He returned home and the next day tried to work the farm. Marie-Angélique* and the children with the help of old Joseph had done a good job and Jacques* and Henri-Pierre had been foraging for game with good success. Pierre was further dismayed when he realized he had become almost too weak to farm.

Chapter 17

HMS Harwood - August 20, 1759:

The discouraged Wolfe again addressed his troops. The last few days had been the same, constant shelling and frequent raids with no results. "Men, we have scarcely two months to finish this battle. When I fought with Braddock in the Scottish highlands, we had a similar circumstance. Braddock ordered what he called a 'walk-around'. It was not pretty but it did succeed. A group of rangers will go to the north shore. Start at Montmorency and gradually work your way to Québec city.

"You will start sporadic fires as you go. Try not to kill any more civilians than necessary. Try to spare the churches, but everything else is fair game. We shall defeat them with terror." When the men left he looked at his failing face in the glass. He appeared twenty years older. "God help me," he muttered, "What am I doing?"

The following day it began. A few fires in Montmorency, houses, barns, stores. Not everyone but many. The effect was devastating. People began to abandon their farms and flee to the woods or the city. The city became crowded. There was no room in the Fort. Sister de l'Assomption took as many as possible. The *habitants* in Charlesbourg and Beauport watched in horror as the flames slowly approached them.

Three days later Beauport began to burn, Pierre* was trying to farm but it seemed hopeless. He muttered to himself, "God help me if I never see another person dressed in red." Suddenly he had a desperate idea. He ran to the field where Jacques* and Henri-Pierre were helping Joseph cut hay. "Henri-Pierre!" You must run as fast as you can and get your grandfather Thomas."

The boy looked puzzled, "What shall I tell him."

"Tell him to come without delay. I think we can be saved but he is the only one who can do it. Jacques*, you come with me to Uncle Franny's."

They parted in a hurry and Pierre* and Jacques* ran as fast as Pierre* could tolerate. His brother Franny lived in their father's old house. When they arrived Pierre* asked. "Where is father's old trunk?"

His brother replied, "Upstairs in the loft, why?"

Pierre* continued gasping for air, "No time, just show me!"

They ran to the loft and found the trunk. Pierre* opened it and began to throw out the contents. "Please God." he whispered. Then at the very bottom he saw the bright red and grabbed the item and flew out of the house. Franny and Jacques* ran with him. As they approached his farm they saw Henri-Pierre with his old grandfather, Jacob* Thomas. Pierre*'s father, Jean-Baptiste*, had captured Jacob* many years ago when he was an English colonist. The man had stayed and prospered in the French community.

He immediately asked Pierre*, "What could this possibly be about."

Pierre* replied still gasping. "Put this on!" He held out the old uniform of a British Colonel.

Jacob* exclaimed, "Johnson's old uniform. I'd forgotten all about it, whatever are you up to?"

Pierre* gasped, "Only you can play the part now put it on and listen to me, all of you."

They headed east in the direction of the flames. Soon they encountered a group of men with torches. Jacob* Thomas hailed them and they came over. In perfect English and with the perfect demeaning attitude of an old British officer, "Thank goodness I've found you men. General Wolfe has sent me to fetch you. We have obtained the co-operation of these locals. They are going to lead us to the city. You are to stop burning at once and return to the clearing by Montmorency. You will be met there. Are there any more of you in the area?"

The leader replied, "No sir, we are all there is. But are you certain we are to stop?"

Jacob* replied with condescendence, "Of course, you fool, now go back before I have you all in the brig!"

With that they returned to Pierre*'s where they found Toussaint. Privately Pierre* explained the scam and told him to meet the men at the clearing. "We must be certain that none of them get back to Wolfe."

That night at the tavern Pierre* explained, "I remembered the old uniform and knew that Jacob* Thomas was the only person who could speak English well enough to be a believable British officer. I must say that he exceeded my wildest expectation."

Old Joseph rose and proposed a toast. "To two generations of Allards who have saved Charlesbourg from devastation, once by Iroquois and once by English."

The joy was short lived as the next week they received news from the frontier. Fort Carillon had fallen July 20th and was now called Fort Ticonderoga. Fort Niagara had fallen July 26th, and Fort Saint-Frederick had fallen August 14th and was now called Crown Point. The sadness in the Allard home grew when infant Louis Allard grew ill and died August 19, 1759, another casualty of war.

Chapter 18

Québec - September 10, 1759:

Wolfe called a meeting to meet with his scouts. They had been searching for a route to the back of the Citadel. The report was not good. "The first opportunity to enter is thirty miles up stream and it is guarded."

Wolfe countered, "Winter could start in the next three weeks. We cannot survive living on the ships. Should we leave today for Louisbourg, there is a chance we would be unable to make port before the ice. Even though we have taken Pointe Lévis, we must end this now! Tomorrow I will go personally with a few scouts, we need our fastest and most maneuverable craft."

The following morning the scouts met Wolfe with a local canoe. They skirted the coast until they arrived at a small almost hidden inlet about one mile west of the citadel. It led to a cliff, imposing but possibly passable. He ordered two scouts to explore it. They returned four hours later. "It is a difficult climb but possible. It took almost two hours. It leads to a long field, which leads to the back of the fort. It could be done but the group would be exposed for two or three hours."

Wolfe remarked, "If we start at night perhaps it could be done. It is a great risk but I see no other option but retreat."

The following day, spies leaked word of the planned attempt. Montcalm called a meeting of his officers and some locals. "It appears General Wolfe believes he has found a way to our back, what do you think?"

Louis Jacques spoke, "It must be l'Anse-aux-Foulon on the south shore of the city. It is a tight cove with a terrible climb, but given enough time it could be done."

Montcalm replied, "Then we must begin to guard it vigorously." Conditions in the colony had reached crisis stage. Many homes had been burned along with half the town. Many people had nowhere to stay and the makeshift hospital was filled to overflowing. There was little food now and winter was approaching. "If only we can hold a few weeks longer, we shall have won."

The local militia and some soldiers began to watch the cove. It seemed impossible that anyone could get by while it was guarded. On the night of the 12th of September, Wolfe's men made their move. The evening had started with a full moon and good visibility for both sides, but the wind shifted abruptly and the cold wind brought a dense fog. The French felt that Wolfe would not try this night and if he did, they would still apprehend him in this narrow cove.

Wolfe's men were on their way when the fog rolled in. By the time they reached the shore they could see no more than a few feet. They inched their way along until they found the cove entrance, entered and began their ascent unimpeded. The terrible ascent that tonight seemed even more grueling. They made their way however, and by nine o'clock on the morning of September 13th they stood on the Plains of Abraham still masked by the fog. Wolfe instructed the men to set columns two deep rather than three deep to appear to have greater numbers and not to fire until they were within twenty feet of the enemy.

They began to march, and by the time the fog lifted at 10 o'clock, Montcalm was presented with the horror of the British army lined one mile wide on his only unprotected flank. He gave the order to attack instantly and the French mobilized into their own columns and set to fight a traditional European battle.

To their horror, the men guarding the cove heard the first shots. Confused as to what had happened they began to climb the cliffs. When they arrived two hours later, the battle and the war were over. The French had been overwhelmed and forced to surrender. 1300 men from both armies lay dead on the farm of old Abraham Martin. Included in the dead was the Marquis de Montcalm who died of a musket shot. Wolfe died a short time later from injuries combined with the ravages of his disease. The impregnable fort of Samuel Champlain had fallen.

The following day they would realize that lost in the fog, the British had missed their target and happened on a smaller inlet with a much more difficult ascent two miles up stream. Although they took all night to scale it, the error turned a certain defeat into victory for the British. Québec had been betrayed by her own bad weather.

Chapter 19

Québec - September 1759:

The British lost no time in occupying the fort and the city. General James Murray was named Provisional Governor. He proved much less hostile and more reasonable than Wolfe. As many French soldiers as could be found were rounded up. Many escaped with Bougainville to join Vaudreuil at Batiscan to plan a new attack. Those who remained were imprisoned or released after signing an oath of allegiance. The British fleet departed for England as soon as possible to avoid becoming trapped by the impending ice.

Sister de l'Assomption was overwhelmed with the wounded of both sides. She went directly to Murray who was quite congenial and agreed to help wherever possible. Life in the city was confusing. No one knew what to expect or how to respond, but the colonists continued as best they could. None of them actually believed that this British occupation would last. Although over 1400 farms had been destroyed, the *habitants* in the country did reasonably well. Those without homes made do with neighbors or relatives. Crops had been respectable in spite of the siege, and the men could now concentrate on hunting and trapping.

Winter descended early and with a vengeance. The British soon realized how precarious life could be in a Québec winter. Scurvy, frostbite, dysentery and other maladies were rampant. Nearly one-third of the British would die before spring. The winter, however, demanded a level of cooperation between the two peoples as nothing else could. The British controlled the buildings, but the French had the know-how to survive. With the encouragement of Marie de l'Assomption, caring and sharing became a way of life that would not have been expected by either side a few weeks before.

<u>The Blue Goose Tavern and Inn - October 1759:</u>

Pierre*, Toussaint, and Louis Jacques sat together discussing the end of the harvest. Toussaint had seemed pensive all evening. Finally he spoke, "Now that the siege is over and things appear to be stable, I have decided to make the move to Détroit. Nicolas* Reaume is in town and I plan to leave with my wife and son tomorrow.

Pierre* had been expecting this but was crushed nonetheless. Before he could speak, Louis Jacques entered the conversation, "I am going too. Not to Détroit, but I have purchased a farm on l'Ile Dupas. Things are still normal there and I've dreamed about it since the days we spent building the cannon boats."

Before Pierre* could reply, Toussaint added, "Joseph will be staying and he's still good help. Your boys can work like men, and maybe you'll see the light and follow us next year."

Finally Pierre* had his chance, "I don't know if I have the strength to go anywhere, but I understand and wish you both well. No man has ever had better friends."

The following day they departed amid tearful farewells. Pierre* put his arm on his son, Jacques*'s shoulder as they each watched their best friends paddle away.

Montréal - three weeks later:

The men had stopped en route at l'Ile Dupas to inspect the new property of Louis Jacques. Jacques would buy supplies and hire two men in Montréal, then return to Ile Dupas to begin his work. Toussaint and his family would meet with Nicolas* Reaume and leave for Détroit. Montréal remained untouched by the ravages of war. People came and went as before, the crops had been very good and there were few hardships.

That evening the group dined at the tavern in the fort. After dinner they saw their friend Jean-Louis Dandonneau who had escaped to Montréal with Bougainville. He entered the tavern with an older officer and joined the men. He introduced the older man. "General Levi is the head of the military in Montréal. We are preparing to meet with Vaudreuil at Batiscan in the spring to retake Québec. We could certainly use you men. We have written to France asking the King to send more troops."

The lack of enthusiasm was overwhelming. Toussaint replied, "I am sick of war. I am particularly sick of the French inability to use the Indians properly."

Dandonneau countered, "General Levi is not Montcalm. He and Vaudreuil have every intention of using the Indians to their best advantage." Toussaint remained silent.

Louis Jacques entered, "I intend to start my farm at Ile Dupas in the spring, but I may come see you." With that the party from Québec rose and left for the evening. They parted ways in the morning.

Québec - December 25, 1759:

Christmas Mass was well attended. Even the bells were chimed. Governor Murray was wise enough to realize it would be folly to interfere with the church at this sensitive juncture. Pierre*'s condition continued to deteriorate. He required the help of his boys getting on and off the wagon. After mass conversation was subdued, and everyone held to the usual topics. The thought of an invasion of French in the spring was on everyone's minds but they dared not to speak of it.

The next morning Pierre* asked Jacques* if he would go for a short hunt with him in the woods near the farm. The boy accepted gladly but knew that there was some other agenda. After a while Pierre* said he needed a rest, and they sat on an old log. It was a beautiful clear winter day. There was a soft falling of the type of snow that comes from a clear sky on a day such as this.

Pierre* took his grandfather's old beaded Iroquois sack out of his pack and handed it to his son as he looked into the boy's strange eyes. "I know that you have heard these stories, but you are going to hear them one more time.

"When your great-grandfather, François* Allard came from France, he took this from an Iroquois brave he encountered not far from here. It has been passed down to the son deemed most adventuresome and most needing of luck. I have known almost since your birth that you would be that son." Then he removed his necklaces and held up the medallion first.

After a brief spell of coughing he continued, "The family legend tells that this medallion was found by an ancestor of ours in France around the time of Jean d'Arc. It is said to have powers. I know you have felt it before. François*'s father gave it to him at the time he left for Québec over 100 years ago. The wooden Indian necklace is wampum. There is said to be an identical piece that fits exactly with this one.

"This was given to François* by an Abenaki Indian when François* helped to save the man's son. In turn, François* gave the medallion to the Indian. Later François* gave the second half of the wampum to a girl he met onboard ship. It has not been seen again. The Indian's son inherited the medallion and gave it to an English girl who his people kidnapped and sold to the nuns in Québec. One day, by chance, she met François* and returned it to him. As he placed the two necklaces on his son he said, "I pray they will bring you luck. I know you yearn for adventure as did I, but for now you must help care for your mother and the children."

Pierre* Allard died that night in his bed, yet another casualty of war. He was buried the next day with his ancestors in the chapel cemetery at Saint-Charles de Boromée in Charlesbourg. No one knew that he would be the last person of his line to be buried in this place.

Chapter 20

Bourg-Royal - April 1760:

The Allard farm was in full swing with early spring planting. Old Joseph, now eighty-four years old, was full of energy. Pierre Jr. and Jacques*, now sixteen and fourteen, were as strong and productive as any man. Young Marie-Angélique, now eleven, was as strong as her namesake mother and worked beside her brothers. Their three young siblings: Marie-Anne 7, Louis 5 and Michel 4 did their part picking up brush and other small jobs.

Their activity stopped as a man approached on horseback, no longer a common scene in Charlesbourg. Marie-Angélique* dropped her hoe when she realized who it was. She rushed almost too quickly to greet her old neighbor. He dismounted and they embraced for some time. When they broke, Louis Jacques said, "I just heard. We get no news from Québec. I could not be more pained. He was a wonderful man and the best friend of my life."

Regaining her composure Marie-Angélique* asked, "Can you stay for dinner? We are ready to quit for the day."

Obviously pleased, "Yes, but I should go inside now. It is best if no one knows that I am here."

Once inside, the family gathered around the table to hear what news there was.

"I am here with General Lévi, we are camped at Saint-Foy just west of the city. We have seven-thousand men and are here to retake Québec!"

Pierre Jr. jumped up and interrupted, "May Jacques* and I join you? We can fight as well as any man."

Louis replied, "I am certain of that, but you must stay and help your mother and the family. Your father would haunt me forever if I allowed you to go." The disappointed boys sat down and he continued. "Half the men are French Army and the rest colonists and Indians. We are certain we can defeat Murray. Vaudreuil sent for reinforcements from France in the fall. When they arrive, the colony will again be secure."

The rest of the evening was spent discussing current events and old times. Louis spoke eloquently on the quiet virtues of l'Ile Dupas. Finally Louis said, "I fear I must return to the men."

Marie-Angélique* walked him to the porch, "Please be careful, we have lost enough men already in this awful war." And she gave him a surprisingly passionate kiss. She stood in the moonlight and watched until he was out of sight.

Québec - April 28, 1760:

The second siege of Québec came as a greater surprise than the first. From the town of Saint-Foy, the Canadians were able to simply march to the Plains of Abraham. General Murray was aghast at their numbers. Fully one-third of his men had died over the winter and another third were too feeble to fight. The attack lasted only slightly longer than the first battle on the Plains of Abraham. At the end of the day, the French had retaken the Citadel. Murray's tattered army retreated to the outskirts of town among the chiming of bells and shouts from the crowd.

Murray set up camp. He too expected re-enforcements from the motherland. It was now a question of who arrived first. Occasional brief Indian raids amplified Murray's problems.

Eventually in late May, the first ship arrived. To the dismay of the colony, it flew the Union Jack. Within a week the British had retaken the Fort and the city. Lévi was compelled to surrender the Citadel to the British again, this time for good. The French fleet never arrived. Louis XV had abandoned his American Colonies.

Montréal - September 8, 1760:

Vaudreuil stood on the ramparts of the fort. Three British armies surrounded him. The futility of the situation was apparent. He called his aide-de-camp and gave the order. He surrendered Montréal and for all purposes, all of Canada east of the Mississippi without firing a shot.

General Jeffrey Amherst arrived in due time and after the usual formalities of protocol, Vaudreuil began to maneuver for the best possible terms. Amherst cut him short, "Monsieur, I have come for Canada and nothing else."

Realizing his plight, Vaudreuil began to negotiate and at the end of the night he had managed to allow the French to keep their farms and their religion, nothing more. Amherst's thoughts were already in the future. "Once this place is secure, we can return to the Ohio country and run off those savage Iroquois."

The South Shore of Lake Erie - November 25, 1760;

Major Robert Rogers carefully landed his canoe on likely stretch of beach. As his men landed in turn he announced, "I believe this is as good place as any. We will set watches at each end of the beach and began to make camp."

The weather had taken a turn toward winter. Ice was on the shores in the morning and there had been traces of snow. The autumn colors lay entirely on the ground. Although it was as cold here as in his native New Hampshire, the ground was flat and the waterway was, with few notable exceptions, easily crossed.

As the camp took form, he saw a lone canoe approach. It carried two Chippewa braves, they signaled peace, but he kept his musket handy. They greeted him in Algonquin. As most New England frontiersmen and traders, Rogers spoke Iroquois and some French. His Algonquin was poor, but he had fortunately acquired an Algonquin guide in Montréal. His guide exchanged words with the men and reported they were inviting him to come to their camp and meet with their chief. They produced a small beaded belt as a sign of peace. Rogers accepted it and agreed.

He appointed a few of his men to accompany him, and they headed their canoes to the west. Rogers was confident of his men. All colonists from New England with considerable frontier experience, they had fought bravely against the French along the upper regions of the Saint-Laurent leading up to the fall of Québec. His group now known as 'Rogers Rangers' had been sent to take control of the French fort at Détroit. Rogers expected no difficulty but knew that it was always best to always prepare for the worst. A party had preceded him to Détroit from Montréal with word from Governor Vaudreuil that the fort should be surrendered peacefully.

They proceeded for a mile until they reached a small river. They traveled a short distance up it to a small clearing with an Indian camp of some note. They were escorted to the central fire and invited to eat and drink. Soon a man appeared who was obviously in charge. He was about Roger's age and size. His dress was a mix of Indian and frontiersman. He wore a single blue feather in his hair. Rogers realized immediately who he was and but did not make this apparent when Pontiac was introduced through his guide.

Rogers gave an appropriate response to the guide and was taken aback when Pontiac said in perfect English, "The interpreter will not be necessary, Major Rogers." The men sat and Pontiac produced a pipe. In typical Indian fashion the conversation skirted all issues and only served for the two men to evaluate each other subtly. Rogers assured Pontiac that the British would not interfere with the Indian trade, and Pontiac indicated that he was willing to co-operate in turn. At the end of the evening, the men parted amicably and both left with a better feeling than the one with which they had arrived.

Later Pontiac met with his chiefs, "I have a good feeling of this man, Rogers. He is more like the French traders than the British soldiers. Perhaps old Saint-Aubin was correct. Perhaps we can do business with them. We shall see…"

At the same time, Rogers met with his officers, "As I had been forewarned, this man is more educated than any Indian I have encountered. Perhaps if the British can refrain from their heavy handed ways, we can work with him."

Fort Pontchartrain, Détroit - November 29, 1760:

Captain François-Marie Picoté de Bellestre stood in the southeast turret. He had planned for a fight, but the events of the past several weeks left him no choice. The man before him held a paper from Governor Vaudreuil ordering him to surrender the fort. The British leader, Rogers, was a charismatic gentleman, a true frontiersman and a colonial native. His men were all native frontiersmen as well. The appearance of such a group gave some hope to the Détroit colonists that perhaps this would not be the British occupation they had feared. The document from Vaudreuil did assure them that their lands and church would go undisturbed.

Boston, Massachusetts - The Same Day:

Samuel Adams paced the tavern floor studying the letter. Looking at his friend, Samuel Price, "It seems that the King arose the evening of October 25, fell to the floor and is no more. His son is now King George III. He is said to be a simpleton, given to fits. This along with the French defeat may play nicely into our plans. 'The King is dead, long live the King.'"

They moved to a larger room next door. Ten colonial men sat quietly nursing mugs of beer. Adams rose to read the letter, "Gentleman, we have good news from England. Tonight we start our plans." Then lifting his own mug, "Gentlemen, to us. May we live free or die!"

Bourg-Royal - The Same Day:

Although autumn had been mild, winter was clearly beginning to descend on Québec. The crop had been respectable in spite of the political upheavals. The Allard farm had just finished the early preparations for winter. As Marie-Angélique* stood on the porch looking at the western sky, she noticed a visitor on horseback. She soon realized it was Louis Jacques. She rushed to embrace and welcome him.

They had met only briefly after the final fall of Québec the previous spring. Jacques had quickly returned to his farm on l'Ile Dupas to avoid capture by the British. They spent the day visiting and walking about the farm. After dinner, Marie-Angélique* rose, "Children, Monsieur Jacques has asked me to marry him and I have accepted. You know he was a close friend of your late father and I am certain that your father would approve.

"We plan to marry after Noël. We will load what we can take, sell the rest, and move to his new farm at Ile Dupas once the weather permits. I hear it is lovely."

There was a commotion among the children. Louis Jacques rose, "I know you have friends and ties to Charlesbourg. However your mother and I believe that we shall be safer on the Ile and less threatened with British interference." The discussion continued into the night. In the morning they began to plan.

Fort Pontchartrain du Détroit - The Same Day:

As Jack Hopson crossed the courtyard, he reflected on how hard winter would be in this end-of-the-world place. He entered the office just as a dark-skinned man in typical colonial dress but for a blue feather tied to his hair, exited the room. Hopson addressed Captain Campbell, "Who was that sir?"

Campbell looked closely at his aid-de-camp. Donald Campbell had replaced Major Rogers as commandant of Fort Détroit, as the British now called it. Rogers had left with his men to take official control of the fort at Michilimackinac. "A very interesting man, an Ottawa Indian chief actually. His name is Pontiac. He dresses as a colonist, speaks French better than I and speaks English better than anyone else in this place. He has business interests aside from the typical trading of the Indians, and he is highly respected by the locals. He claims that he is here to make peace and protect his interests. Quite difficult to read if I might say."

Nodding, Hopson continued, "I see sir. Mr. Campau is here with Mr. Saint-Aubin to discuss some details regarding the mills."

Campbell answered, "Very well, send them in."

Charlesbourg Chapel - January 7, 1761:

Père Morisseaux looked much older than he did when he married Marie-Angélique* to her first husband several years before. At thirty-nine, Marie-Angélique* was as beautiful and sturdy as ever. The congregation was a tapestry of the friends and neighbors the Allard family had enjoyed for the last eighteen years. Following the ceremony, neighbors welcomed the new couple with congratulations and farewells, for in the early spring, they would begin their journey to their new home.

Later in the afternoon, when the well-wishers had departed, Jacques* Allard came to speak to his mother, "Father asked me to stay as long as you needed me. With Monsieur Jacques, this is no longer the case. You know that I have little use for farming and yearn adventure. Monsieur Charbonneau has asked Louis* Renaud to go with him to Détroit. They have asked me as well. I believe this is my destiny."

Marie-Angélique* looked into her son's strange eyes and replied, "Let me think about it and I will give you my answer in the morning." Later that evening she went to see Joseph.

At eighty-five the old Indian remained bright and spry. Since the death of his wife, he had returned to living in a simple Indian camp by the Allard farmhouse. As Marie-Angélique* approached him, he was sitting by a very small fire smoking his pipe. Marie-Angélique* sat and before she said anything, Joseph looked up, "Your son does not wish to go to the farm at Ile Dupas." Marie-Angélique* was always amazed at the old man's ability to see the question before it was even asked.

"He is meant for the backcountry and adventure, as were his father and grandfather." Then leaning to empty his pipe in the small fire, "I was not much older than he when the man Cadillac invited Jean-Baptiste* and me to go with him. My own grandfather, the first Henri, went with us for a while to help and keep us safe. He left us in Michilimackinac. It was the last time any of us ever saw the old man.

"If you approve, I will accompany Jacques* and his friend at least as far as Détroit. It will allow me opportunity to see Toussaint and Henri-Pierre for a last time." Smiling he added, "Who knows, perhaps there is still one more adventure left for me. Allow the boy to go and do not grieve. It is his destiny."

They stood and Marie-Angélique* gave Joseph a long embrace and the kiss of a granddaughter. "I shall miss you both terribly."

Chapter 21

Québec - Winter 1761:

Jacques* Allard and Louis* Renaud spent most of the winter foraging for game in the Québec backcountry. Louis*, at twenty was five years older than Jacques* but the younger boy was as strong and capable as the older. The excitement of their upcoming adventure was overwhelming. The fact that Joseph was coming made it even better. Although they knew their family histories, the boys gave little thought to the fact that their great grandfathers, François* Allard and Guillaume* Renaud, had made a similar journey together on a boat called *l'Aigle d'Or* from Normandy in France to Québec one hundred years before.

Although he lived in Québec and traded out of Détroit, the boys knew Jean-Baptiste Charbonneau. His grandfather, Michel, had gone with Jean-Baptiste* Allard and Joseph to Louisiana. His father, also Michel, had gone with Pierre* and Toussaint to the Yellowstone River and the Rocky Mountains. Jean-Baptiste Charbonneau and his father had also fought with Pierre* and Toussaint at Fort William Henry. Jean-Baptiste Charbonneau was now a prominent voyageur and had a reputation of traveling to the extents of the frontier and beyond. The boys expected nothing but the most wonderful of adventures.

May 1, 1761:

The day of departure had arrived. The family had spent the winter selling and disposing of goods too large to travel, and making the rest transportable. For larger items Joseph and Louis Jacques had fashioned a barge from two canoes, much like that built by Toussaint and Pierre* for the cannons. The animals were all sold and new ones would be purchased in Montréal or Trois-Rivieres. Many friends and neighbors gathered to help and say tearful farewells.

The party consisted of Marie-Angélique* and her new husband, Joseph, Louis* Renaud, and the six Allard children ranging in age from Pierre at sixteen to Michel at four. In addition, Louis Jacques had hired two voyageurs and an Indian to help with the canoes. The trip was tranquil as the river was clear and the weather remained fair. They camped each night, but at the end of the first week they stopped for the night in the village of Trois-Rivieres. The children were thrilled at the prospect of rooms and a meal at the tavern.

After dinner Marie-Angélique* took the young children to bed, while her husband and Joseph stayed with Pierre, Jacques*, and Louis* Renaud in the tavern. They were joined by an acquaintance of Louis Jacques's, named Boucher. Boucher's family had been the first settlers of Trois-Rivieres and he was up to date on everything, "I hear two of these boys are going to Détroit with Charbonneau. They say things are quiet in Détroit but no one ever knows what Pontiac is up to. I hear he is now at Pittsburgh at the forks of the Ohio talking with the Iroquois and some of the British colonists.

"At any rate, you boys are in for adventure with Charbonneau. He keeps going farther into the wild every season. He says he thinks he has found the Northwest Passage north of where his father was with Vérendrye years ago. But now there are others who say the British are going to take the trade away from the French. So who can say? Well, anyway, good luck to you."

The next day they entered the widest part of the Saint-Laurent between Québec and Montréal. Called Lake Saint-Louis, it could be rough in high winds. Fortunately, the weather remained fair. Two days later the river narrowed. The main channel followed the southern shore and two smaller channels entered marsh. Louis Jacques explained, "This is the northeastern tip of our island. The canoes could take the northern channel, but it might be tight for the barge so we will take the main route."

Later in the day they saw a village with a church steeple on the southern shore. "This is Sorel, many voyageurs live here in the fair season. We are now at the other end of our island and we will turn right here and go to the northern channel where our farm is located." The southwestern tip of the island was beautiful with large maple, oak and willow trees on high ground. As they entered the northern channel, they saw the clearing and the farmhouse. Two men ran to the shore to help. Louis introduced them as his two hired men, "Between the three of us, we have the house and farm in good order. They have already begun the planting and we can all get to work as soon as we are settled."

Ile Dupas was truly idyllic. There were only four farms, two on this island and two more on the center island. There were a few farms along each side of the mainland and the village of Sorel was quite close on the southern shore of the river. The hands and the boys started to unload while Louis gave Marie-Angélique* a tour of her new home. The younger children began to explore.

By dinner things were coming under control. Everyone had a story from the day; excitement of the new home was apparent. The next day they began to finish the planting. Jacques*, Louis* and Joseph would stay one week and then leave to meet Charbonneau in Montréal.

As the week progressed, Jacques* was taken by the beauty of the area. He almost began to regret his decision, but when the day to leave came, the promise of adventure won out. When the family gathered at the bank as they loaded their belongings, Marie-Angélique* gave Jacques* a board wrapped in cloth. "Give this to Toussaint. I have always treasured it, but I believe it should again belong to him."

After a long tearful goodbye, the two boys and the old Indian pushed off in Joseph's canoe. After they were out of sight, Louis and Marie-Angélique* headed back to their new home. Louis remarked, "I only hope that there is something out there for them. I fear our way of life and its adventures are coming to an end."

His wife reflected, replying, "My grandmother Tessier used to say that when one thing ends, something new always begins and it is almost always for the better. Who is to say, perhaps they are embarking on the greatest adventure of all."

Marie-Angélique* Bergevin-Allard-Jacques would live another 27 years on l'Ile Dupas. She would give birth to and raise four more children before she would die peacefully and be buried there at the age of 65. She would never, however, fully appreciate, the prophetic nature of her words on this day.

TO BE CONTINUED

EPILOGUE

The Peace: The more than forty years of relative peace which surrounded the Peace of Utrecht allowed French colonies time for exploration and prosperity. It also gave French colonists time for fun and events like canoe and sled races. These and other festivities abounded.

The Ice Boat: I remember my first ride in my father's iceboat. It was a sensation of incredible exhilaration and fear the likes of which I have never again experienced. No one actually knows who invented this wonderful craft or when. Some say it came from North America and others from Holland. At any rate, no one seems to know of a time when they were not around. They will be seen again in other books about the Allards.

The Epidemic of 1728: Now believed to have been diphtheria, it killed many Québecois, mainly children, including the three Allard brothers.

Niagara Falls: The early voyageur tales are filled with stories of this wonder of the world. I don't know how many are true but I included a few here.

Pierre Gauthier de la Vérendrye: This man and his sons did spend many years exploring the west. After he was recalled, his sons claimed to have gone with a few other French voyageurs up to the great mountains. Their story was suspect until the Vérendrye plaque was discovered. Historians now believe their journey did end in what is today Yellowstone National Park.

The Buffalo: From the many stories of these creatures, only a few are included here. The Allards have not seen the last of these wonderful creatures.

The Tremblay, Laforest Migration to Détroit: The basics of this story are true and taken from a wonderful article in "The Michigan Habitant Heritage."

The Milk River Settlement: As this will be a setting for the next three books, I have chosen to introduce it here.

The War: While the Peace of Utrecht allowed the French leisure, it allowed British colonists time to search for new lands for their crowded colonies. The resulting Seven Years, or French and Indian, War is arguably the most important conflict in the history of North America. Not only did it change the culture of Canada to British, it laid the seeds for the American War for Independence and greatly affected its outcome, as will be seen in the next book.

Ohio: The war was in great part about control of this territory. The main players, Washington, Braddock, Montcalm, Wolfe, etc. are depicted from historical accounts.

The Battles: Braddock's fall, Fort William Henry, etc. are also taken from historical accounts. The fall of Louisbourg and the flight of the Acadian refugees are accurate.

The Fall of Québec: Is taken from a marvelous daily diary kept by one of Wolfe's soldiers.

DESCENDANTS OF FRANCOIS* ALLARD
THREE GENERATIONS

1. **Francois* Allard**, b. 1637-1642, Blacqueville, France, (son of Jacques* Allard and Jacqueline* Frerot) occupation farmer. He married Jeanne* Anguille, Nov 1, 1671, in Beauport, QC, b. 1647, Artannes-sur-Indre, Tours, France, (daughter of Michel* Anguille and Etiennette* Toucheraine) d. Mar 12 1711, Charlesbourg, QC, buried: Mar 12 1711, St Charles de Boromée cemetery, Charlesbourg parish. Francois* died Oct 25 1725, Charlesbourg, QC, buried: St Charles Boromée Cemetery, Charlesbourg.

   Children:

   2. i **André Allard** b. Sep 12 1672.
   3. ii **Jean-François Allard** b. 31 Jul 1674.
   4. iii **Jean Baptiste* Allard** b. Feb 22 1676.
   5. iv **Marie Allard** b. NOV 1 1678.
   6. v **Georges Allard**.
   vi **Marie-Renée Allard**, b. MAY 16 1683, Bourg Royal, QC, d. OCT 10 1684.
   7. vii **Marie-Anne Allard** b. 1685.
   8. viii **Thomas Allard** b. 17 Mar 1687.
   9. ix **Jeanne Allard**.

2. **André Allard**, b. Sep 12 1672, Notre-Dame de Québec. He married Anne LeMarche, Nov 22 1695, in Charlesbourg, QC, b. 1668, Montreal, QC, (daughter of Jean LeMarche and Catherine Hurault). André died Dec 05 1735, Charlesbourg, QC.

Children:

i **Marie Catherine Allard**, b. Nov 16 1696, Charlesbourg, QC. She married Nicholas Jacques, Nov 05 1719, in Quebec, b. 1691, Charlesbourg, QC, (son of Louis Jacques and Antoinette Leroux).

ii **Marie Genevieve Allard**, b. Oct 31 1698, Charlesbourg, QC. She married Pierre Chalifou, Nov 07 1718, in Charlesbourg, QC, b. 1692, Charlesbourg, QC, (son of Pierre Chalifou and Anne Magnan).

iii **Jacques Allard**, b. 1700, Bourg Royal, QC. He married Marguerite Brosseau, 1723, b. Feb 02 1698, Charlesbourg, QC, (daughter of Joseph Brosseau and Marie Anne Gaudreau).

iv **Pierre Andre Allard**, b. Dec 21 1702, Bourg Royal, QC. He married Madeline Paquet, Nov 15 1724, b. 1702, Charlesbourg, QC, (daughter of Philippe Paquet and Jeanne Brosseau).

v **Thomas Allard**, b. Jul 20 1705, Bourg Royal, QC. He married Marie Agnes Belleau, Nov 25 1731, in Ste. Foy, QC, (daughter of Guillaume Belleau and Suzanne Robitaille) d. 1762. Thomas died Jun 26 1762.

vi **Jean Charles Allard**, b. Feb 06 1708, Bourg Royal, QC. He married Madeline Danet, Nov 12 1731, in Ste. Foy, QC, (daughter of Charles Danest and Madeline Bertheaume).

vii **Jean Baptiste Allard**, b. May 28 1710, Bourg Royal, QC. He married (1) Marie Elizabeth Pepin, Sep 30 1732, b. 1715, (daughter of Louis Pepin and Elizabeth Boutin). He married (2) Marie Auclair, Aug 01 1746, in Charlesbourg, QC, (daughter of Francois Auclair and Charlotte Martin) d. 1751, Quebec. Jean died May 28 1751.

viii **Marie Joseph Allard**, b. Jun 22 1712, Bourg Royal, QC. She married Francois Dion, Jan 09 1736, in Quebec, d. 1760, Pointe Aux Trembles, QC. Marie died May 29 1735.

3. **Jean-François Allard**, b. 31 Jul 1674. He married (1) Marie Ursule Tardif, Nov 05 1698, in Beauport, QC, b. 1678, Beauport, QC, (daughter of Jacques Tardiff and Barbe DÓrange) d. Apr 23 1711, Beauport, QC. He married (2) Genevieve Dauphin, Aug 03 1711, in Beauport, QC, b. 1692, Beauport, QC, (daughter of Rene Dauphin and Suzanne Gignard). Jean-François died 1746, Quebec.

Children:

i **Jean Baptiste Allard**, b. 1699, d. 1699.

ii **Jean Baptiste Allard**, b. 1701, d. 1701.

iii **Jean Baptist Allard**, b. Sep 29 1702. He married Agathe Meunier, Feb 28 1729, (daughter of Mathurin Meunier and Madeline Meneux).

iv **Marie Charlotte Ursula Allard**, b. 1704. She married (1) Louis LaMothe, Oct 29 1727, in Lorette qc, b. 1699, Beauport, QC, (son of Francois Lamothe and Marie Anne Leroux). She married (2) Pierre Protot, 1745.

v **Jacques Allard**, b. 1706, Charlesbourg, QC. He married Charlotte Godin, 1731, b. 1683, LÁnge Gardien qc, (daughter of Charles Godin and Marie Boucher) christened widow of Vincent Guillot.

vi **Pierre Noel Allard**, b. 1708. He married Catherine Meunier, Jul 30 1736, in Quebec, (daughter of Mathurin Meunier and Catherine Bonhomme).

vii **Genevieve Allard**, b. Nov 25 1712. She married Jean Baptiste Cantara Deslaurier, Jan 15 1732, ref: ? 196 rjd.

viii **Gabriel Allard**, b. Aug 03 1714, ref: see note, occupation coureur des bois. He married Elizabeth Proulx, Feb 12 1748, in Baie du Fevre, Qc, (daughter of Claude Proulx and Elizabeth Robidas Manseau). Gabriel died Apr 30 1777, Quebec.

ix **Andre Allard**, b. Mar 22 1716. He married Jeanne Giguere Despins, Oct 20 1749, (daughter of Antoiene Giguere Despins and Francoise Jutras).

x **Rene Allard**, b. Feb 02 1718, d. Feb 06 1736.

xi **Marie Louise Allard**, b. Feb 20 1720. She married Joseph Couturier-Labonte, Oct 28 1741.

xii **Marie Catherine Allard**, b. Feb 26 1722. She married Gabriel Dany, Jan 13 1744.

xiii **Marguerite Allard**, b. Feb 23 1724.

xiv **Louis Allard**, b. Feb 22 1726, d. Nov 14 1749.

xv **Marie Ursula Allard**, b. Nov 28 1727, Beauport, QC. She married Francois Proulx, Feb 17 1749.

xvi **Suzanne Allard**, b. Apr 12 1730. She married Joseph Gagne, Feb 05 1759.

xvii **Joseph Allard**, b. 1732, d. 1732.

xviii **Marie Angelique Allard**. She married François Joseph Prou, Feb 17 1749, b. 1724, (son of Claude Prou and ...).

xix **Joseph Allard**, b. May 19 1734. He married (1) Madeline Harel, Oct 12 1761, in St Michel d Yamaska, (daughter of Pierre Harel and Madeline Tessier) d. 1764. He married (2) Amable Gagne, Oct 01 1764, in St Francois du lac qc, (daughter of Rene Gagne and Gabrielle St Laurent). Joseph died Mar 27 1764.

4. **Jean Baptiste* Allard**, b. Feb 22 1676, Quebec. He married Anne Elizabeth* Pageot, Feb 23, 1705, in Charlesbourg, QC, b. Jan 16, 1686, Charlesbourg, QC, (daughter of Thomas* Pageot and Catherine* Roy) d. Dec 22, 1748, Charlesbourg, QC. Jean died Dec 22, 1748, Charlesbourg, QC, buried: Dec 23 1748, Charlesbourg, QC.

Children:

i **François Allard**, b. 10 Feb 1706, Bourg Royal, QC, d. Aug 28 1728, Charlesbourg, QC.

ii **Thomas Allard**, b. 31 Jan 1708, Bourg Royal, QC, d. Oct 22 1728, Charlesbourg, QC.

iii **Jean-Baptiste Allard**, b. 18 Jan 1710, Bourg Royal, QC. He married (1) Genevieve de Rainville, Jan 22 1731, in Beauport, QC, b. 1712, Beauport, QC, (daughter of Paul Rainville and Marie Anne Roberge) d. Mar 27 1743. He married (2) Marie Plante, b. 1715, (daughter of Francois Plante and ....) christened died at childbirth, d. 1756.

- iv **Marie Therese Allard**, b. 26 Mar 1712, Bourg Royal, QC. She married Francois Roi, Jun 04 1731, in Charlesbourg, QC. Marie died Aug 19 1759, St. Michel, QC.
- v **Andre Allard**, b. 11 Mar 1714, Bourg Royal, QC, d. Oct 12 1728, Charlesbourg, QC.
- vi **Pierre* Allard**, b. Apr 28, 1716, Charlesbourg, QC. He married Marie Angélique* Bergevin, Nov 5, 1743, in Charlesbourg, QC, b. Oct 10, 1722, Charlesbourg, QC, (daughter of Ignatius* Bergevin and Genevieve* Tessier) d. Mar 18, 1788, Isle Dupas, QC. Pierre* died Dec 27, 1759, Quebec.
- vii **Francois Allard**, b. 3 Feb 1719, Bourg Royal, QC. He married Barbe Louise Bergevin, Nov 13 1741, in Charlesbourg, QC, b. 1724, (daughter of Ignatius* Bergevin and Genevieve* Tessier) d. 1794. Francois died 1801, Charlesbourg, QC.
- viii **Jacques Allard**, b. 17 Aug 1721, Charlesbourg, QC. He married Ursula Agnes Denis, May 10 1750, in St Michel, (daughter of Joseph Denis and Jeanne Labonte).
- ix **Marie Madeleine Allard**, b. 26 Aug 1723, Charlesbourg, QC. She married Germain Bergevin, Nov 05 1743, b. 1719, (son of Ignatius* Bergevin and Genevieve* Tessier).

x **Marie Charlotte Allard**, b. 28 May 1726, Charlesbourg, QC. She married Pierre Bergevin, Jan 28 1743, b. 1727, (son of Ignatius* Bergevin and Genevieve* Tessier).

5. **Marie Allard**, b. Nov, 1 1678, Bourg Royal, QC. She married Charles Villeneuve, May 07 1703, in Bourg Royal, QC, b. 1681, Charlesbourg, QC, (son of Mathurin Villeneuve and Marguerite Lemarche).

Children:

i **Marguerite Villeneuve**, b. 1704, Charlesbourg, QC, d. 1720, Charlesbourg, QC.

ii **Marie Charlotte Villeneuve**, b. 1706, Charlesbourg, QC.

iii **Michelle Francoise Villeneuve**, b. 1707, Charlesbourg, QC. She married Michel Magan.

iv **Marie Madeline Villeneuve**, b. 1709, Charlesbourg, QC.

v **Marie Renee Villeneuve**, b. 1710, Charlesbourg, QC.

vi **Marie Teresa Villeneuve**, b. 1712, Charlesbourg, QC. She married Francois Marie Bergevin, 1732, in Charlesbourg, QC, b. 1710, Charlesbourg, QC, (son of Ignatius* Bergevin and Genevieve* Tessier).

vii **Marie Angelique Villeneuve**, b. 1714, Charlesbourg, QC, d. 1730, Charlesbourg, QC.

viii **Charles Pierre Villeneuve**, b. 1716, Charlesbourg, QC.
ix **Joseph Francois Villeneuve**, b. 1718, Charlesbourg, QC.
x **Francois Xavier Villeneuve**, b. 1720, Charlesbourg, QC.
xi **Germain Francois Villeneuve**, b. 1721, Charlesbourg, QC.
xii **Jean Marie Villeneuve**, b. 1723, Charlesbourg, QC.
xiii **Louis Villeneuve**, b. 1725, Charlesbourg, QC.

6. **Georges Allard**, baptized Feb 10 1680. He married (1) Marie Marguerite Pageot, Jan 07 1710, in Charlesbourg, QC, b. 1693, Charlesbourg, QC, (daughter of Thomas* Pageot and Catherine* Roy) d. 17 Mar 1711, Hotel Dieu, QC. He married (2) Catherine Bedard, Jan 30 1713, in Charlesbourg, QC, b. 1680, Charlesbourg, QC, (daughter of Jacques Bedard and Elisabeth Doucinet). Georges died 1755.

Children:

i **Marie Francoise Allard**, b. 1710, Charlesbourg, QC. She married Joseph Collet, 1728, in Charlesbourg, QC, b. 1707, Charlesbourg, QC, (son of Joseph Collet and Marguerite Courtois).
ii **Marie Anne Allard**, b. 1714, Charlesbourg, QC, d. 1714.
iii **Marie Josette Allard**, b. 1715, Charlesbourg, QC.
iv **Marie Louise Allard**, b. 1717, Charlesbourg, QC.

v **Marie Charlotte Allard**, b. 1719, Charlesbourg, QC.
vi **Marie Madeline Allard**, b. 1721, Charlesbourg, QC.
vii **Genevieve Catherine Allard**, b. 1723, Charlesbourg, QC.

7. **Marie-Anne Allard**, b. 1685. She married (1) Pierre Boutillet, Jul 23 1714, in Charlesbourg, Quebec, b. 1677, St. Sauveur Rouen FR, (son of Pierre Boutillet and Jeanne Lemoine) ref: rjd 157, d. 1715, Charlesbourg, QC. She married (2) Jean Renaud, Nov 18 1720, in Charlesbourg, Qc, b. St.Aumario,Perigueux,Perigord(DordogneFR, (son of Jean Renaud and Marguerite Anne ...).

Children:

i **Francois Boutillet**, b. Jun 09 1715, Charlesbourg, QC.
ii **Jean Charles Renaud**, b. 1721, Charlesbourg, QC.
iii **Jeanne Elizabeth Renaud**, b. 1723, Charlesbourg, QC, d. 1730, Charlesbourg, QC.
iv **Joseph Renaud**, b. 1725, Charlesbourg, QC.

8. **Thomas Allard**, b. 17 Mar 1687, Bourg Royal, QC. He married Marie Charlotte Bedard, Jul 11 1714, in Charlesbourg, QC, b. 1696, Charlesbourg, QC, (daughter of Etienne Bedard and Marie Jeanne Villeneuve).

Children:

i **Francoise Allard**, b. 1716.
ii **Thomas Allard**, b. 1718.

iii **Nicholas Allard**, b. 1720.

iv **Jacques Allard**, b. 1722. He married Marie Madeline Bergevin, 1751, in Charlesbourg, QC, b. 1734, Charlesbourg, QC, (daughter of Ignatius* Bergevin and Genevieve* Tessier).

v **Charlotte Allard**, b. 1726.

vi **Marie Allard**, b. 1728.

vii **Elizabeth Allard**, b. 1735.

viii **Pierre Allard**, b. 1737.

9. **Jeanne Allard**. She married Guillaume Longpre, b. Quefille New England.

Children:

i **Guillaume Longpre**, b. 1697, new England, christened went west 1721. He married Catherine Bleau, 1720, in Montreal, QC, b. 1699, Montreal, QC, (daughter of Francois Bleau and Catherine Campau).

DESCENDANTS OF JEAN-BAPTISTE* ALLARD THREE GENERATIONS

1. **Jean Baptiste* Allard**, b. Feb 22 1676, Quebec, (son of Francois* Allard and Jeanne* Anguille). He married Anne Elizabeth* Pageot, Feb 23 1705, in Charlesbourg, QC, b. Jan 16 1686, Charlesbourg, QC, (daughter of Thomas* Pageot and Catherine* Roy) d. Dec 22 1748, Charlesbourg, QC. Jean died Dec 22 1748, Charlesbourg, QC, buried: Dec 23 1748, Charlesbourg, QC.

Children:

- i **François Allard**, b. 10 Feb 1706, Bourg Royal, QC, d. Aug 28 1728, Charlesbourg, QC.
- ii **Thomas Allard**, b. 31 Jan 1708, Bourg Royal, QC, d. Oct 22 1728, Charlesbourg, QC.
- 2. iii **Jean-Baptiste Allard** b. 18 Jan 1710.
- iv **Marie Therese Allard**, b. 26 Mar 1712, Bourg Royal, QC. She married Francois Roi, Jun 04 1731, in Charlesbourg, QC. Marie died Aug 19 1759, St. Michel, QC.
- v **Andre Allard**, b. 11 Mar 1714, Bourg Royal, QC, d. Oct 12 1728, Charlesbourg, QC.
- 3. vi **Pierre* Allard** b. Apr 28 1716.
- 4. vii **Francois Allard** b. 3 Feb 1719.

5. viii **Jacques Allard** b. 17 Aug 1721.

ix **Marie Madeleine Allard**, b. 26 Aug 1723, Charlesbourg, QC. She married Germain Bergevin, Nov 05 1743, b. 1719, (son of Ignatius* Bergevin and Genevieve* Tessier).

x **Marie Charlotte Allard**, b. 28 May 1726, Charlesbourg, QC. She married Pierre Bergevin, Jan 28 1743, b. 1727, (son of Ignatius* Bergevin and Genevieve* Tessier).

Second Generation

2. **Jean-Baptiste Allard**, b. 18 Jan 1710, Bourg Royal, QC. He married (1) Genevieve de Rainville, Jan 22 1731, in Beauport, QC, b. 1712, Beauport, QC, (daughter of Paul Rainville and Marie Anne Roberge) d. Mar 27 1743. He married (2) Marie Plante, b. 1715, (daughter of Francois Plante and ....) christened died at childbirth, d. 1756.

Children:

i **Jean Baptiste Allard**, b. Apr 13 1732. He married Francoise Legault, Oct 23 1757, in Pointe Claire QC, (daughter of Charles Legault and Josephte Dubois).

ii **Marie Genevieve Allard**, b. Sep 25 1733. She married Joseph Antoine Jekimbert, Oct 27 1753.

iii **Louis Allard**, b. 1735, d. 1735.

iv **Francois Allard**, b. Sep 13 1736.

v **Marie Charlotte Allard**, b. Nov 14 1738, d. May 12 1744.

vi **Michel Jean Allard**, b. Jul 09 1740.
vii **Paul Joseph Allard**, b. 1742, d. 1743.
viii **Francois Allard**, b. Mar 28 1745. He married Marie Louise Bacon, Feb 09 1767, (daughter of Eustache Bacon and ...... Bacon).
ix **Paul Allard**, b. May 08 1746, d. 1760.
x **Marie Louise Allard**, b. Jul 31 1747.
xi **Angelique Allard**, b. Sep 04 1749. She married Jean Mathieu, Oct 17 1774.
xii **Simon Allard**, b. Oct 24 1750.
xiii **Joseph Allard**, b. 1752, d. 1753.
xiv **Marie Madeline Allard**, b. May 25 1753.
xv **Marie Joseph Allard**, b. 1754, d. 1756.
xvi **... Allard**, b. Mar 26 1756, christened, mother and son died at childbirth, d. Mar 26 1756.

3. **Pierre* Allard**, b. Apr 28 1716, Charlesbourg, QC. He married Marie Angélique* Bergevin, Nov 5, 1743, in Charlesbourg, QC, b. Oct 10, 1722, Charlesbourg, QC, (daughter of Ignatius* Bergevin and Genevieve* Tessier) d. Mar 18, 1788, Isle Dupas, QC. Pierre* died Dec 27, 1759, Quebec.

Children:

i **Pierre Allard**, b. Dec 23 1744, Charlesbourg, QC. He married Elizabeth Lariviere Chapdelain, Feb 03 1772, in Quebec, (daughter of Jean Seraphin Chapdelain and Josephte Brisset). Pierre died Oct 26 1795, Quebec.

ii **Jacques* Allard**, b. Oct 14 1746, Charlesbourg, QC, occupation Voyageur, Farmer. He married Marie Genevieve Magdelainne* Laforest, Feb 7 1780, in Detroit, MI, Ste. Anne, b. June 16 1764, Detroit (now windmill Pointe GP), (daughter of Guillaume* Laforest and Marie Marguerite* Tremblay). Jacques* died 1814, Detroit, MI.

iii **Marie Angélique Allard**, b. Oct 02 1749. She married (2) Antoine Amable Dutaut Vilandre, Oct 27 1777, in Isle Dupas, QC, (son of Pierre Dutaut and Marie Louise Hus). Marie died Jun 16 1832.

iv **Joseph Allard**, b. Apr 12 1752, Charlesbourg, QC, d. May 04 1752, Charlesbourg, QC.

v **Marie-Anne Allard**, b. Sep 16 1753. She married (1) Noel Penisson, Aug 18 1777, in Isle Dupas, QC, (son of Jean Marie Penisson and Catherine Monet). She married (2) Raphael Desorcy, Jan 30 1786. Marie-Anne died Feb 17 1839.

vi **Louis Allard**, b. FEB 11 1755, Charlesbourg, QC. He married (1) Marie Levron, Aug 18 1806, in Quebec. He married (2) Marguerite Malbeuf, Aug 14 1780, in St Cuthbert QC, (daughter of Jen Baptist Malbeuf and Dotothee Cloutier). He married (3) Louise Masse, Feb 25 1790, in St Cuthbert QC, (daughter of Jean Baptist Masse and Louise Larose). Louis died Apr 02 1825, Quebec.

vii **Michel Allard**, b. NOV 20 1756, Charlesbourg, QC. He married Marie Louise Plouffe, Jul 25 1785, in Berthierville qc, (daughter of Pierre Plouffe and Angelique Hamel). Michel died Sep 28 1832.

viii **Louis Allard**, b. Oct 12 1758, Charlesbourg, QC, d. Aug 29 1759, Charlesbourg, QC.

4. **Francois Allard**, b. 3 Feb 1719, Bourg Royal, QC. He married Barbe Louise Bergevin, Nov 13 1741, in Charlesbourg, QC, b. 1724, (daughter of Ignatius* Bergevin and Genevieve* Tessier) d. 1794. Francois died 1801, Charlesbourg, QC.

Children:

i **Marie Louise Allard**, b. 1742. She married Jean Ariail, Jul 13 1761.

ii **Marie Angelique Allard**, b. 1744. She married Guil Leroux, 1764.

iii **Pierre Francois Allard**, b. 1746.

iv **Therese Allard**, b. 1748. She married (1) Jean Baptist Bouet. She married (2) Benoni Couture, Jul 15 1782.

v **Jean Baptiste Allard**, b. 1751. He married Marie Angelique Jacques, Feb 07 1774, in St Cuthbert, (daughter of Joseph Jacques and Josephte Groinier).

vi **Louis Allard**, b. 1752.

vii **Louis Charles Allard**, b. 1755, d. 1755.

viii **Charles Allard**, b. 1757. He married Marie Bocage, Jan 07 1783, in St-Cuthbert QC, b. 1763, (daughter of Jean-Baptiste Baillargeon-Bocage and Angélique Sansfaçon-Duhamel).

ix **Marie Joseph Allard**, b. 1759, d. 1760.

x **Antoine Allard**, b. 1761. He married Marie Francoise Morin, Jan 14 1788, in St Cuthbert, (daughter of Louis Morin and Genevieve Couillard).

5. **Jacques Allard**, b. 17 Aug 1721, Charlesbourg, QC. He married Ursula Agnes Denis, May 10 1750, in St Michel, (daughter of Joseph Denis and Jeanne Labonte).

Children:

i **Marie Agnes Allard**, b. 1751, d. 1751.

ii **Marie Clotide Allard**, b. 1752, d. 1756.

iii **Marie Victoria Allard**, b. 1754.

iv **Marie Ursula Allard**, b. 1756, d. 1756.

v **Jacques Allard**, b. 1757, d. 1758.

DESCENDANTS OF HENRI
FIVE GENERATIONS

1. **Henri**, b. c. 1630, Quebec. He married **Angelique**, b. Quebec.

    Children:

    2. i **Philippe** b. 1650.

Second Generation

2. **Philippe**, b. 1650, Quebec. He married **Marie**.

    Children:

    i **Henri**.

    3. ii **Joseph** b. 1676.

Third Generation

3. **Joseph de Baptiste**, b. 1676, Quebec. He married **Monique de Baptiste**, (daughter of ... and ...).

    Children:

    4. i **Toussaint** b. 1716.

Fourth Generation

4. **Toussaint de Baptiste**, b. 1716, Quebec. He married **Monique Roy**, (daughter of Pierre Roy and ...).

   Children:

   i **Henri-Pierre de Baptiste**, b. 1746, Quebec.

Made in the USA
Las Vegas, NV
21 November 2022